LORD OF LOYALTY

Trysts and Treachery
Book Two

By Elizabeth Keysian

Dragonblade Publishing, Inc. is an imprint of Kathryn Le Veque
Novels, Inc.
P.O. Box 7968
La Verne CA 91750
ceo@dragonbladepublishing.com

Produced in the United States of America

First Edition August 2020
Mass Market Paperback Edition

ARE YOU SIGNED UP FOR DRAGONBLADE'S BLOG?

You'll get the latest news and information on exclusive giveaways, exclusive excerpts, coming releases, sales, free books, cover reveals and more.

Check out our complete list of authors, too!

No spam, no junk. That's a promise!

Sign Up Here

www.dragonbladepublishing.com

Dearest Reader;

Thank you for your support of a small press. At Dragonblade Publishing, we strive to bring you the highest quality Historical Romance from the some of the best authors in the business. Without your support, there is no 'us', so we sincerely hope you adore these stories and find some new favorite authors along the way.

Happy Reading!

CEO, Dragonblade Publishing

Additional Dragonblade books by Author Elizabeth Keysian

Trysts and Treachery Series
Lord of Deception (Book 1)
Lord of Loyalty (Book 2)
Lord of the Forest (Book 3)
Lord of Mistrust (Book 4)
Lord of the Manor (Book 5)

CHAPTER ONE

Holborn, London, July 1586

I SOBEL MARSTON ROCKED back and forth in agitation, desperate for release from her captivity. Not only was she stuck in this small, stifling room, she was also imprisoned by her mind, forever struggling to remember anything. Each time a memory was in her grasp, it drifted away like thistledown on the wind, and ofttimes, she forgot her own name.

Today was one of the days when she barely felt complete. Her remedy for this was ever the same—to look in her polished steel mirror. She could always find herself in that—gazing into the troubled green eyes that stared back at her from a pale, anxious face. Alas, the mirror gave her no sense of *being*, but at least it confirmed her existence. Which was better than nothing.

She comforted herself with the words of her cousin, Hubert Pike. "You've been ill, Isobel. We're here to care for you while Edward's fighting abroad. None can harm you while we're here to keep you safe."

Her flawed mind managed to picture Hubert—the hard intelligence in his eyes, the ostentatious high ruff around his neck, and his silken clothing. She remembered the face of his pot-bellied manservant, Flinders, too, and the slovenly housekeeper, Goodwife Avice Quill, who administered her bitter-tasting medicine. It wasn't every day she could remember them all, for their faces often blurred, and became meaningless.

The mirror trembled in her hand. "I'm not sure they grant me the loving kindness a caring relation should," she told her reflection. "Take your medicine like a good girl and don't complain. Your brain sickness will soon pass if you do as you're told." She imitated Avice's insidious whine. One day, when she felt strong enough, she'd dash that foul-tasting stuff in the woman's face. Nay, she must not. A well-brought-up gentlewoman would never behave thus.

Next, as an exercise for her faulty memory, Isobel concentrated on Flinders. A thickset man who was a stranger to washing, and whose breath smelled like rotten meat, he was her "special protector". But she was revolted by him and had repeatedly told Hubert she couldn't stand having him near her. Her cousin always gave the same response—it was a symptom of her illness that she should develop delusions about people. She shouldn't trust her feelings.

Her head snapped up, and she dropped the mirror on the bed. She could hear an uneven step on the cobbles below—someone was coming. She hurried to peer through the diamond-shaped panes, hoping for a visitor from beyond the walls, but expecting to see only a servant. It wouldn't be one she recognized, however—they all seemed to be different from those her father had kept when her parents were alive. Mayhap Edward had employed some new ones to manage Marston House in his absence.

How long had her brother been gone, now? It seemed months since he'd last dwelled here. The house had changed in his absence—there were fewer items of quality furniture, not so many decorated jugs and inlaid boxes as there ought to be. Or so she *imagined*—this brain sickness of hers had attacked her memory and twisted everything, like yarn on a spindle.

Why was she looking out the window? Was it for something important, or was it just to see if it was fine enough to go outside and do some gardening? That was a task Hubert was happy for her to do, working in the walled garden—that, or reading quietly in the tiny chamber which had become her world. Not that she had any books other than her Greek mythology. She'd read it over and over, until the characters came to life in her head, steering her thoughts as the gods had steered Mankind in those ancient days.

There was a bubble of excitement in her chest—why? Ah, yes, she'd heard someone at the front of the house. But if it were a visitor, they wouldn't be here for *her*. Hubert had explained he couldn't allow anybody to disturb her in her fragile state of mind.

But that didn't mean she couldn't look, did it?

Cautiously, she tried her door. Not locked! And the chair in the passageway, where Flinders usually sat, was empty. With a brief flash of insight, she realized he must be with the kitchen wench who'd taken his fancy. Nobody knew she noticed such things, but on a good day, she noticed a lot.

Tiptoeing to the gallery above the main entrance into the house, she bent and peered down.

A servant, his broad figure obstructing the doorway, was in a heated discussion with the visitor. The argument lasted but a moment—the new arrival thrust the servant aside and marched in, limping a little. Isobel gasped. She'd never seen anyone shoulder their way in before.

While the stranger stood and looked around him, the harried-looking servant raced to the parlor door and announced the visitor to those within. *Sir William Cavendish.* That was a grand-sounding title—was Hubert in trouble with the authorities? Isobel snorted. She wouldn't mind if he were.

Cavendish removed his high-crowned hat and placed it on the carved chest in the entranceway, then—after a moment's hesitation—unbuckled his sword.

She stared down at him, anticipation stealing her breath. Cavendish was a tall, broad-shouldered man, with a short cloak worn on one shoulder, and tightly-fitting doublet. His upper hose were paned and padded, and his stockings clung to well-muscled calves. Not as finely dressed as she might expect a knight of the realm to be, but perhaps he'd been traveling. Or mayhap she'd forgotten what a peer should look like.

Tawny gold hair framed the kind of face a classical sculptor would have adored, and there was an air of virile decisiveness in Cavendish's movements. It made her breath catch.

"What a beautiful man—it must be Apollo. No, foolish girl—the gods don't come to earth any more. It could be a demi-god—Orpheus perhaps. But then, where's his lyre?"

He was out of view now, but by leaning her head as close to the handrail as possible, she could overhear every word spoken down below.

"Sir, permit me to introduce myself. I'm Sir William Cavendish, a friend of Edward Marston's. We fought together overseas."

"Hubert Pike, at your service. Any friend of Edward's is a friend of mine. Have you journeyed long this day?" The stiffness in Hubert's tone belied his words of welcome.

"I disembarked yesterday, at cockcrow, and rode directly here."

"What reason had you for such haste?" Hubert's voice held disapproval. Isobel pressed her forehead against the carved wooden banister and tried to recall where she'd heard the name "Edward Marston" before.

"I considered my news urgent. I would have arrived ere now but, alas, I had a wound that festered, then bad weather held back my sea crossing."

She liked the sound of the man's voice. It had a resonance to it that was strong, commanding. But then, if he was Orpheus, his songs could calm the hearts of savage beasts, so he was bound to have a good voice.

"Sir, I bring ill tidings, I fear."

"Bad news? Not about poor Edward, I hope." That name again. Why was her mind so muddled when she tried to remember anything? She knew Edward, surely?

"I regret to inform you of his death. I

hope it will soften the blow of his loss to hear that he died nobly and bravely. I was with him to the very end, so I can vouch for everything. His family may be justly proud."

"Oh, dear! Excuse me. I think, mayhap, a drop of sack to calm my nerves. Sir?" Hubert sounded horrified.

Isobel heard the clink of glass from below. "Oh, my poor darling Isobel. This could be the end of her."

She froze at the sound of her name. Hubert rarely sounded so concerned about her.

Cavendish asked, "The *end* of her?"

There was a hard edge to his voice. Perchance he cared no more for Hubert than she did herself. Nay, she should not be so ungrateful. Her cousin was trying to make her better, and he kept away ignorant physicians who didn't understand such maladies as brain fever.

"Edward and Isobel were very close, you understand. She is greatly changed since he went away, care-worn and worried. With good reason, it appears."

"You weren't close to him yourself, sir?"

"Alas, no. Our sires quarreled you see—one of those ridiculous feuds that can take hold in even the best of families. I have endeavored to make amends since their demise, of course. How fortunate that we did, or the girl would have had no one to care for her in her darkest hour. Are you certain Edward is dead? Where did it happen?"

There was a pause before Cavendish answered. "I watched him die—I cannot tell you where. I've barely slept the night through since."

"Cannot, or will not tell me? Edward never *did* say where he went to make his name as a soldier."

"My lips are sealed. You must appreciate that youngbloods seeking favor at court are wont to get themselves into mischief—I would not harm his memory by revealing his secrets. But if you don't trust my veracity, I have here the seal ring he gave into my keeping. And a signed note—it's in my baggage, and can be fetched if required."

Had Orpheus been fighting? Perhaps in Greece, or at Troy? Isobel shook her head—this was very confusing.

"Where *is* Isobel? I was charged to give her my news in person."

She sat bolt upright. Was she going to be

allowed into the parlor? That was where her harpsichord was—how she'd missed being allowed to play it!

"As I said—she has not been herself since Edward went away. I fear for her sanity. It is neither meet nor proper that she should come down and receive these tidings in her present state. I shall tell her when I deem 'tis right."

No! Hubert was going to deny her. Tears pooled in her eyes.

"You're welcome to stay the night and recover from your journey. You'll soon see we have nothing to hide."

She dashed the tears away. Orpheus was staying the night? There was hope yet she might meet him face-to-face.

"Most hospitable of you, sir, but I *must* see Mistress Marston. 'Twas a deathbed promise I made to her brother, and thus cannot be broken."

Hubert made no answer—he hadn't expected the stranger to be so persistent, had he? Isobel clenched her fists—it was as much as she could do not to fly down the stairs and tell the stranger how desperate she was for company.

"Mayhap I've not made myself clear enough," Hubert said. "The young lady is barely in her right mind. Her wits have been addled for some time now, and the information you bring could unhinge her completely. I'm sure Edward would not have wished you to take such a risk, had he known."

She heard a chair scrape back as someone got to their feet. "Perchance I've not made *myself* clear. I wish to see Isobel Marston in the flesh, forthwith."

"Very well. On your head be it if she falls into a rage or a swoon, and all the goodness we've lavished on her these last few weeks is wasted." Hubert was clearly irritated. "Be warned—you'll not care for what you see. But be assured we know her mind well enough and will tell you if she's likely to strike you."

Yes! Hubert had given in. Isobel scuttled back to her room, closed the door and sat on the bed, heart pounding. Soon, the heavy tread of Flinders' feet could be heard on the stairs—he'd be angered at being torn away from his kitchen wench. Hopefully, he'd not revenge himself on *her*.

Moments later, Isobel was ushered into the parlor, Flinders' thick fingers gripped tightly around her elbow.

CHAPTER TWO

S IR WILLIAM CAVENDISH spun around, his breath catching as he stared at the woman he'd waited so long to see. He'd been expecting a well-bred, proper young lady, not this wild sprite who looked as if she'd just stepped out of the madhouse. Tall and willowy, Isobel Marston moved with grace, keeping her elfin chin up. But her raven-black hair was unconfined by coif or hat and straggled about her face and shoulders. Disturbing green eyes stared at him intently beneath dark, lustrous lashes. Her flawless skin was pale, with shadows around the eyes and beneath the cheekbones, and she wore a worn skirt and bodice, haphazardly laced and with several of the waist tabs hanging off.

No wealthy young lady, this. More like a guttersnipe. Will could barely keep the astonishment from his face. Astonishment laced with anger.

"Had we expected you, Sir William, we would have made her more presentable. 'Tis pointless bedecking her in finery on an ordinary day—as you see, she tends to ruin clothes."

Fie on the fellow for discussing Edward's sister as if she were less than a person! Will had learned a lot about her, and about his friend's home, Marston House, during those grim days in the Lowlands. He'd been eager to meet the accomplished young woman whom Edward held in such high esteem.

He stood before her and proffered his hand. She stared at it as if it were some new kind of vegetable, then raised her bewitching green eyes to his.

Master Pike cleared his throat. "My apologies. Since her illness began, she has forgotten her manners. Shake hands with Sir William, Isobel."

She cowered, then took Will's hand. And failed to let go.

What thoughts passed behind those beautiful, unfathomable eyes? She had no polite smile for him, no maidenly blush. Mayhap, after all, he should *not* have insisted on seeing her when she was so clearly not in her right mind. He gently disengaged his hand.

"It's Orpheus, returned from the underworld." She sounded like some actor in a Greek tragedy, proclaiming their lines. "Don't look behind you, or Eurydice will sink back into the depths, and you'll never see her on the earth again."

Baffled, Will looked at Pike.

He smiled sympathetically. "Be not alarmed. She rarely speaks two words of sense together. When she's like this, I doubt she'll understand the tidings you bring—though you may attempt it if you wish. Sit down, Isobel." Pike raised his voice when he spoke to her, enunciating every syllable clearly. "Sir William has something to tell you."

The young woman settled herself obediently onto the high-backed settle, and continued to stare silently at Will. Then she gazed around the room, a slight frown between her brows as if she were looking for something.

"Mistress Marston, let me make myself known to you." He was determined not to lose face in front of Hubert Pike, nor to fail in his quest. Not when he'd come so far, and been through so much. "I am Sir William Cavendish. I served as a soldier with your brother."

There was no response. She looked to have forgotten his existence. He approached the settle and crouched before her, ignoring the protest from his injured leg. "You remember your brother, Edward, Isobel? It must be around seven months since last you saw him."

She focused on him again. Encouraged, he continued, "I regret—I bring you bad tidings. Your brother died during a raid. I got him to the surgeon, did what I could, but his injuries were too severe."

He paused and swallowed hard. The scene of carnage after that raid at Venlo had never left him. The blood, the sickly color of Edward's face, the sheer horror of it all. He'd been so shocked by his friend's wounds that he'd not even noticed his own. Until the surgeon had pointed it out—after which point, he remembered but little.

He cleared his throat. "Before your brother died, he bade me take good care of you."

A sharply indrawn breath from Pike distracted him. Of course, the man would not welcome any interference in his dealings with Isobel. But Will was bound by a deathbed promise, and too hardened by his recent experiences to give a farthing for Pike's feelings.

Still no response from Isobel, who continued staring dazedly around her, as if she knew not where she was. Had she any idea of the significance of what he'd just said?

He turned to Pike. "I have Edward's rapier outside, strapped to my horse. Mayhap *that* will push the message home. Shall I have my saddlebags brought in at the same time, if your offer of a bed for the night still stands?"

Not that he had any great desire to spend more time in the company of Master Pike and his insane patient, but weariness and pain were starting to take their toll.

The gigantic manservant fetched his belongings, but Will refused to entrust Edward's sword to him. He'd had a box made to accommodate it, and carried it reverently into the parlor, like a sacred relic. He set the box down in front of Isobel.

She stared at him, avidly. "Sir—what, pray, have you done with my harpsichord?"

"I—" He caught Pike's attention, but the man just shrugged. "I've done nothing. I didn't come here to speak of musical instruments. Isobel—"

As he looked into her blank but delicate face, his gut twisted. Was he attempting the impossible in making her comprehend her brother's death? Was *he* the only one left to mourn Edward's passing? Pike's sympathetic expression was unconvincing, and Isobel was trapped in a world of her own—unknowing, unseeing.

Seating himself on the settle beside her, he made a final effort. "Mistress Marston—Isobel—your brother, Edward, is dead. He charged me to give you this, in remembrance of him."

When she reached for the box, optimism stirred. Until she smiled and exclaimed, "Pandora's box! I have always wondered what Hope looked like." She opened the lid.

A tragedy that a woman so clearly out of her wits—and with little in the way of genuine hope—should look to an ancient myth in search of that valuable thing.

Jaw set, Will looked at Pike. "Wherefore does she cite so many classical references?"

Pike shook his head. "There may be reason or connection in what she says, but I have yet to understand it."

"*No!*" Will grasped Isobel's wrist in time to stop her pulling the sharp blade from its scabbard. She seemed startled for a moment, then reached out slowly, and stroked the side of his cheek. He gazed, transfixed, as her face fell. Did she understand what had happened, at last?

"After the Maenads tore him limb from limb, his head floated singing down the river."

Will recoiled and removed himself to a chair.

"Another classical reference, to Orpheus, I believe."

"Yes, yes, Master Pike. I know that." What he didn't understand was *why*. Why was she talking in riddles? Why had this lovely woman been reduced to this state, and how? Edward had said nothing of any sickness of the mind. Indeed, he'd portrayed his sister as a handsome, lively, witty and accomplished young woman.

Will had seen too much illness during the Earl of Leicester's disastrous campaigns in the Lowlands to fear it. He was fascinated by Isobel, while at the same time, consumed with pity. Did anything of the woman Edward had described remain behind those tortured green eyes?

Suddenly her head shot up, her face even whiter than before. "Oh, oh, help me, I beg you!" Her entire body shook with a sudden burst of tears.

He was by her in an instant—had his message about Edward's death finally penetrated her clouded mind? The urge to take her in his arms was powerful, and deep compassion clutched at his heart. Only—he must remember he had an audience.

"Flinders, fetch Avice. It's time for Isobel's medicine. Apologies, Sir William—this is never pretty to witness. But needs must—hysteria will ensue if we fail to calm her this instant."

An unpleasant scene then followed, in which Isobel's arms were pinned behind her by Flinders while the woman, Avice, poured some dark, sticky-looking nostrum down her throat. Isobel coughed and choked, then fought with her captor before she was eventually subdued and carried from the room.

Will folded his arms across his chest and raised an eyebrow at Pike, but said nothing. How fortunate he'd agreed to stay the night. The loyalty he owed his friend now belonged to Isobel.

And it looked as if she was damned well going to need it.

CHAPTER THREE

ONCE UPSTAIRS, THE noisome Flinders shoved Isobel into her room. Then Avice's rough hands took over, tugging at her laces, wrenching off her shift, petticoat, and shoes. Shivering, miserable and confused, she was forced into her nightgown and made to lie down.

No sooner had Avice left the room, than Isobel threw off the covers and ran over to wrestle with the door. There was a reason she mustn't be shut away, something she needed to tell someone. But whom? And why could she not remember what it was so imperative she say?

Relief came when the door opened, but it was Flinders who stood there, not Avice.

She quailed, and backed away. His blotchy face was twisted by an evil leer. He terrified her so, she should scream—but she'd tried that before, and no one ever came.

"I'll brook no trouble from you tonight, girl." His voice was a growl.

She couldn't help herself. "But something terrible has happened. I must go… somewhere, do something." The tears were back, but the fight within her was ebbing away.

"Get back into your bed, wench." Flinders took an ominous step closer.

"Don't you come any nearer. Don't dare lay a finger on me." She fought the drowsiness in her limbs and her head.

"Shut your noise." Flinders dealt her an open-handed slap across the cheek. As she wilted, sobbing loudly now, he picked her up and threw her onto the mattress. Terrified, she readied herself for battle, but he didn't touch her again, only tucked the covers so tightly around her that her arms were trapped by her sides.

Coffins. Her mind was filled with images of corpses bundled in their winding-sheets, trapped in coffins as she now was in her bed.

Fury lashed at her. She spat curses as

Flinders left and locked the door behind him, wishing she could free her hands and throw something. But gradually—as it always did—the medicine took hold of her mind, soothed her pain and lulled her into peaceful oblivion.

Only—she wasn't quite asleep. Or if she was, she had a wonderful dream.

Orpheus came. He brought a lamp and held it aloft, gazing at her. She wanted to tell him to go away, not to look at her when she was like this. Her tangled hair was spread across the pillow, as they hadn't bothered to tie her coif over it. Her eyes stung from her tears and must be rimmed with red, and the pain in her cheek portended a bruise. He shouldn't look at her so intently, so softly, when she was at such a disadvantage, but even though her lips moved to chastise him, no words emerged.

He leaned in close, the dream so real, she could feel his breath on her face. Was he going to kiss her? Had she somehow turned into Eurydice? Seldom did her soporific medicine give her so glorious a dream.

He eased away without touching her, and said, "I could almost believe myself bewitched. Or enchanted—I know not. I care not. I swear on my life, I will do what I can to ease your suffering."

Her heart was full. This glimpse of happiness was no more than a cruel torment. She would awaken in the morning, and all would be as it was before—her room empty of all her things but her precious book of Greek and Roman myths, her blurry mirror, and her comb.

And her memory of the night Orpheus came to earth to visit her. If only there were some way to keep that memory alive. Because some oracular inner sense told her he was going to be incredibly important to her.

CHAPTER FOUR

I SOBEL WAS IN the walled garden, enjoying the July sunshine and transplanting a batch of colewort seedlings from the potting shed. Her eyes were inexplicably sore today—had something happened yesterday to make them so? Perhaps the demon nightmares had brutalized her sleep again, as they so often did. But all was well now if only she could keep her thoughts on what she was doing.

A man was coming towards her, down the gravel path from the house. It wasn't Hubert, and it wasn't Flinders—she knew that because neither of them had the poise or physique of this man. Then something struck a chord in her memory.

"It's Orpheus!" Delighted, she struggled

to get up, but her skirts were a muddle, and the strength had left her limbs. Puzzled, she gazed at him as the man smiled and hunkered down beside her.

"God give you good day, Mistress Marston. What are you about?"

She peeped into her basket. "Planting coleworts, it seems." Only, her fingers were all a-tremble. How could she separate out the tender seedlings without damaging them? It must be Orpheus' influence.

She shaded her eyes. There was something she was meant to be telling him. Wasn't there? "They're poisoning me, you know."

"What, the coleworts?" He looked amazed.

"Nay, foolish fellow, coleworts aren't poisonous."

Ah. That wasn't the way to talk to a demi-god—he looked taken aback. She flushed.

"What I mean is—it's good to see you so well-recovered. With your body intact, I mean." By the rood, she was making a midden of this!

The man appeared to ponder her words

for a moment, then nodded. "Thank you. Pray, let me assure you that I am *not* Orpheus, and I have not been ripped limb from limb by a group of crazed Bacchantes. I'm William Cavendish, your brother's friend. Just 'Will', if that's easier for you to remember."

He paused, his aspect softening. "Do you remember what I told you last night? About Edward?"

She shook her head to clear it, with little success. "Edward was dark." How did she know that? "You are fair. Are all Greeks fair?"

No. That was not what she meant to say at all. Turning away in frustration, she jabbed at the ground with a sharpened stake, making holes for the seedlings. She heard the rustle of the man's movement, felt his shadow pass over her as he rose and walked away. Her hand stilled, and she watched him.

He had a limp, much in evidence as he patrolled the garden, giving the gardener a passing nod and looking around with apparent appreciation at the well-tended brick paths and herb beds. He paused by a raised bed which was displaying a magnificent range of purple, pink and crimson poppies. She knew if the new gardener didn't cut the seed heads, the whole garden would be full of poppies, with no room for anything else. Which would be a pity, as you couldn't eat poppies—she remembered that. She also knew she disliked the poppies, though she couldn't recall why.

Will, Orpheus—whoever he was—stooped to examine the dried seed heads that remained from the previous autumn, tracing a finger over the even series of scratches which had bled a dark brown resin. He straightened abruptly and beckoned the gardener across.

What was the gardener's name? She used to know it. Why did he look so different now, as if he were a stranger?

"What do these scrapes mean?" Orpheus asked.

The gardener wiped a sleeve across his forehead. "Avice—Goodwife Quill, I mean, uses the poppy juice for her potions. I don't know how, sir. I believe her husband, God rest his soul—was an apothecary. Poppy juice is good against pain and promotes sleep. I guess she takes it herself—the other servants say she snores like a hog, but she never wakes herself up, so it works. Oh, forgive me, sir. I didn't mean to speak out of turn."

Isobel bit her lip. She shouldn't be listening to someone else's conversation, but she couldn't help herself. It lightened her heart when Orpheus… no, *Will*, laughed lightly and shook his head.

"'Tis no concern of mine," he said. "I barely know Goodwife Quill. Did *you* plant the poppies?"

"Nay, sir. I only came last month. The last gardener was a good one, by all accounts—I'm surprised they let him go."

Isobel saw their visitor stiffen. "Wherefore did they let him go?"

"I know not. He didn't please Master Pike, mayhap. I was glad enough of the work, as my wife has been brought to childbed again. Another mouth to feed."

Another mouth to feed. She was meant to be planting coleworts for everyone to eat, wasn't she, not eavesdropping. Hurriedly, she stuffed some plants into the holes she'd made.

Yet, if one couldn't help overhearing, that was no sin, was it? She kept her head bent over her task, ears straining.

"I came with news of the young master's death. Did you know Edward Marston?"

"Not I. 'Twas afore my time. I sorrow to hear it—the young lady won't take it well. If she takes it at all."

"Are there any old retainers I could talk to about Master Edward? He was a good friend, and I should like to have someone join me in mourning him."

There was that name again. Edward. It meant something she couldn't quite grasp. She gave up all pretense of gardening and stared at the two men.

The gardener frowned down at his mud-clogged boots. "I can't think as how there is. So far as I know—and they don't all talk to me, of course—but I think everyone's been hired recently by Master Pike. On the young mistress' behalf, as she can't manage it all herself."

"Hmm. Thank you. I'll disturb you no longer. Ah." Orpheus had caught her staring, and she ducked her head, but he walked across and held out his hand to help her up.

It was an honor to touch his hand. She felt the spark of his divinity and wondered how Leda, and Europa, and all those others, had avoided being charred to ash when they were chosen by the all-mighty Zeus.

She was escorted to the furthest corner of the garden, where the man put his head close to hers.

"Orpheus." She touched his cheek.

"Nay." He pressed her hand down but retained it in his own. "Will, remember? Will Cavendish. Your brother's friend."

"I have a brother?"

"Once, you did, aye. But that can wait. It strikes me that anyone who knew Edward—or yourself, before your illness—has been removed from the house. Your cousin, Master Pike, has a free hand here, with the aid of Goodwife Quill and that walking megalith, Flinders. I fear you may need protection from your own relation. But how is it to be accomplished? I have no right to intervene, no right at all."

She chewed on her lip again. The man was profoundly troubled—she sensed it. What could she do to help?

"There's a clerk, my father's man of business, Master Bradshaw. He has a room at Gray's Inn."

Orpheus—nay, *Will*, dropped her hand

like a hot coal. "What did you say?"

She didn't know why he was so surprised. She repeated the name and address.

He grasped her shoulders, gazing deep into her eyes. "I know you're still in there, Isobel Marston. I shall bring you out of the darkness, whatever it takes."

She beamed back at him until a male shout made him drop his hands and step away. Hubert was scurrying down the path. Her smile vanished.

"Isobel. I hope you've not been goading our visitor." His voice was that of a strict schoolmaster, contemplating use of the birch. She shrank back, and Will stepped in front of her.

"Nay, sir, she has troubled me not at all. I have tried, and failed, to get any word of sense out of the lady."

Ah. She'd thought she was managing to make herself understood—a forlorn hope.

Hubert looked relieved. "I'm not surprised. We had such a time of it last night— she could hardly be restrained at all." He threw up his hands with a dramatic flourish. "Did you know the insane can fight with the strength of ten men?"

"Perhaps we could use a few of them on the battlefield." She could hear the smile in Orpheus' voice. It made her feel warm inside, but she still cowered at his back, hoping to avoid Hubert's spite.

Will bowed. "I thank you for your elegant hospitality, sir. You have a well-stocked physick garden here, as well as flower and vegetable beds, and an attentive gardener. The house is in good order. Is it true the servants are but lately come into your service?"

"Thank you, thank you. I pray you will break bread with us again before you leave?"

"I shall be glad to. Mistress Marston had better go in and wash her hands before she breaks her fast."

"Oh, she won't be joining us."

Of course, she wouldn't. Pike treated her like an animal sometimes. It wasn't as if she'd forgotten how to use her knife, or her napkin, or drink without spraying water all over the table.

When Will cocked his head at Hubert, her cousin continued, "I mean to say, her conversation sits not well when one is at one's meat. You do recall what she was saying about Orpheus yesterday?"

Will made a dismissive gesture behind his back, and his broad shoulders shook. Something flared to life in Isobel's belly—he was laughing at Hubert, and letting her see it. But Hubert was oblivious. She stifled a snort—she couldn't remember the last time she'd wanted to laugh. A strong instinct warned her not to give in to it now.

As Hubert bustled away with her newfound friend, Isobel meandered back to her basket, then sank to her knees and began woodenly planting coleworts, her mind busy. Could she trust the fair-haired man, whose name she couldn't remember? He hadn't gripped her painfully, like Hubert and Flinders did, nor dealt her a slap, as Avice did when she became overexcited.

The handsome stranger had given her his time and attention, had tried to speak with her. But could he *help* her? Did he know any physicians who could improve on the treatment her cousin was providing?

Sometimes, when her thoughts were less clouded, she questioned the way she was dosed for her brain fever. When she needed the medicine most, they didn't give it to her.

But when she felt at her most lucid, they reveled in pouring the stuff down her throat.

She stared at the soil on her hands. This wasn't right. She must go in and wash. There should be a bowl of water in her room, with sweet rose petals floating in it, or lavender. She hurried inside and headed for her bedchamber, keen to cleanse herself in the scented water. But suddenly, Flinders was there, blocking the passageway. He steered her into a tiny cell of a room and locked the door on her.

Feeling stifled, she hurried across to the window and saw a man emerging from the front of the house, placing a high-crowned hat on his tawny-gold head. A massive wave of despair drenched her as she saw he was leaving, striding away with a peculiar crooked gait. She tried to throw open the window and call to him, desperate to see Orpheus' startling blue eyes looking up at her. But a frantic fumble had no effect—the window was nailed shut.

Subsiding against the cold stone mullion, her tears wet the glass panes, already misted by her sobbing breaths. Would he ever come back? He *must* come back. There was something of great import she must tell him, something to do with Hubert, and poison and—oh, he'd know what she meant when she told him.

But nothing in Hubert's behavior suggested the man was *ever* likely to be invited to Marston House again.

CHAPTER FIVE

AS HIS HIRED mount cantered away, Will tried to put his unsettling encounter with Edward's sister from his mind. He'd discharged his duty, and proved his loyalty to his dead friend. Now, he must pick up the shattered pieces of his life, put the disastrous Dutch campaign behind him, and find the peace he so desperately sought.

War did terrible things to a man. The wounds went deeper than the flesh. Yet, how could he have remained at home, lazing by the fireside, knowing the Spanish scum who'd killed his younger brother, Simpkin, were advancing relentlessly on the fiercely Protestant Low Countries? England had a duty to her allies, to her fellow Protestants—

it was how the world worked these days.

And what better way for a young man—two young men, in fact, as he'd persuaded Edward to accompany him after one cup too many in a tavern—to make their fortunes? What better way to make a name for themselves, to find favor at court under the aegis of the queen's favorite, the Earl of Leicester, than to accompany the English troops sent to assist the Dutch?

Will sniffed at the air. It wasn't fresh, exactly, as this was London, but at least it didn't stink of black powder, unwashed bodies, sickness, and blood. The Dutch campaign had been doomed from the start. Troops were starved of support from Queen Elizabeth, and went unpaid for months, suffering the leadership of a man unable to navigate the choppy waters of Dutch politics. But there was no point bemoaning the miseries he'd experienced—Will was back in England, no one knew where he'd been, his family's reputation was intact, and he must be grateful for what he had.

His surroundings took on a familiar aspect, the timber-framed houses packed more closely together, leaning drunkenly on their neighbors, jettying over the street like zealous gossips trying to whisper in each other's ears. He was almost home. He could slide out of his traveling clothes and into a delicious tub, soak his aching limbs, and rub some arnica salve into his damaged thigh.

"Cavendish? Hold there, Cavendish, it *is* you. Stay a moment."

Someone had hold of his horse's bridle. Without thought, Will's hand flew to the hilt of his sword.

The man released the leather strap. "Whoa, there, sirrah, do you not know me? Thy neighbor, Mathieson. I beg you, kill me not, as I mean you no harm."

Will's hand relaxed, and he dismounted carefully, keen to conceal the stiffness in his leg. "Forgive me, Mathieson—my mind was elsewhere."

"As have you been. I've not seen you in a good six months or more—we thought you were dead. Poor Paulina has been weeping her eyelids raw for worry over you."

Will bowed. "Your daughter is a sweet lady, but there was no need. I've been in no danger."

Mathieson, a grizzled former courtier

fallen from grace, was no great friend. Used to the in-fighting that went on around the queen, he was utterly untrustworthy, continually contradicting himself, and forever involved in dubious money-making schemes. These—thus far—Will had managed to avoid.

"I'm glad to hear it." The man's eyes scanned Will's horse, his clothes and saddlebags. "You've been traveling, then. I assured Paulina that was all it was, but she swore you'd have told her if you were going away. She was certain some ill had befallen you."

"No ill." Will frowned. They shouldn't be talking like this in the street, especially not about Paulina. He'd never given the woman any reason to worry over him, had done nothing to secure her interest. Now Mathieson was making it sound as if she'd set her cap at him—which was the very last thing he wanted.

"I'm weary, sir, if you'll forgive me. I'll just walk my horse along a little way and rouse my servants to heat me some water. Mayhap I'll call on you upon the morrow when I am more myself."

Mathieson's smile didn't reach his eyes. "Ah, but I have something for you. A messenger came a few days ago with a packet. A sealed package. I've seen the seal before, so he didn't need to tell me it was from the Earl of Leicester. Of course, I did the neighborly thing and took it in, as we'd no idea when you might return, and we all know servants are not to be trusted. The messenger wasn't keen to give it up but a shilling persuaded him. I shall not charge you for that." Mathieson sniffed and looked smug, then added, "Now, why don't I send a boy to alert your staff you're on your way, while you come to my house, sup with us, and retrieve your packet?"

Will didn't like the way the man narrowed his eyes, or the touch of those fingers, digging into his shoulder. A serpent of doubt slid down his spine. Mathieson had that look about him, the subdued excitement of another scheme, a brightness to his eyes like that of a hound on the scent.

"From Leicester, you say? That does surprise me. I wonder what he can have sent me, and why." It wouldn't do for Mathieson to know Will was Leicester's man. He who had once been Queen Elizabeth's favorite had blackened his own name by taking the title of Governor of the Netherlands against her wishes, and later, he'd executed the Governor of Grave for surrendering to the Spanish. It had been a grim affair, sickening both Will and Edward, but their loyalty to Leicester remained steadfast. What else could they do? They'd been in an impossible situation.

Of course, Leicester's detractors had made the most of it, whispering lies and deceit into the queen's ear. Consequently, now was not a good time to be openly supportive of Robert Dudley, Earl of Leicester. Particularly not in front of scheming neighbors like Mathieson.

But if Will didn't accept the man's invitation, he'd never get his packet.

He made a gracious bow. "Most generous, sir. Send a boy if you will. I may not stay long—I'm not dressed for company and, as I said, am weary from riding."

Mathieson dispatched a messenger, along with Will's horse for stabling, and opened the heavy oak door that led into his plot. Larger than most on the street, it boasted a cobbled courtyard, an herb garden, and small fishpond. The building itself was a towering three stories high, allowing much-needed access to light and air from the top floor. As the men entered, some doves fluttered noisily up from the yard to perch on the roof of their rickety dovecote.

A young woman, blonde and rosy-cheeked, glanced up from scattering seed. As soon as she saw Will, her eyes lit up, and she hurtled towards him across the cobbles, then bobbed a breathless curtsey.

"Sir William! I cannot believe 'tis you. We had given you up for dead. I asked your housekeeper whenever I saw her but she swore to me she'd heard nothing of the kind."

She linked her arm with his. "Why so secretive? Why depart without bidding us farewell? I should chastise you, I truly should—should I not, Father? I have quite broken my heart over you."

Ah, Paulina Mathieson. His memory of her had faded in his time abroad. He'd forgotten how pretty, but not how garrulous she was, nor how inclined to be a nuisance. Most women would have matured in over half a year but she, it seemed, was reluctant to relinquish her girlish behavior.

"I regret you have done so. As you can see, it was needless." As Paulina bounced him towards the house, he made sure to conceal his limp. The family was too sly, too apt to ask awkward questions.

She hugged his arm tightly. Yes, very pretty, but he knew her rosebud mouth was quick to pout or droop when she failed to get her way. He'd seen her pinch a female servant on more than one occasion, and whenever she walked abroad, her nose was held so high, it surprised him she wasn't forever stepping in something. As soon as they were within the home, he disentangled himself.

The commodious parlor housed Goody Mathieson, Paulina's mother, working a square of cutwork embroidery in her lap, and one other person, a gentleman who was leaning against the empty stone fireplace. As Will doffed his hat and handed his cloak to a manservant, the man came forward.

"Good morrow." The stranger spoke with the hint of an accent.

"Good day to you, sir." In the dim light that filtered through the window, Will could see the man was short in stature, though well-made, sporting a doublet with the fashionable peasecod belly he himself despised. He'd far rather his clothes fitted him—padding was a foolish frippery, and impractical withal.

"You are thinking me a suspicious Spaniard, or one of the deplorable Dutch." Dark, intelligent eyes twinkled at Will. "I assure you, I am merely a compatriot of your queen's 'Little Frog', God rest him, but have lived here so long I no longer feel myself French. The Comte de Velors, at your service."

Will had heard of the French count. After Elizabeth's rejection of her French suitor, the Duke of Anjou, the disappointed peer had taken himself off to stir up trouble in the Low Countries, before dying of a tertian ague. De Velors had been in the duke's retinue while he was in England and having—so he claimed—an English mother, had elected to remain here rather than follow his benefactor. He'd spent the past few years borrowing, gambling, and speculating to secure his financial position. Rumor had it that much of his small fortune consisted of gifts from grateful widows and single ladies. However, the comte was allegedly too handy with a sword for anyone to suggest this to his face.

What was this handsome, capricious creature doing in the Mathieson household? Courting Paulina, mayhap? But not for gain, surely—the Mathiesons were middling folk at best, despite their ambitions. He must have been tempted by Paulina's good looks—Mathieson had better watch out, lest his daughter become more of a burden than she was already, by getting with child.

Only… only Paulina was hanging on *his* arm once more, gazing up adoringly at *him*, not at the comte. And both her parents looked on benignly, neither of them castigating her for her impropriety.

Will cleared his throat and extricated himself from Paulina's grip. "I am honored, monsieur." He turned to Mathieson. "Sir, you said you had a packet for me?"

"Aye, here it is." Mathieson held out a package tied with thick ribbon and sealed with the Earl of Leicester's distinctive bear and ragged staff device. Will felt its weight—it was a box, probably containing coin or jewels, the personal payment the earl had promised him for his loyalty.

His heart lifted, but he forced all expression from his face. "Ah, yes, I recall now, he promised me a pair of fine bollock daggers I once admired. Thank you for taking care of them for me."

"How splendid it must be to be friends with an earl!" Paulina clapped her hands together.

"I wouldn't say we were that, in truth."

"Nay, indeed." Mathieson inclined his head, giving Will an oily smile. "Particularly not when he is out of favor at court. The queen's favor means everything, does it not?"

He felt forced to defend the man by whose side he had fought. "Her favor may change."

"It may. But currently, to be associated with the Earl of Leicester is to be at a great disadvantage. The stain of his failure will spread to his associates, and those whose characters are damaged may find their reputations never recover. Unless they are well-supported by powerful friends, relations, or advantageous marriages."

Will stared at Mathieson, who returned his look with one of innocent disinterest.

"Then it is as well he and I have no more than a passing acquaintance."

"He knows you well enough to give you a brace of fine… um, *daggers*." Mathieson nodded meaningfully at the packet.

Aware that everyone in the room was looking at him expectantly, Will huffed out a laugh. "I assure you—I admired the daggers as a politeness when I encountered the man at court and, on a whim, he offered them to me, but I refused. He said he had another, lesser pair in his lodgings I might appreciate. I never expected he would adhere to his promise."

His story sounded weak, but it was the best he could concoct at short notice. The last thing he wanted was for all of London to know what he'd been doing the past seven months. As Mathieson had pointed out, a tarnished reputation meant doors were slammed in one's face. He couldn't allow the ancient name of Cavendish to be sullied thus. No one must ever know the truth.

He bowed. "Forgive me, gentlemen, ladies. I'm keen to return home and unpack my belongings. Pray, dine without me. I shall be but poor company in any case, being wearied and saddle-sore."

"Paulina will be so disappointed." There was a hard edge to Mathieson's voice. A *very* hard edge. The comte looked merely bored, yet something about the atmosphere in the room smacked of conspiracy.

"My apologies again. I shall endeavor to make recompense for my bad manners upon the morrow. Thank you for taking care of my packet. Good day to you."

Will gave them his deepest bow, pretended not to see the hand Paulina held out to him, and beat a hasty retreat. A few quick steps brought him to his own front door, and he entered it with the relief of a man who has just escaped an ambush.

But what had been the purpose of that ambush? And in exactly *how* much danger was he likely to find himself?

CHAPTER SIX

ISOBEL WAS SITTING in the walled garden, admiring the budding fruits on an espaliered apple tree. No one was forcing her to do anything at present, so she could luxuriate in the perfumed air and let her thoughts wander where they would. Hubert had gone out—she'd seen him go, dressed in all his slashed and silken finery. Avice Quill had also left the house, with a basket over her arm and, if she stopped at the Three Tuns as was her wont, she'd not be back for an hour.

Isobel had heard Flinders lock the door between the garden and the house—doubtless so he could be with his kitchen wench again. There was a second door, from the garden to the street behind, but she'd never yet found it unlocked. It was of no matter—she liked the garden, and time spent by herself within it was rare, special. However, melancholy was never far away. In winter, most of the plants would fade and die, as would she if she didn't escape by then.

Her mind and her memory were failing. She was sliding away into nothingness—what had gone before was a blur. What was to come was ceasing to have any importance.

Little wonder she was unsettled. With great effort, she'd pieced together snatches of conversation from the past few days, and now knew—most of the time—that Edward, her brother, was no more. But how could she mourn him as he deserved, when sorrow and love had died within her?

Despite his protestations, she couldn't believe Hubert cared about either her dead brother or herself. He had plans of his own, and she wasn't expected to interfere in them. If only she had the wit or wile to escape! Yet whenever she tried to concentrate, her thoughts drifted away, to be overlaid by immaterial things. Why were the drapes red when she recalled them being blue? Where was her harpsichord, if she'd ever had one?

What had happened to the sword she'd been given, or had that been a dream?

Leaving her turf seat, she strolled towards the poppy bed. They were pretty and colorful, but deep down, she hated the flowers, wanted to wrench them from the soil and trample them underfoot. But she would suffer if she harmed the poppies. *That* had been made abundantly clear by her cousin.

A scrabbling noise made her look up, startled. It was coming from the other side of the creeping pear tree that trailed up the old brick wall. Before she could react, a man had leapt down onto the path and clamped his hand over her mouth.

Instant rage made her bare her teeth to bite, but a voice spoke in her ear, one she thought she knew.

"Isobel. It is I. Be not afeared—I'm a friend, not a foe."

She stilled, forcing herself to calm, and was released. Turning around slowly, she recognized the handsome face that went with the voice, the light blue eyes and tawny hair beneath the rakishly-angled velvet cap.

"Orpheus! You're wearing a different hat

today."

His face brightened. "You remembered. That was well done, Mistress Marston."

She lowered her eyes. "An insignificant detail. Forgive me—I have no recollection of your name."

The man swiped brick dust from his upper hose, then doffed his cap, bowing low. "Sir William Cavendish. It is a lot to remember for a lady with the brain fever. I answer to Will. Much simpler."

She imagined burning his name in her memory, like a brand mark. Hopefully, it would then stay there.

"Why did you jump over the wall?" She could remember seeing him with a limp. Or had she imagined it?

He grinned broadly. "Demi-gods never use gates. Nay, pay me no heed. We both know I'm no Greek hero. In truth, I was told by that man, Flinders, you were out, but I was unconvinced. So here I am." His smile faded. "I wanted to ask you some questions and see how you fared."

Her heart raced faster. If only she could keep her mind clear long enough to tell him. In a massive feat of concentration, she managed to say, "Help me." She repeated the words silently to herself, lest she lose them, or forget the urgency of her need.

"Of course. What sort of help do you need?"

"Help me—" She rolled her eyes, infuriated with herself. It shouldn't be this hard to convey an important request. "Help me… to escape."

He'd laugh at her now, for sure. She wore no chains, and no ropes bound her. Yet she'd made herself out to be a prisoner.

Will whistled out a breath. His face darkened. "It is as I feared. A thousand poxes on that slimy toad, Pike."

Merciful heavens! It sounded as if he believed her. She must drive her point home. Gazing around for inspiration, she spotted the billowing ranks of poppies. Grasping Will's hand, she dragged him towards them.

"There." She pointed. "The poppies are poisoning me."

She clung to his hand, searching his face, willing him to understand what she could not explain.

And then it didn't seem to matter anymore. Whatever had aroused her feelings of urgency diminished, and she looked out across the garden, at nothing in particular.

Will's warm hand closed over hers. "If I have this aright, Pike has some reason for deliberately driving you out of your wits. What manner of man would prey on a helpless, harmless female? None that deserves the name of gentleman, that's for sure. Tempted as I am to throw him in the nearest horse trough, I must get you somewhere safe while I get to the bottom of what is afoot here."

Being somewhere safe sounded appealing, but this fair man was a stranger. Or was he a friend, and she'd just forgotten?

Suddenly his head snapped up. She heard the sound at the same time, the front door of the house slamming, followed by heavy footsteps on cobbles.

Flinders.

The man called Will took her hands and looked deep into her eyes. "We have to go. Now. Do you trust me?"

An impossible question to answer when she was so confused. But if it came down to a choice between Flinders and this man…

There was only one answer she could give if she wanted to escape.

"I trust you."

CHAPTER SEVEN

LETTING HIS BATTLE instincts take over, Will hurried Isobel towards the street gate.

It was locked. Well, if the worst came to the worst, he'd heave her on top of the wall, and scramble up after her. They'd land in the gutter on the other side—unpleasant, but it wasn't too far to drop. Unsheathing his dagger, he tried to prise the door open, and realized the wood around the catch was rotten.

It took but a moment to free the door. Stepping onto the street, he whistled for his mare, Jennet. The hired beast he'd ridden to London had been sent home—a relief, for his own horse had the sturdier back, and was more amenable. The street urchin he'd told to look after her came running up. Feeling in his purse for a coin, Will found a groat and handed it over, then hefted Isobel onto Jennet's back and mounted behind her.

His injured leg protested at his haste, but there was no time to lose. As he urged the mare into a gallop, he heard the distinctive sound of the opposite gate to the walled garden being unlocked. With any luck, Flinders would search awhile before realizing Isobel was gone, which would give them a head start.

Good. One day, he'd like to put his sword through that villain's belly but, for now, he must take care of Isobel and put her beyond the reach of Hubert Pike. As he wheeled left onto Gray's Inn Road, he glanced over his shoulder, but no one had, as yet, emerged through the street gate of the walled garden. If he was lucky, any pursuit would turn towards town, rather than away from it.

As he made another turn, onto Clerkenwell Road, he found the highway filled with laden vegetable carts and packhorses traveling into London. Uncomfortable-looking carriages swayed past with a jingle of harness and the clatter of hooves. If he could put the busy crowd of people between himself and Flinders, all the better. However, to ride on at breakneck pace would attract attention, so he slowed Jennet to a trot and tried to appear as if riding along with a wild-looking woman in his lap were an everyday occurrence.

They'd reached Farringdon now, and the houses were thinning out. Soon, they'd be in open countryside, and no one would look twice at an ardent swain, taking his lady-love for a gallop through the landscape.

Isobel was starting to look around her more, sucking in great breaths of air, her ribs expanding against his hand, where he held her pressed against him. His saddle wasn't made for two—the only way he could ride with her was to have her on his lap. She must be so uncomfortable, yet she uttered not a word of complaint.

She was wearing a coif today, but her raven-dark hair escaped it and hung over her shoulder. With her elfin chin elevated, and her green eyes fixed on distant views, she looked as if all the gloss of society had been rubbed away from her, leaving an untamed creature, free to experience life in a primal, animal way. The thought disturbed him. It excited him too—how he envied her freedom from the chains of a stifling world.

He took the first road he could find heading north, which he assumed must be in the general direction of Hertford. At this stage, he had no idea where he was going, or what he was going to do. His only thought was to put London behind them, and place as many miles between himself and Hubert Pike as possible. His purse was full with some of the coin contained in the package sent him by Leicester, so he should be able to keep them fed and housed for the foreseeable future—if he could think of anywhere Pike wouldn't come looking for them.

Isobel shifted and twisted her head to stare at him. She looked anxious, no longer a wayward sprite enjoying the pulse of nature.

"Who are you?"

Lord, no. Had she forgot him already?

"Isobel, 'tis I, Will Cavendish. Orpheus, if you will. You wanted me to help you escape, remember? That's what we're doing. You're safe now. You're with me."

Her eyes widened. "The journey back

from Hades is never safe. Did the gods not warn you?"

He slackened his fist on the reins and wiped beads of perspiration from his brow. What a fool he was, to confuse her by mentioning Orpheus. The sooner she let go her peculiar fancies and returned to the real world, the better. He must be firm and not encourage her.

"Let us pretend I didn't say that. I am Will Cavendish, and you are Isobel Marston. That's all you need to think about at present."

She pressed her teeth against her lower lip, then nodded. It might have been his imagination, but she seemed to push closer to him then, fitting more tightly into his arms. Then her head drooped and rested against his shoulder.

His heart pounded, even as he felt a new strength flow through his limbs. Whatever the legality of the case, *he* had her now, and she was his responsibility. He would discharge his duty to Edward by caring for her, restoring her to what she once had been, no matter the cost.

So, what was his next move to be? He

dare not go home, lest Pike discover his address. His name was well-known in London—it wouldn't take anyone long to track him down. At present, he feared he was on the wrong side of the law, having abducted Isobel from the care of her nearest relation, even though it *had* been at her own request.

What resources did Pike have at his disposal, what influence, which friends in high places? If he raised the hue and cry, the group of well-meaning citizens would scour the main roads out of London first. That put wayside inns out of bounds, so what were he and Isobel to do for rest and refreshment? Jennet would soon tire of carrying two. Perhaps he *should* have ridden deep into the metropolis, after all.

This was a challenge. In his mind, he was back in the field again, trying to find a billet for his troops, living off the land when their provisions and wages failed to come through. They'd lived on hope and air then, and had survived. But with Isobel, it was a different matter.

Relaxing his speed, he steered off the highway and onto a lesser road. Jennet picked her way around the potholes, but suddenly she lifted her nose to the wind. Will tilted his head and heard it too—the chattering of a brook. God be thanked—the horse could be watered while he and Isobel rested.

Reining in, he lowered the drowsy woman to the ground, then jumped down beside her, gritting his teeth at the pain in his injured thigh.

She followed him meekly about as he led the horse to drink, and knelt to splash some cool water over his face. Her expression was blank, her mind trapped in her own private world. What was she *really* like? Hot-headed, courageous, and noble like her brother? If she ever regained her full senses, and recovered her personality, would he like her? Not that it should matter. He owed her his loyalty, whether he liked her or not.

There was a costrel attached to his saddle. He drained the remaining drops of Malmsey from it, rinsed and filled it, and brought it for her to drink

"How do you feel?"

She took a few gulps from the costrel. "Well enough. Only weary and jogged and jostled. It is a long time since I've been out for a ride in the country. Edward used to take me often. I wonder who will take me now."

His eyebrows shot up. "You remember? I wasn't sure you'd understood—you seemed so *distrait*. I am sorry."

Her face betrayed no emotion. "Sometimes, I remember he is gone. But 'tis hard to picture his face, and my memories are so scant, I find it difficult to grieve. When I am myself again, I shall mourn him properly. When my mind has returned—if it ever does."

Unable to lament her dead brother? How cold-blooded that sounded. Mayhap madness killed off the finer feelings first—mayhap insanity drained the emotions. But what if she *weren't* mad? What if the poppy juice they'd been giving her was the cause of her sickness, not the cure? When she came to her full senses again, her suffering would be great indeed.

He would be strong for her when that moment came—he had enough strength for both of them. But for now, practical considerations were of the greatest import.

"Isobel, listen to me. I must find us a place we may rest and refresh ourselves where we can't be seen. Do you understand?"

She nodded and handed him the costrel.

"Nay, keep it. Sit ye down and stay here with Jennet." He indicated the mare, and Isobel nodded again. "Speak to no one—I shall be back directly."

She sat, wrapped her arms around her knees, and rested her chin on her hands, quiet and trusting as a child. But he felt in his gut he couldn't expect this situation to last for long. A storm would come—he'd seen her start to fall apart without her medicine.

And as he had no intention of ever allowing her near poppy juice again, he knew that storm would break over *him*.

CHAPTER EIGHT

WHEN THE MAN was gone, Isobel rose and went to stroke the horse's rough nose. She hoped it might bring back memories of days when she'd been out riding with her brother and friends. What had become of those friends? Had Hubert kept them away because she was ill?

She stopped struggling with her untrustworthy memory. Her mind was closing down again, and there was nothing she could do to stop it. Not knowing what to do with herself, she sank to the ground and started plucking long grass stems, plaiting them together until her fingers ached. When she tired of that, she looked around her, wondering how long she'd waited, and trying to recall what exactly she was waiting *for*.

She was sitting by a shallow stream in the middle of the countryside. Did that make her a naiad? If so, she ought to be dancing to the pipes. But there *were* no pipes. Didn't naiads wear garlands? She must make one forthwith. Ivy would bend and twine easily, but hadn't she been told not to leave the horse? What if she were to take the horse with her? That would serve, surely—they couldn't punish her then.

"Isobel! Where are you going?"

The man had returned, flushed and out of breath, limping a little. A truly handsome fellow, with hair the color of ripe straw. She flogged her memory to life again, knowing this was important. *He* was important.

"Orpheus. I mean, Will. I was going to look for ivy to make a garland."

"I told you to stay here." He sounded annoyed, but there was pity in his blue eyes. It bewildered her.

"Forgive me."

"No matter. Here." He flung off his short cloak and drew it around her shoulders. It was warm from his body, and she clutched it to her neck, relishing the softness of the fine wool.

"Won't you be cold?"

His mouth quirked up. "I'm a soldier. I'll survive the light breeze of a July day, I imagine. But your clothes are poor and worn—we'll find you something better. Until then, pray, keep the cloak."

She looked down and picked at the skirts of her kirtle. He was right—why was she dressed like a servant? She flushed, ashamed.

Will tipped her chin up with his finger. "Don't despair. Lady Fortune has favored us. We are hard by a large estate. The gates are shut, and I can neither see, nor smell, smoke. There's a cottage in the grounds, the windows of which are all shuttered. 'Tis well screened from the house and the view of any servants who might be looking after the place, so we could lie low there for some time to come. I've found an old dew pond with bushes around it in a neighboring field, thick enough to keep Jennet hidden for the time being. We must climb a wall to reach the cottage unseen, however. Could you manage a climb?"

His excitement conveyed itself to her. Or was it his proximity? Something was making her heart perform a gavotte in her chest. Flustered, she took a step back.

"If we must climb, we must. But I may need help."

He smiled. "You're doing very well, Mistress Marston. Just don't forget what you're doing halfway up. Come."

He led her to a spot where a thick-trunked maple tree overhung a mossy brick wall. Taking her about the waist, he hoisted her onto the lowest branch. "Shuffle along until you come to the wall, then grasp the top of it. You should be able to find some footholds where bricks have weathered away. I'll stay below to catch you if you slip."

She hid her grin as she hitched up her skirts and tucked them into her belt. He might think her a pale, delicate creature, but Edward had taught her to climb trees as a girl. If only there'd been one tall enough for her to escape the walled garden at Marston House! But where would she have gone? She hadn't had Will to help her before. Now, everything was changed.

Will had chosen the spot well. Below the point where she sat atop the wall was a springy-looking evergreen shrub, a laurel, mayhap. She hung for a moment from her fingertips, then slid down into the bush.

As she let her skirts down, Will joined her, wincing as he landed. There was something wrong with him, wasn't there? But her mind had blurred again, curse it! She really must try harder—she'd remembered about Edward and tree climbing. A small start, but a start nonetheless.

As Will brushed bits of bark and twig from his hose, she saw bloodied scratches on his hands. "Oh, you're hurt!"

"Shh!" He raised a finger to his lips. "It's nothing. Prickles from the hawthorn bushes where I hid Jennet."

"Let me see." She took his hand, and stroked a finger gently over the wounds. He recoiled violently, pulling away as if she'd just stabbed him.

"But you said it was nothing." She didn't understand his reaction.

He was looking at her strangely, his body tense. She'd done something wrong, broken some code of manners. Was she going to have to rediscover how to behave once she was better?

Then she remembered something he'd

said, or she'd dreamed he said. He'd called her a witch. A shiver coursed through her.

"Come, Isobel. 'Tis of no importance. The scratches sting a little, is all. Now, have you a pin? We have a cottage to break into."

Her pins, as it turned out, were no use at all on so large a lock, but a bent nail was eventually found with which to pick it. The dexterity Will exhibited as he broke into the cottage was impressive. She wondered how often he'd had to do it before. Had he said something about being a soldier? If so, he might have had to break into places while on campaign, in search of a billet. In fact, hadn't Edward mentioned such a thing in one of his letters?

What had happened to those letters?

Once inside the building, she stayed by the door while Will ignited the kindling in his tinder box and lit a couple of candles. The room was plainly furnished, featuring an oak settle with a carved back, a chest, a linen press, and a chair with an upholstered seat. The fireplace was deep, with a small bread oven tucked on one side, and a separate space for smoking meat on the other. Several mice scuttled about in the corners, and a cobweb draped the gap between the two mulling jugs on the hearthstone.

There was a small press containing a few books. Was there anything there beyond the usual Bible and Book of Common Prayer? She hoped so. Most of the books at Marston House had disappeared. Stored away for safekeeping, Hubert had told her.

"I daren't light a fire, as that would signal our presence." Will was poking about, opening doors, lifting the lid of the chest, peering in the linen press. "There may be some blankets somewhere. I can manage without, so there'll be more for you. I'll light another candle, and see what can be found in the pantry."

While he explored the house, she examined the book press. She chose a volume at random, pulled the candle closer, and settled to the comfortingly familiar task of reading.

Will gave her a broad grin when he returned. It revealed healthy, white teeth and a dimple in either cheek, bringing warmth to his handsome features. It had not been fanciful to compare him to a Greek hero—that strong jaw, those sensuous lips, were just the sort of attributes she would imagine one to have.

"I could only find some dried apples. But when it gets darker, I may be forced to take the horse and see if I can find a hostelry. Hopefully, there'll be one not far off, as I hate to leave you alone. But you'll be hungry, so I must bring something back for us, and get some oats for Jennet as well."

Not exactly nectar or ambrosia. But dried apple slices washed down with well water were most welcome. Part of Isobel urged caution as she ate—she needed to be sure she could trust whatever she consumed. But was she in danger from Will, or someone else? She couldn't remember.

Best to lose herself in the book she'd picked, which was a copy of *Aesop's Fables*. She would face whatever peril was to come when she felt better—and Will would help.

He sat down opposite and gazed at her, the empty fireplace between them. But he said nothing, just left her to her reading.

Gradually, she felt a familiar pressure behind the eyes, and the words melted together on the page. Her heart beat faster, filling her veins with an uncomfortable urgency. Something was amiss.

Her head shot up as the book thumped to the floor. Daylight had faded from the chinks around the shutters, and the man watching her from the other side of the hearth was a shadowed creature of candlelight and darkness.

"Isobel? Do you sicken for something?"

Where was she? Who was the stranger?

"I don't know you." Her hands shook, so she twisted them together in her lap.

"You've forgotten me, but only for now. You asked me to take care of you, remember? I'm Will. Orpheus?" His voice was gentle, and his face looked kind. "You're safe. We're hiding from Master Hubert Pike and his henchman, Flinders."

Hiding? That sounded amusing. She willed her heart to slow. "Is this some manner of game?"

Was that compassion in his eyes?

"Aye, a game, if you will. We cannot allow them to find us."

She nodded her understanding, then realized there was a book by her feet. What was so precious a thing doing on the floor? Opening it, she discovered it to be *Aesop's Fables*. She flipped the book open, then glanced up. "Is there aught to eat?"

"Ah." He drummed his fingers on his knee. "Only more dried apples, alas."

A pity. She'd have loved a mouthful or two of cheese. Pressing a hand against her empty stomach she gazed down at the book.

"Isobel, I fear I must go out to get vittles for us—but I daren't take you with me. You may not stir from the house or make any noise."

She flipped over another page and admired a handsome woodcut of a wily fox. "Was I reading this?"

"Aye. Pray continue to do so until I return. Remember, don't light the fire, or open the shutters or windows. I must lock the door when I go."

Lock the door? She didn't like locked doors. A locked door made a chamber, or a garden, into a prison. But it was too late—he was gone. And she couldn't get out, because they had no key, only the bent nail that he'd taken with him.

She became agitated. Will had bidden her be quiet but how could she be when her feelings were coiled inside her like a snake about to strike? Flames licked up from her vitals and entwined her limbs, making her sweat, exhorting her to panic.

It was impossible to keep quiet and she couldn't remain still. There was a crisis coming, and it would tear her asunder if she didn't do something.

A familiar shape in the far corner of the room caught her eye. She hurried over and flung off the sheet that covered it. A harpsichord—the perfect distraction from disquiet and an empty belly! Dragging up a stool, she flexed her fingers and began to play.

CHAPTER NINE

WILL THANKED LADY Fortune he'd found an inn that was no more than half a mile from the cottage where he'd left Isobel.

Where he'd left Isobel. He should never have abandoned her in her confused state, for who knew of what she might be capable? She'd grabbed at Edward's sword as if it were a toy—what if she should find a sharp knife in the cottage or—God forbid—an ax?

Perspiration broke out on his forehead as he scrambled up the maple tree by the wall of the manorial estate. If Isobel had injured herself, he'd need a physician—then awkward questions would be asked. What if she'd decided to climb out through an upstairs window, so she could make her way back to Marston House? He'd find her in a pathetic heap, with her neck broken, and Edward's ghost would torment him the rest of his days.

Foolish fellow—he'd be jumping at shadows next. He'd left her quietly reading, and had returned as soon as he'd bought provisions, and fed and watered Jennet. Isobel would most likely be asleep and his fears unfounded. But he must take care, and plan more thoroughly next time.

As he pushed through the darkened bushes, struggling not to lose his way in the twilight, a sound made him prick up his ears.

He stopped in his tracks, heart thumping. *Music?* The resonant notes of—what was it? A harp? Nay, a harpsichord. And the noise was coming from the direction of the cottage.

Jupiter almighty! She'd have the whole countryside roused up—at very least, the servants from the manor house would be able to hear. Forgetful of his injured thigh, he ran the final yards and fought with the lock, cutting his hand in the process.

Bursting into the room, he dragged Isobel's fingers from the keys and pulled her to her feet.

"What did you do that for?" She slapped at him, growling, so he seized her wrists in one hand, and when she sucked in a breath, clamped the other hand over her mouth. Then he blew out her candle, and stood in the deep shadow behind the door, listening intently.

For several minutes he held his captive inert, exerting his superior strength, answering every wriggle with a tightening of his grip until the message finally sank in.

No sound. With her body still clamped to his, he moved to the door, closed it softly and locked it. All was silence and darkness. Until Isobel sank her teeth into his bleeding hand.

He bit back a yelp and yanked his hand away. Taking her by the shoulders, he hissed, "Listen to me. You must be *quiet!* Remember the hide-and-seek game? If you make any noise, any sound at all, they'll find us, and there'll be Hell to pay. Now, nod your head if you understand."

His eyes were getting accustomed to the gloom. Every nerve, every sinew was tense, ready to subdue her if she threatened to scream or cry—though he had no wish to hurt her. Closing his eyes, he offered up a silent prayer. And eventually, was rewarded when he felt her nod.

"Splendid. It sounds as if there is no damage done. Now, we may eat. I just need to relight that candle."

His tinderbox was tucked into his doublet, and he found the candle from the acrid smell of tallow smoke. By its flickering light, he unpacked the basket of vittles he'd obtained from the nearest tavern.

"Sit down, Isobel. Here's a crock of hogget stew—though I fear I spilled some getting over the wall. We have bread, a leg of ham, and a dish of butter. There's a costrel of strong ale as well. Feast well—I must return the crocks to the inn come daybreak."

He watched with satisfaction as she filled her stomach. She ate robustly, more like the countrywomen he'd seen in the Low Countries than an English gentlewoman, but he was certain she hadn't always been like that. How long had her conniving cousin been feeding her poppy juice and treating her like a drudge?

He took but little, still recovering from the shock of her making enough noise to give away their illicit presence. Speaking of illicit, they would have to spend the night together. He must remain awake and watchful, lest she attempt to escape, or do something else that revealed their presence.

The cottage had two stories. He'd reconnoitered the top floor, finding a bed and a few linens. Isobel must have the bed, of course—but then, where would *he* go?

Before he'd resolved the issue, she was on her feet, pacing up and down like a caged animal. When he blocked her path to stop her, the look in her eyes sent a shiver down his spine.

"Why do you not sit down, and digest your supper?" He kept his tone calm but firm.

She made a gesture of impatience. "I can't—I need to move. My body gives me no rest. At times like this, Avice's nostrum was the only thing that would calm me."

He set his jaw. "You'll never touch that foul stuff again. Your body and mind must heal themselves."

"How can they without the remedy? You have to fetch some from somewhere—there must be an apothecary hereabouts." She glared at him balefully.

He gentled his tone. "Nay, no more of that. 'Tis for the best, I swear."

Her expression darkened and he sensed her control starting to slip. "What do *you* know about it? You're no doctor. I *must* have my medicine soon, I tell you, or I shall not sleep this night."

"Then neither shall I. It will not be pleasant for either of us. But there will be no more poppy juice while you're under my care."

"Oh, you hateful man, to make me suffer so! *I'll* go and find some if you refuse to."

He folded his arms across his chest. "You're going nowhere." This was harder than he'd imagined. He hated to deny her anything, but the die had been cast the instant he stole her from her garden. He'd always been taught that death would be preferable to defeat, so he was going to be more immovable than the most stubborn of asses. Defeat was not an option.

She shoved against him, so he stepped back against the door and planted his feet farther apart.

This only served to infuriate her more. "Out of my way. I've had enough of your company and your foolish games. I want to go home."

With a composure he was far from feeling, Will gave her a gentle shake. "You're not in your right mind, Isobel. You must fight this urge. We both must."

He felt her shoulders relax, and she gazed up at him, head angled, the anger having mysteriously vanished. It was replaced by a look he'd seen many times before—and to which he'd ofttimes succumbed. But this time, a woman's wiles were *not* going to get the better of him.

"If you are kind to me, I could be kind to you," she suggested.

Not so nicely brought up after all then—or was this what Pike and Flinders had done to her, between them? The thought brought bile into his craw, and he prayed she was just aping the behavior of a serving wench, or some character in a play.

"You won't get around me that—"

Suddenly, she was pressed against him, clinging to his arms, her cheeks stained with color, green eyes feverishly bright. A shudder of desire lanced through him. It came as a complete shock, and he reeled with the power of it. As if propelled by an exterior force, his arms lowered, wrapped around her, welcoming her into his embrace. Her small breasts pushed hard against his chest, and her soft thighs pressed against his own.

Her hands clutched savagely at his hair as her gaze focused on his lips. He fought for control, his breath coming in painful gasps. If only this passion of hers were inspired by desire! How he could enjoy such a woman—his defenses were barely proof against the excitement she aroused.

"Isobel." He kept himself rigid, holding her firmly by the arms. "This is not *you*. 'Tis the drug—or the lack thereof—that makes you behave thus. You don't have to fight with me, and you don't need your medicine. Trust me—it's been destroying you. Combat your desire for it with all the willpower you possess. I will help you—I promise."

Her eyes still darted back and forth, but she went limp in his arms. No sooner did he relax his grip, than she tensed, and tried to heave him away from the door.

Enough was enough. If he had to continually restrain her like this, one or both of them would be hurt. "I regret having to do this, Isobel, but you give me no choice." He untied her woven girdle, ignoring the kicks and blows aimed at him, and bound her hands behind her. Then he hefted her onto the settle, undid his belt, and secured her feet as well.

"Don't even *think* about screaming, or I shall gag you, too. Until you behave, I must make you my prisoner."

She glared at him furiously but kept her lips clamped together. He watched as a tear moistened her eye, but she shook it violently away.

Collapsing into the seat opposite, he ran his hands through his hair. How was he supposed to deal with her in this unhinged state? Had Isobel been a man, he'd feel no guilt about restraining her, but this—this was *wrong*.

"What am I to do when I need the privy? Or will you deny me that as well?"

His head snapped up, and he met her glare. "I hope you don't have supernatural powers, Mistress Marston, for if you did, that look would fell me in an instant."

Not that he was afraid—he didn't believe in witchery or magick. But there was something unearthly about Isobel that fundamentally disturbed him.

"I'll fetch the pot, and leave the room while you use it." He wasn't going outside the cottage again unless she came with him. He'd learned *that* lesson.

"How may I use it when my hands and feet are tied?"

He sighed. Ah, well—at least she was trying to reason with him, not kick or bite. But he knew better than to trust a desperate woman. "I'll untie your feet, but I'm not undoing your hands. You'll just have to manage."

"You brute! You're no better than Flinders. What kind of gentleman debases a woman so cruelly?"

"This kind, evidently." Setting his jaw, he went upstairs, found a pot, and set it by her feet. He untied her ankles and returned aloft.

When he came back, the pot was empty, and Isobel's lips were pale with anger. He raised an eyebrow.

"I can't perform when *made* to."

He hid his frustration. "Very well. We shall go upstairs and prepare for bed. The pot can come with us. And I'll leave a light burning, in case you need anything in the night."

Her face blanched still further. "I'll not share a bed with you."

"You won't have to—not exactly. I don't intend to sleep."

"You mean you'll watch me, like a jailer. I know I asked you to take me away, but I've changed my mind. I want to return to Marston House, forthwith."

He rolled his eyes. Despite being in the most terrible coil, he couldn't make himself regret it. There was a challenge in their situation that roused his blood. And if he didn't hold firm, his efforts thus far would have been for nothing.

"At this hour? We're going nowhere in darkness. Besides which, Jennet needs her rest, as do I. Up the stairs with you."

Muttering, she preceded him above, then sat on the bed, scowling. "I can't undress myself without use of my hands."

Despite the temptation to offer to do it for her, just to see the shock on her face, he realized even *that* wouldn't be possible without untying her. "I suggest you sleep in your clothes. Should anyone discover us here, we'll need to make a hasty departure."

"I do believe, Sir William Cavendish, I have never hated anyone more than I hate *you*."

He turned his back, reaching for a pillow, and pulled the linen chest close to the bed. Her words, though not spoken in her right mind, seared a line of pain through his breast. It was the ingratitude, that was all. This woman must not be permitted to breach his defenses, however much she tried to hurt him. His strength must be enough for two.

"Keep still while I remove your shoes. I'll tie your hands in front now, so you may sleep more comfortably. You know there's no point in struggling, don't you?"

As soon as she was settled, he collected some twine and a pitcher of water from below. Tucking his bent nail under the pillow upon which he intended to sit, he tied the twine between Isobel's wrists and his own. And watched her fall asleep.

Now that all was still and quiet, his thoughts jumped about like chestnuts roasting over the fire. Mostly, they were concerned with the damage he was doing to Isobel by simply being alone with her. If anyone ever discovered they'd shared the same chamber, she'd be pilloried, and her good name ruined.

There was a further problem. His body was all too aware of hers, and the unfathomable attraction he'd felt for her when she'd pretended to seduce him. He was bitterly ashamed of how close she'd come to breaching his defenses. His self-control would be sorely tested if they spent much more time alone together.

It would take little less than a miracle for them both to escape their situation without *someone* getting badly hurt.

CHAPTER TEN

PERFECT! THE MAN had fallen asleep. Using her teeth, Isobel worried at the knot in the girdle, careful not to rouse him. It seemed to take forever but, eventually, she managed to undo it, and untie the cord that ran from her wrists to his. He shifted, and she stilled, but he didn't wake.

The next task was to remove his knife—not easy when it was secured to its sheath with a peace string—but eventually, she succeeded. She meant him no harm, but a knife was always a useful thing to have.

Now all she need do was put on her shoes, and see if she might climb out through a downstairs window. There was confusion about what she'd do once that was achieved.

Some idea of riding back into town and finding an apothecary had entered her head, but that was as far as she'd managed to plan. Getting the next draft of her medicine before her fever rose any higher was her principal aim.

The man let out a moan. She froze, then edged closer to where he sat on the carved press, head lolling towards his chest. He twitched then, one fist clenched as if he clutched a sword, and his head went up.

She must go now—she must run before he awoke. She knelt to lace her shoes, and heard him say, quite distinctly, "No, Edward! Stay with me. Send for a surgeon, make haste!"

She knew that name. Didn't she? Why was her memory so clouded? No matter. She dare not tarry.

He groaned, his head moving from side to side. "Too much blood. There's too much blood."

Her gaze was fixed on his face. If he opened his eyes and saw her, all would be lost. A tear slid slowly down his cheek, and his whole body writhed and trembled, like an animal in its death throes.

No. Don't stay. Go now. This is no concern of yours.

Only—she couldn't bear to watch his suffering. She grasped his shoulder and shook him firmly.

His eyes flashed open, and he focused on her, his jaw slack with surprise.

"Isobel? What is it? You look unwell."

"You were having a dream. Not a pleasant one—I had to wake you."

He straightened, reached for the candle that flickered in the sconce behind him, and raised it, running his eyes over her.

"You've freed yourself." His voice was level, his face unreadable.

"I know."

"And you didn't run, because I was having a nightmare?" He stood, taking her gently by the elbow.

She'd been a fool—she didn't need him to tell her that. "You spoke in your sleep. Of Edward. I have a brother by that name."

Placing the candle back in its sconce, he drew her close, enfolded his arms around her and took her in an embrace so tender it stole her breath.

"My poor girl. You still don't truly understand, do you? But when you do, I fear it will hit you as hard as it hit me, as the hammer strikes the anvil. The pain is excruciating—and I know I'll never forget what I saw. It tortures me often in dreams."

She understood more than he knew—she'd seen that revealing tear. That a man so strong, so determined, could weep for the loss of a friend, was a revelation.

Her hand rested over his heart, reassured by its firm beat, by the powerful muscle that protected it. Without volition, her head nestled against his shoulder.

She *should* feel something. Her brother was no more. This man mourned for him—she must do so, too—yet, the fever, the urgency within her, refused to let her. Each time she tried to concentrate, it was as though her mind were slipping on ice.

"Isobel. By Jupiter—you're burning up. This won't do at all. I'm taking you out of here—I was a numbskull to bring you hither in the first place. We'll find some distant tavern, feather beds for both of us, and a physician. I don't care if Pike finds us—I'll make him regret having done so."

No sooner had he made this decision,

than she was lifted up, wrapped in a cover from the bed, and carried downstairs. Not long thereafter, she was bouncing uncomfortably on horseback through the black of the night, clinging to the horse's neck and fighting the nausea and stultifying brain fog that assaulted her.

After an agonizing eternity, there were lights, careful hands, warmth—and a hot, throat-searing drink that made her cough and sent her into merciful oblivion.

But not for long. It felt as if she slept and woke, and woke and slept, and couldn't be sure exactly which was which. How long this delirium lasted, she'd no idea, but eventually, the sweating abated, she was bathed in cool water, and the panic in her breast eased.

"Goodwife? Madam? How do you fare?"

Isobel groaned. "My head." She'd never felt so ill before. What was it? The sweating sickness? The plague?

Someone prised her lips open with a spoon. Expecting the familiar draft of poppy juice, she was surprised to taste something salty.

"What's this? Who are you?" Her voice was croaky, petulant.

A woman leaned over her, a few grey curls escaping her linen coif. Not someone she recognized.

"Goodwife Franks. The innkeeper's lady. This is bone broth—you may have meat when you're stronger. We're trying to keep the fever down."

Isobel struggled to sit up. "Why can't I move?" She was seized with horror. She was imprisoned again, as in her nightmares. Only this time, there were no serpent-haired women glaring at her, or many-headed dogs lolling their enormous tongues as saliva pooled at their feet. This looked like a perfectly normal person. And yet... she was still held captive.

"You mustn't exhaust yourself. We've just tucked the covers in to stop you thrashing about, lest you be hurt. Here, open wide. The broth will do you good."

As the panic died away, the warm goodness of the soup suffused her body, and drowsiness returned. Mayhap this time, when she slept, the terrifying visions would not return.

The room lightened, darkened, and lightened again. She slept, she woke, and drank broth—which seemed thicker each time she tasted it. On occasion, she was helped from the bed to relieve herself. She hated these times—her bones ached, she could barely stand upright, and she shuddered at the touch of the hands that held her steady, fearing at any moment they would grip and tear into her flesh like the talons of a harpy.

Sometimes there were others in her sick-room, her cell, or whatever it was. One was a man, who stood by her bed and gazed at her with sorrowful eyes, but forbore to touch her. Occasionally, she sensed his presence in the room, but couldn't see him. There was someone else, clothed in black, who terrified her, but his voice was soft, and often, during his visits, she'd be given a drink that calmed and made her feel better.

Gradually, in her waking moments, she felt the strength flow back into her limbs. She was confused, forgetful, not sure of the difference between nightmare and reality, but the fear ebbed, and the turmoil of mind and body eased. She was permitted to sleep however long she wanted, and when no ill dreams assailed her, she always felt better on waking.

After a deep sleep that felt as if it might have lasted days, she opened her eyes and stared for a long time at the ceiling, taking in the detail. The ceiling had remained constant for some time now—it was there when she slept and there when she awoke. It was a simple plaster one—peeling, pitted by the passage of time—and an orange flicker of lamplight danced over its surface, making a play of light and shadow. She felt calm today, and almost content. Yet despite the obvious reality of the ceiling, a powerful sense of unreality cloaked her, as if she were still in a dream.

To test out whether or not she was awake, she stretched her limbs, then noticed how lumpy and uneven her mattress was—like the ceiling, it must have seen the passage of many years. Turning her head, she found herself facing a wall of crumbling wattle and daub—not a brick or stone to be seen. Had she traveled back in time in this particular dream? If so, how could everything seem so real?

She blinked. Her eyes, her head, and her stomach were sore. In truth, her whole body ached as if she'd tumbled from a horse and been trampled. There was a foul taste in her mouth as well. Groaning at the discomfort, she rolled over to inspect the rest of the room. And discovered she was not alone.

Alongside the door, on a crudely carved settle, lay a man, sleeping. His tousled fair hair and striking features stirred memories. A dark stubble roughened his jaw and cheeks, and even in sleep, he exuded a powerful masculinity. Truly, an exceedingly handsome fellow—but how came he to be in the same room?

Staring around in increasing perplexity, she discovered she had *not* traveled back in time. The high-quality doublet and cloak hanging behind the door were cut in the latest fashion, with a multitude of expensive embroidered buttons down the front of the doublet. A pair of paned hose was flung across a chair, along with nether hose and a brace of garters.

Merciful heavens! Had the man discarded *all* his clothing? Slipping out of bed, she tottered across the room to see. Why was she so unsteady on her feet—had she imbibed heavily last night? It felt as if she'd drunk a whole cade of wine.

He was attired only in his shirt, with a blanket over his lower half. The shirt was open at the neck, and loose-sleeved—the material was so fine, it clung to his broad chest. She was sure she could see the hue of his skin beneath it.

Blushing furiously, she took a slow breath to still the racing of her heart. And then looked down at her hands.

She wore a ring—one she'd never seen before. She held it up to the light. It was gold and bore a backwards impression of the letters C and W, surrounded by curlicues. A seal ring, but not hers. Nor her brother's.

She gasped, her hand flying to her mouth. Edward was dead. *That* was why she felt a gaping hollow in her chest where her heart should be. She'd known for many days—weeks, even—had she not? Yet she'd not been able to comprehend it. Now, she believed it. Now, she understood she would never see him again. A gulping sob escaped her as hot tears stung her cheeks.

"Isobel?" The man sat up and swung his legs to the floor. She remembered his voice, she thought, and his face, as in a distant dream. She sensed she need not fear him.

He held her gaze, pale eyes scouring her face. "Have you been restored to us?"

She looked down at herself, at the unfamiliar ring, and the coarsely-woven nightgown. "I know naught of these things. Who put them on me? And why am I not at Marston House?"

"A subterfuge. I feared I'd be courting scandal and undue attention if I didn't claim you as my wife. It was the only way I could share your chamber and watch over you in your illness."

What nonsense was this? "Who the devil *are* you, sirrah?"

Keeping the blanket tightly around his waist, he rose and bowed deeply. "Will Cavendish, knight, at your service. As I've told you on numerous occasions." His lips twitched.

She lifted her chin. "I shall endeavor to remember it. What has befallen me? You have much to account for."

He drew a hand through his hair. "'Tis a lengthy tale. Pray, sit." He indicated the bed, and she sank dizzily onto it as he resumed his place on the settle.

"What do you remember of the past few

days, or weeks even?"

She searched her memory. Aye, she knew this man. And remembered how he'd treated her. "What leaps to mind is the fact that you humiliated me, tied me up like a piece of baggage, and tossed me about on a horse. Oh, and seemed not overly fond of my playing."

He gave a wry grin. "Only the bad bits, then. I assure you, I'm not such an ogre as you believe. I did what appeared meet and proper at the time—be assured, I'm your friend, not your enemy."

Meet and proper? When they were sharing a chamber, and she wore only a nightgown?

"No need to look so cross. You've been under the care of Goodwife Franks, the innkeeper's lady, and her daughter. I come here only to sleep, lest it be commented on that I lie not with my lady wife."

She shook her head. What had happened, that he had to pretend they were married? He'd abducted her, for the sake of her dowry—it was not an uncommon occurrence. But from the look of his clothing, he had no need of coin, so why take her at all?

His next words mirrored her thoughts. "You must be strong now, Isobel, in case you have to prove you're of sound mind to reclaim your home and chattels from Hubert Pike. Forgive me, but I assume you're Edward's heir?"

Her beloved brother, Edward, was dead. She needed no reminder. "I'd been telling myself it was all just one of my hideous nightmares."

The man's knuckles whitened where he clenched the arms of the settle. "Are you well enough to hear this, Isobel? I don't want to send you back into delirium."

She chewed on her lip, relishing the pain. Images of Hubert Pike and the massive bully, Flinders, chased one another across her mind's eye. Potions and punishment, being locked in, a garden burgeoning with colorful poppies, and an ugly woman forcing something down her throat—it was a lot to assimilate.

"Tell me." She straightened her spine—it was better to know than not.

"You know of the conflict in the Low Countries?"

She nodded.

"Good. Now, you must swear to speak to no one else of what I tell you, do you understand?"

She nodded again. Why was he being so secretive?

"You may have heard of the siege of Grave. Leicester was ready to relieve the place, but the mayor surrendered to the Spanish, and was executed for his perceived treachery. An action not sanctioned by the queen, nor approved of by either your brother or me. Indeed, we were so eager to remove the taint of association, we joined a contingent of six-score-and-ten English lances in a raid. Our aim was to lift the siege of Venlo. It was a daring mission—foolhardy, you might say—to breast our way through the Duke of Parma's encampment at night."

He paused, his eyes focusing on a point beyond her head, his expression grim.

"Many were slain or mortally wounded, including your brother, Edward, felled by a shot from a matchlock. I carried him to safety—we survivors took refuge in nearby Wachtendonk. But there was no hope—I held him as his life ebbed away. There was a look in his eyes as he understood the inevitability of his death. How can one imagine what it's like, to know your life is closing down, that the darkness will descend on you in minutes rather than years, and that the whole process is irreversible? He showed indomitable courage at the end, and his last thought was for you."

A lump came to her throat, making her voice catch. "I understand I've been unwell in Edward's absence, and am only just recovering. You're my friend, you say?"

"Always." Suddenly she was in his embrace, cradled against his chest. It seemed the most natural thing in the world to rest her head against his shoulder as his arms tightened around her. The temptation to sob out her sorrow and bewilderment against the soft linen of his shirt was almost overpowering—but he was too much a stranger to her newly awakened self. She knew they'd spent a considerable time in each other's company, yet she'd been barely aware of what was happening for most of it. She'd have to start again, from the beginning.

"I must apologize." He released her and moved to the far side of the room.

She hovered uncertainly for a moment,

then retreated to the bed. "So, what do we do now, Sir William Cavendish? Shall you tell me what my evil cousin, Hubert Pike, has done? And why?"

His brow darkened. "Don't sully your tongue with the name of that blackguard. He has, as far as I can tell, taken over your home, dismissed all your loyal servants, and kept you subdued by feeding you copious amounts of poppy juice."

Ah. She'd asked for poppy juice, hadn't she? Nay, *begged*. But Will Cavendish had refused to give it to her.

"Is that why I've felt so ill? Because Hubert was poisoning me?"

"Making you dependent upon it and poisoning you at the same time, according to the physician. Don't worry!" He put up a hand as her face fell. "He said you'll make a complete recovery, given care and time. I will do whatever is needed."

There was a pain under her heart. "But why would my cousin treat me so? I have done him no harm."

"For financial motives, no doubt. He saw a vulnerable young woman, and took advantage."

She pondered this, chewing on her lip. "But what if Edward had come home? Hubert would have been found out."

"Not before he'd emptied the coffers and sold all the valuables. A criminal and his cronies can vanish easily enough in the alleys and rookeries of London. He must have been certain he'd not be caught."

Anger made her cheeks grow hot. What would she find when she returned home? Would there be anything left?

"I want him punished. Either in this life, or the next. My brother is dead, and my nearest relation prepared to leave me with nothing." Her voice caught.

Will held her gaze, his expression solemn. "I'll not see you bereft. I swore an oath to Edward the day before we undertook that final, perilous mission to look after you. I have his ring, and a signed letter allowing me to deal with your attorney. But if all else fails, I have an alternative solution—so, pray, do not distress yourself."

She wasn't distressed. She was boiling with a rage she struggled to suppress. Her fists clenched in the bedcovers.

Will came closer. "Master Pike shall pay

his dues—I'll see to that. We need proof of his felonies—but I'll not have you go back to Marston House. Not straightaway, at least. Are you well enough to travel? I can hire you a mount from the stables here."

"Aye." The fresh air would do her good and calm her temper. "But if we can't go to Marston House, where shall we go?"

"Back to London—you shall reside with me. I have some matters of my own to resolve, but I can keep you safe while they're sorted, then restore you to your rightful inheritance. And your place in society, for society is where you belong."

"Only if no one finds out about this escapade." She knew enough about tittle-tattle to understand its power, even though it was infuriating.

Will cleared his throat, then took a turn about the room. "I have an answer to that as well, should it be necessary. We can marry. You're not already betrothed, I take it?"

She was too overcome by his outrageous suggestion to answer right away. How dare this virtual stranger be so presumptuous! She yanked savagely at a loose stitch on her nightgown. "I think I'd remember something as important at that. I am not betrothed. Hubert gave me to understand that in Edward's absence, he stood as my guardian. There was no hint of any other interested party."

"I hope Master Pike is *not* your guardian. But if he's condemned for his crimes, it will be of no account. He cannot stand in our way."

What did Will Cavendish mean by pacing about the room, deciding on her future? *She'd* quite like a say in it, too. To immediately exchange the prison of Hubert's devising for the shackles of matrimony was unthinkable. There had to be another way.

"Sir William, let me assure you, I have no intention of marrying you. I'm not ungrateful for having been rescued from the vile machinations of my cousin, but I have no intention of exchanging the power of one man for that of another. And that's my final word on the matter."

CHAPTER ELEVEN

OFFERING HIMSELF TO Isobel to save her good name had seemed the perfect solution. Once they were married, he would be her protector officially, and could guard her against any attempts Pike might make to steal Marston House from her.

Hubert Pike. Hah! If the man had any sense, he'd have taken himself off long since, for fear of being thrown into a cell. As soon as Will had the chance, he'd go to Marston House and see how the land lay—and if Pike had flown the coop, he'd use all his resources to find him and see him punished for the damage he'd done to Isobel.

Alas, Isobel's haughty rejection of his suggestion they marry wounded him deeply.

Much to his surprise, for he'd thought himself hardened by war and misfortune—her blunt refusal was a blow to his pride. Not that he'd set out to win her heart—far from it. He wished only to fulfill his promise to his dying friend, and take care of the woman. Her vulnerability had affected him, and her courage impressed him.

He should have no need of her gratitude—and if she decided she no longer wanted his help, what did it matter? He'd done his duty, hadn't he?

He found he had nothing to say when they went downstairs to break their fast. She was quiet also, and afterwards, as they readied themselves for the short journey back to London, they talked of practicalities only. Gone was the warmth that had sprung up between them when he'd comforted her in his arms. Gone was the close bond he felt they'd forged at the beginning.

As they mounted their horses and rode onto the sunlit highway, his mood lifted a little. He could observe her without her knowing, as she was concentrating on riding the unfamiliar hired horse. Her face showed none of the wildness he'd first observed in her—she was the model English gentlewoman now. Dressed in a new gown he'd procured with the help of Goodwife Franks, and a decent traveling cloak, she gazed straight ahead, her eyes on the road. Her rampant mane of hair had been tamed, brushed and bound, and now resided beneath a lace-edged coif and a very dashing hat which kept the sun from her skin. No one looking at her today would have guessed at the thoroughly unorthodox nature of her story.

If only he hadn't made that ill-judged mention of marriage! He hated how lukewarm she was towards him now. Not entirely unfriendly, but she was keeping him at a distance. Mayhap this was normal to the nature of the *real* Isobel—how was he to know, having only ever seen her in a drugged and unstable condition? The passion he'd glimpsed in her had been inspired by anger, and her attempt to seduce him fed by her desperation to escape. None of her behavior then had reflected the true Isobel. If he wished to soften her heart, he'd have to be circumspect, and start afresh.

Whatever the outcome, he would never

regret this adventure. It had given him a fire in his gut again, the urge to progress with his life, to put aside the ignominies of Leicester's failed campaign in the Netherlands. It was unfortunate his rich benefactor was currently out of favor, as Will would love to go to court and present Isobel. The queen enjoyed a good tale, and she'd have to agree that Isobel Marston, though only the daughter of a wealthy merchant, deserved the opportunity to share her story and to shine at court. Indeed, she'd be one of the brightest jewels in Elizabeth's retinue. She was striking, poised, and graceful—and exuded a magnetism no man could resist.

Jealousy gnawed at him. The idea of any other man wooing Isobel—no. He must not allow himself such thoughts. He should follow the dictates of his head, not his heart. First, he must ensure she was safe in his house, after which he'd consult the lawyer she'd mentioned, and speak to a magistrate on how best to bring Pike to book. This had to be done without dragging the Marston family name through the mire—a difficult thing to achieve, especially with neighbors as inclined to pry as the Mathiesons.

Isobel's cheeks had reddened, and he realized he'd been staring at her unashamedly far longer than was proper. Dragging his gaze away, he saw a rider approaching, followed by a brace of serving men. He made to raise his hat, but his hand stalled in midair.

"Jupiter's bones!" The man reined to a halt, his rounded face wreathed in smiles. "Cavendish, by my kidneys! I haven't seen you since Oxford."

"Aloysius Maybury."

How agreeable it would have been had he managed to get Isobel back to London unnoticed. The gods were *not* smiling on him today.

"You look well, sir." The man had put on a little weight—but from what he'd heard, Maybury had invested in some lucrative privateering, so little wonder if he was plump from good living. A dangerous and deadly business—he'd lost his younger brother, Simpkin in such a venture when an attack on a Spanish treasure ship had gone awry.

"As do you." Maybury reined in, ignoring the scowls of a youth struggling with a heavy barrow of beets who almost collided with him. The road was busy today—not a good place to speak of private matters.

"It has been too long. Is your business in town urgent? I would relish sharing a jug of ale with you in the nearest tavern. And being properly introduced to your enchanting companion." Maybury twinkled at Isobel, who looked down her nose at him.

Taverns had ears, and Will didn't want to entrust Maybury with his story in any case—he had no wish to entrust it to *anybody.*

Seeing Isobel's fingers tense on her reins, he pasted on a jovial smile. "Alas, old friend, we have no time to tarry. This lady is entering my service as a… a seamstress. I would not advise flirting with her." His mind raced. "She is Portuguese and has, as yet, no knowledge of English."

"Indeed." Maybury's smile slipped a little, as his gaze fell to Isobel's fingers. Will looked, too. Saints—his ring! But Isobel had slid one hand over the other, and the gold seal ring was no longer visible. Bless the woman—*she* had more wit than he.

Now, Maybury was running his eyes over Jennet, with the intensity of a man who knew good breeding stock when he saw it. But what he said next chilled Will to the marrow.

"Curious, Cavendish, but just such a horse as this was seen galloping hastily away from my property in Hampstead, bearing both a man and a woman. It was several days since, I grant you, so I doubt it could have been this mare. However, if it *was* you and your Portuguese acquisition, you owe me a blanket and a handful of dried apples. Not to mention the price of a ruined lock."

Maybury's stallion pranced sideways, eager to be on its way. This distracted the man just long enough for Will to compose his features.

"How very disturbing for you, sir. Had you no servants or watchmen to guard your property?"

"The main house, aye, for I was away from home. But the cottage had no such guard upon it as it was considered to contain naught worth stealing. It housed my late steward—not yet replaced—who died there of the sweating sickness. The place has yet to be aired and properly cleaned, lest any contagion remain."

Will repressed a shudder and exchanged a glance with Isobel, who pressed her lips together and paled.

Maybury grinned broadly. "So, it *was* you. Nay, look not so pained. I do but jest. There was no contagion, nor vengeful shade haunting the place. But I must tell you—I know the reason for your subterfuge."

This time, Will could not prevent the shiver that scuttled through him. Was he to be found out so soon, before he'd even put his new plan into action? Saying Isobel was a Portuguese seamstress who spoke no English had not, admittedly, been a part of the plan. He'd panicked when he saw Maybury.

He tilted his head to one side. "What do you mean by that, sir?" He made sure there was an edge to his tone that Maybury couldn't mistake.

"Only that a few days after the felonious entry into my cottage, a man came calling. I'd not give him the name of gentleman, for all that he dressed like one. Called himself Pike, and said a person had recently abducted his ward."

Keeping his face averted from Isobel's, Will said, "I'm sorry to hear it. But I don't understand why you're telling me this."

Maybury leaned forward in his saddle, eyebrows raised.

"Because, like my woodsman, he described a horse matching that which now you ride. One of his servants caught a glimpse of it disappearing up the road."

Found out, so soon. Will hadn't bargained on Pike's tenacity. There must be a great deal at stake for him to be scouring the countryside for Isobel. Suddenly, anger got the better of him.

"That man is a villain, and I'll move heaven and earth to prove it. This lady is his victim, but I'll not say more, as I know not whom to trust. You will forgive me, sir."

"At last!" Maybury's face brightened. "I can see the truth in your eyes, Cavendish, and written in the blush on yon fair damsel's face. You may trust me, I assure you. As soon as I saw that horse, and the lady, I knew you to be the guilty party. You always were one to hurtle around, courting danger and righting wrongs. And I would have crushed that snake Master Pike beneath my heel had I known. Now, why don't you invite me back to your lodgings for a private discussion over a glass of Canary, and see what I may do to help you?"

Will caught Isobel's eye. And was surprised to read amusement where he'd expected dismay.

She inclined her head towards Maybury. "Sir, you have the advantage. Hubert Pike is my cousin, and just such a serpent as you describe. If we may trust you, then I, for one, would be grateful for another ally."

"A wise decision. I like her, Cavendish— we must both take good care of the lady. I cannot wait to hear your tale. In any wise, 'tis best I return with you to your dwelling, for who knows what reception party awaits you there?"

As it turned out, Will had cause to be grateful for Maybury's company, for when he returned to Giles Street, there was, indeed, a reception party.

But not the one he was expecting.

CHAPTER TWELVE

WHILE WILL WAS in conversation with Maybury, Isobel had been subtly trying to remove his ring. This, to her horror, proved an impossible task. He'd put it on her while she was in one of her deliriums—had he used a vise and a lever? The thing would need a blacksmith to get it off.

Learning that Pike had pursued her, and had a description of Will's horse, was a further blow. The final cut was the way Master Maybury had uncovered their secret so easily—it did not bode well for their situation. Would all London know of their escapade? Would she be forced to wed Will after all, despite her refusal to countenance the idea?

As the jettied buildings crammed closer together, she realized they must be heading into one of the closely packed residential areas of the city. There was little room here for gardens such as she was used to at Marston House—Londoners had to purchase their provisions, not rear or grow them. There were costermongers on every corner, flower sellers crying their wares, and peddlers pushing through the throng of pedestrians with brightly beribboned baskets.

The smell had intensified, too—with this many pannier-laden donkeys, horses, and closely crammed humanity, 'twas hardly surprising. A kite flapped lazily away from a heap of something dead as they approached, and she wrinkled her nose. One of the first things she'd ask Will for was a pomander. Or an orange and some cloves, so she could make something for herself.

Maybury coughed loudly. "Why do you take us along this street, old friend? I thought the Cavendish house was in a less noisome neighborhood."

"It is." Will leaned closer to Maybury, but Isobel was close enough to hear. "I would prefer not to attract the interest of my neighbors by bearing the lady in through the front door. If I'm to continue with the deceit that she's a Portuguese seamstress, we ought to enter via the service lane. I must introduce her to my housekeeper first, and get her accepted into the household before I risk any of my neighbors seeing her."

Maybury turned to Isobel and pulled a face. "Best cover your nose, Mistress. This is the place from whence the night soil is collected, and we shall no doubt be passing the Cavendish midden. How charming of Sir William to take us in via such intriguing landmarks."

She smiled. There was sense in what Will was doing, and now that Maybury was a co-conspirator, she felt more at ease. It was not that she didn't trust Will, but she felt herself always off-balance in his company. Maybury caused her no unease at all.

They dismounted in the cobbled lane, and Will let out a powerful whistle which, after a few minutes, brought out a middle-aged gentleman wearing a stained apron, whose face brightened when he saw Will.

"Good day, Hagger. Pray, take these horses to the stables and see they're given a good rub down. And if you could endeavor to keep Jennet between the others, I'd be most grateful. I have reason to keep her out of sight for the moment."

He then took Isobel's elbow and leaned his face close to hers. "And you, if you will, had best keep your eyes lowered submissively. Aye, I know." He waved a hand at her. "You don't approve of any of this, but please, if you would do as I say for now, it would serve us both well. Pretend you don't understand the language. I'll give you into the care of Goody Cooper, who keeps house for me. She'll give you refreshment and find you a bed. Once Maybury has had sufficient Canary and departed, you and I will talk."

She nodded. Will's servants couldn't question her if they couldn't speak her supposed tongue. It would be a hard part to play, but do it she must, for exposure could be the ruin of them both.

She walked beside him as they traversed a small vegetable plot, entered a narrow passageway, and emerged onto a cobbled courtyard.

And immediately ran into trouble.

"Aha, Sir William!" A well-dressed gentleman with white hair and beard had just emerged from the main door of the house, followed by a small entourage. Isobel froze, but Will quickly whispered something to Maybury, who pulled her off to the shadowed side of the courtyard.

"We have no role in this masque, lady. Best give Cavendish the stage. I wonder who that golden-haired beauty is?"

She'd been wondering the same thing. A young woman, with a plump bosom and small mouth was fawning all over Will. A short but well-made gentleman stood on one side of her, looking sour, while the white-haired man—her father, mayhap—spoke to Will in slow, deliberate tones, loudly enough for his words to reach her where she stood with Maybury. Although, she must remember not to appear to understand what passed between them.

Alas, the blonde lady had noticed her, and the thin lips were pressed close together. Isobel shuffled and stared at her feet, then drew out her handkerchief and blew her nose loudly. She hunched her shoulders, too, for added effect, and eventually, the woman lost interest.

"You've been on your travels again, Sir William," the older man was saying. "I'm disappointed. I thought we had business to discuss."

"What kind of business?" Will's manner was reserved, even cold. He didn't look at the young woman or the fellow at her side.

The older man glanced over at Maybury, who was paring his fingernails with his dagger, a pursuit requiring a good deal of concentration.

"Concerning the packet I received on your behalf. Most particularly the personage from whom it came. A person with whom an ambitious man would not wish to be associated."

"You already know the contents of the package. And a passing whim of Robert Dudley's hardly bears the brand of treachery. What more is there to say on the matter?"

The white-haired man's face darkened. He waved at his younger companion. "Take my daughter back home if you would, Comte. I shall return shortly, after a brief discussion with my neighbor here."

The rosy-cheeked young woman was borne off, pouting, but as she departed, she subjected Isobel to intense scrutiny, then tossed her head haughtily as she sailed through the gateway to the street beyond.

Will had claimed to have no betrothed. But that didn't mean no one had a claim on *him*. Isobel realized, with an unexpected twinge of her heart, that the woman had more than a passing interest in Sir William Cavendish.

Will and the girl's father had vanished into the house, and peace descended on the courtyard, broken only by the odd *coo* and flutter of the doves inhabiting a small dovecote in the corner. Maybury glanced up.

"Ah, it looks as though Cavendish has sent us his housekeeper. She appears to have set a course for you, Mistress, so I'll follow the gentlemen and demand my cup of Canary. And I should like to hear about this packet from the Earl of Leicester, and why Cavendish is so dismissive thereof."

With a wink, he left Isobel and disappeared into the house.

She glanced at the woman before her, then lowered her gaze. For good measure, she executed a curtsey. If Will had, indeed, informed his housekeeper she was a seamstress, the woman was a cut above her, and she must remember her place.

But how did one pretend to be Portuguese? She had no idea what the language even sounded like. Best to mutter and mumble, and signal with her hands. Mercy—could Will not have come up with a better disguise for her?

"I am Goodwife Cooper." The housekeeper, neatly dressed in a tan bodice and skirt, with a generous rouleau to accentuate the width of her hips, spoke each word with exaggerated clarity. "Follow me."

When Isobel pretended not to understand, she beckoned. Smiling and nodding, Isobel followed her through another doorway into a narrow passageway. She was taken into a small paneled parlor with a decorated plaster ceiling and invited, with exaggerated hand gestures, to sit down, wash her hands, and help herself from a charger bearing bread, cheese, a brace of cold chicken legs, and a slice of sweet onion tart.

This was good fare for a servant. Did all Will's people dine so well, or only the higher ones? She was grateful for the vittles—her stomach had misbehaved ever since she'd been deprived of her poppy juice, and the only way to quiet it was to fill it.

She was given no instructions, no duties, but left to her own devices as the housekeeper vanished into the depths of the building.

Looking around, she surmised she must be in the preserving room. A carved dresser bore various pots and ceramic bottles either corked or covered with pigs' bladders. A sugarloaf stood on a high shelf, partly covered with a muslin cloth, and a spice chest had its own shelf further down. Salt and candle boxes hung from hooks in the paneling, and a large bunch of dried lavender was suspended from the ceiling, along with other flowers and herbs she didn't immediately recognize. A chafing dish stood near the fireplace, on the hearthstone.

This would be a pleasant place in which to work. She could make simples, sweetmeats and conserves, tussie-mussies, and bowls of dried, scented petals—such as roses, stocks and lavender—to set about the house.

What was she thinking? This was a mere island in the storm, a temporary refuge while her perilous situation was resolved. She needed security, coin, and her own house back. She had to assume it *was* her house, and that Hubert hadn't already found some way to deprive her of it. Her sojourn with Will would be but brief. It had to be, for who would marry her if they knew she'd dwelled in another man's house, especially a gentleman as handsome and eligible as Will?

She took a swig of small beer to cool herself. Since when had she thought of him as *available?* She'd banished all thought of marriage—but then, he hadn't suggested it for the right reasons. A marriage of convenience to Will Cavendish would be a misery—unless she could tempt him into making it something *more*. Merciful heavens, she was confused!

The door into the housekeeper's room slammed back against the wall, making the paneling reverberate, and Will stalked into the room.

Desperate to hide the flush on her cheeks, Isobel stood and backed away from the light.

Will's fist hit the table with a thump. She had never seen him look so furious before—rage boiled in his pale eyes, and a muscle worked in his jaw.

She came forward and laid her hand over

his. "Whatever is the matter?"

He rolled his wrist and clutched at her, his grip strong enough to hurt.

"That accursed scoundrel Mathieson is blackmailing me into marrying his daughter, Paulina."

CHAPTER THIRTEEN

"FORGIVE ME. I should control myself better. This is not the behavior of a gentleman."

Will looked down as Isobel rubbed her thumb across his clenched knuckles. Her touch was sensuous, tender, too. Yet, it made him feel worse.

"It is of no matter. You must tell me what this Master Mathieson said."

He collapsed onto a bench and ran a hand through his hair. "He took in a packet addressed to me, sent as payment for my assistance to Leicester. And, in some sense—though the earl ought to know he can trust me—to buy my silence over that issue with the Mayor of Grave. Leicester somewhat foolishly used his own seal, which, of course, Mathieson recognized. Apparently, he's been making inquiries in my absence, and has proof positive I was with the earl on that ill-fated expedition."

"As were my brother and many others. Does your neighbor mean to threaten them all?"

Will heaved out a sigh. There was comfort in holding Isobel's hand, though he knew she could do naught to help him.

"Nay, only me. His daughter, he claims, has expectations where I'm concerned, and he'd be heartbroken to see her disappointed. I swear to you—I never gave her cause to hope."

Isobel settled on the wooden bench beside him. "I'm sure you didn't. I could tell from watching her, she was making calf's eyes at you, but there was nothing in your aspect to suggest you were encouraging her. She must be besotted, however, if her interest hasn't dimmed in over half a year."

"I can take no responsibility for that." He'd never paid any attention to Paulina beyond the usual courtesies, as far as he was aware. He'd thought her little more than a child, despite her curves, because she so often behaved like one—eager for attention, mercurial in her moods, and the possessor of a high-pitched giggle that would send his wits begging if forced to cope with it for more than a few minutes.

"You wouldn't even consider plighting your troth to his daughter? You have no wife, and are of an age where you might think of acquiring one."

He resisted the urge to leap from his seat and pace around the room. Isobel would let go of his hand if he did. "The devil I will! I mean—I have no objection to wedlock. But my spouse must be my own choice, not one thrust upon me by another. I don't mean to be the type of husband that packs his wife off to the country while he pleases himself in town."

"She's very comely."

Not so comely as you. "If I want to attract attention, I'd rather do it with jewels and status than a strumpet on my arm."

Isobel laughed then, a deep, throaty giggle he'd never heard before. His wrath eased.

"Just because she flirts with you doesn't make her a strumpet. However, with what exactly has Master Mathieson threatened you?"

"He'll make it known to all and sundry that I'm Leicester's man. So, I must partake in the man's fall and also bear the brunt of the queen's disfavor. Any hopes I might have of bettering myself by my connections at court would be dashed. My family name would be dishonored and vendors would refuse to offer me credit—should I ever need it. I might even be deprived of my title, which has been in my family for generations."

Isobel returned the strength of his grip. "But favor, once lost, can be regained, can it not? It has long been thought Elizabeth and Robert Dudley, Earl of Leicester, were lovers, so she might carry the candle for him still."

"A woman as strong-willed as Queen Bess? I doubt it. She'll put her throne and her country above any personal consideration. But I thank you for your words of comfort—they mean much to me."

He lifted their joined hands and kissed her knuckles in a salute of gratitude. At least, that's what he told himself it was.

"A solution must, and shall be found. I

apologize—but Mathieson made me so angry I needed to talk to someone."

"What about Master Maybury? Could he not help?"

"I'm not certain." It stung to have to seek help from another—he'd been used to shifting for himself for many a long year. And then he'd let himself become beholden to Leicester. The last thing he wanted to do was be in debt to anyone else.

"You may be right." He released her hand and stood. When his emotions ran this high, he feared he'd do something he might later regret. "Enough of my troubles. How do you fare?"

She rose as well and went to gaze through the window to the street beyond. "Well enough, I thank you. Mayhap a little wearied."

"Unsurprising. Are you still willing to remain here while Pike is found and brought to justice? I don't seriously expect you to work as my servant."

He gazed at her, unsure they would succeed in their deception in any case. Even dressed in an unadorned bodice and skirt, there was no mistaking she was a woman of quality. Isobel Marston simply couldn't help the way she held herself, with straight spine, and shoulders well back. It would be a feat of acting for her to look servile.

"Will these garments serve, do you think?" She looked down at herself. "I worry they're too well-fitting for a servant."

"Many men pay their servants in cloth and have their clothing made for them. To have one's people go about town in rags would not do. So, 'tis meet your clothing should fit." It made the most of her figure which, he thought, required filling out after her ordeal. If only he knew more about how she'd been treated at Pike's hands—if he'd been depriving her of food, it would add to the case against him. Should he use some of Leicester's coin to bribe Pike's servants? Nay, he'd prefer to take his horsewhip to Flinders than put gold in that man's hand.

"You're scowling. We must find me something plainer to wear."

"Nay, indeed. You look so well, were you in any other household, I'm certain you would not be spared the attentions of the master. 'Tis not to say that *I* don't find you tempting... I mean, please don't think I *wouldn't if—"*

He should stop talking. How was it that he'd become so tongue-tied? He was more than experienced in giving compliments to ladies, so why did he feel so unnerved when trying to flatter Isobel?

A smile played across her lips—she was mocking him. He liked it.

"What I'm trying to convey is that you will always look splendid, whatever you might be wearing. No man could be unaware of your attributes… I mean, *charms*. Although it is not my intention to take advantage of you."

He hung his head—he was making a complete mull of this. But at least it was a distraction from the problem of Paulina Mathieson.

Isobel was laughing openly now. "To spare you any further discomfort, let me extrapolate your meaning. I look very well, but should not mistake your compliment as a ploy to seduce me, for you are too much the gentleman to toy with any of your servants, let alone your friends."

Raising his head, he held her gaze. "You're very forthright, Mistress Marston. Or would you rather I called you Eurydice from now on?"

"Are you making fun of me, Sir William?"

"Nay. Only I had to give a name for you to Goody Cooper, and as I was in a hurry, Eurydice was the best I could come up with. I know 'tis not Portuguese, but they must have an interest in the classics there, too, so I hoped it would serve. Regrettably, my housekeeper is, as yet, unable to pronounce it. And—and it pains me to say this—I should not be surprised to find the servants assuming you and I are lovers."

His voice cracked on the word "lovers". How had he become so coy all of a sudden? He'd faced down a rank of arquebusiers, by the rood, so he ought to be able to manage a little awkwardness with Isobel.

The air between them charged like a thunderstorm. He'd put her to the blush, but he couldn't be sorry. It made her look hale and happy.

She nodded "Like as not they will. Since I cannot remove your signet ring."

"A pox on't!" He leapt up and seized her hand. The ring was, indeed, held fast, and couldn't be removed without effort and ingenuity. "For the moment, turn the intaglio into the palm of your hand so 'tis less obvious. I'm deeply sorry to have branded you thus."

Her mouth quirked, and his gaze was transfixed by it.

"You'll have to come to me every time you want something impressed with your seal."

"I'll have another one made." Although the prospect of taking her hand on a regular basis was decidedly agreeable.

He took a horn beaker from the dresser, replenished her cup and poured himself some of the small beer. "So, are you content to play your part?"

"I shall do my best. I can only I hope it will not be for long, for every moment I remain here puts you in danger."

"Think not of that. I can look after myself. And remember your brother's dying wish… I'm honor-bound to care for you, for however long you have need of me." He hoped it would be some time, as she intrigued and excited him—this new, lucid woman with her dancing green eyes and tempting smile.

His cup rattled as he put it on the table. "I shall go to that lawyer, Bradshaw, first thing tomorrow, with the letter and ring Edward gave me, as proof of my integrity. I must discover as soon as possible whether or not Pike has any legal claim to either you or your property now that Edward's gone. He gave me no reason to believe there was any heir but you."

"And with what shall I occupy myself in your absence?"

"You need do nothing."

"Nay, I must earn my keep. You told Master Maybury I was a seamstress, so mayhap I can help with the sewing and the linens. I sew a fine stitch. And if your housekeeper is busy now that you are returned, I might assist with making remedies and household necessities. I can remember the recipe for a potent mixture for cleaning glass."

His skin prickled. "Nay. Keep away from the windows, lest Pike sees you. Or one of his henchmen, as he might not want to be caught keeping watch on the house himself."

She looked anxious then, and he could have cursed himself for reminding her.

He moved closer. "Don't feel you have to do any work at all. You're not a slave, and I have no wish to demean you."

"Pray, don't concern yourself." She held his gaze, and the beat of his heart picked up speed. "I shall enjoy putting my household skills into practice and learning new ones. It will stop me being melancholy and brooding over my lot. Besides which, 'tis the least I can do to repay you for your kindness."

"That's not what you said when I bound your feet so you couldn't run away." He grinned, taking her by the elbows, letting his gaze rove over her face. Yes, the blush was there again. Because of what he'd said, or because of *him?*

"Harsh remedies for hard times." Her voice was almost a whisper. He noted she didn't pull away.

The door to the housekeeper's room suddenly opened, and Maybury bowled in. Will took a huge step backwards, away from Isobel.

"Ah, Cavendish—I've tracked you down at last. I just wanted to ask… oh, but I see you are otherwise engaged."

"I'm sure Mistress Marston can spare

me." Hah! As if using her proper title could redeem him.

Because he had, almost certainly, been about to kiss her.

CHAPTER FOURTEEN

THE FOLLOWING MORNING, Isobel discovered how lonely one could feel, even in a house full of servants. Maybury had departed the previous evening, and she'd seen Jennet brought into the courtyard an hour ago, saddled up for Will. Where was he bound? Had he gone to confront Mathieson? Would he give in and become betrothed to Paulina? And could she bear to remain a moment longer in his house if he did?

Her chamber fronted onto the courtyard, so she was aware of the constant to-ing and fro-ing of his household. Occasionally, she'd hear the clatter of hooves filtering through from the main street, along with shouts, laughter, the braying of asses, the high whistling cries of kites, and the caws of carrion birds.

Servants shuffled softly along the passageway beyond her door, occasionally giving away their presence with the *clack* of earthenware pots or the jingling of keys. She must dress herself and brave their company, as she was to become one of them.

She went down and broke her fast with Will's staff, but as she was supposedly foreign, none attempted to speak with her, although their aspect wasn't unfriendly. It was amusing to listen to speculations about herself which she wasn't expected to understand, but it isolated her as well. Will was correct—the consensus among the servants was that she had been a camp follower while he was away fighting, and he'd brought her back because of her superlative skills in the bedchamber.

This suggestion caused much ribald laughter, but her face grew hot as a mulling poker. Fearing someone would notice, and realize her English was as good as theirs, she hastened away without finishing her meal.

Fortunately, Goodwife Cooper found her not long thereafter and took her to the housekeeper's room, where she set her to chopping dried apricots and quinces for marmalade. The fire in the hearth was already lit, and a pitcher of clean water stood ready on the table. Isobel settled herself happily to her task, drawing it out as long as she could, for she found it calming.

She was busy scraping sugar from the loaf when she heard a door slam. Her heart cartwheeled, and she ceased her scraping, ears peeled for any indication Will had come home.

Looking down, she realized she'd scraped sugar all over the table, and Goodwife Cooper was staring at her. An apology leapt to her lips, and then she remembered she wasn't supposed to know the language. So, when Will came through the door and bade her accompany him, she shook her head and frowned her lack of comprehension.

His impatient gesture made it obvious what was required, so she curtseyed, nodded her apologies to Goody Cooper—who was tutting over the spilled sugar—and raced from the room in Will's wake. A few yards brought them to a commodious chamber, beautifully paneled in oak, with an empty fireplace and a large window looking onto the street. It sported some heavy drapes featuring ceremonial scenes, which Will pulled across before lighting the candles.

He stood close, and she could smell the leather of his saddle and riding boots, as well as the soapwort he used for washing, smells that were now familiar to her. Scents that made her feel safe.

"Keep your voice low when we converse—I'll not have my servants catch me in a lie. If anyone comes in, we must speak nonsense to one another but pretend to understand it."

She rather hoped someone *would* come in—it would be highly entertaining. Yet there was an aspect to Will's look that warned her he was not in the mood for frivolity.

"How goes it?" He indicated the settle. "Pray, sit down. How do you feel?" Pulling up a chair, he sat close to her.

"Almost as I used to, although there is an air of unreality—is that a word?—about everything. It is as if the world is blurred about the edges, and the harder I look at a thing, the less I see it. But I've managed to eat something, and my body appears to do as I wish it to." Except when this close to Will. It didn't behave properly then.

"You look hot—are you feverish again?"

Yes, but not for the reason he imagined. She must learn to control this foolish sensitivity to him. He'd be thinking her as obsessed as Paulina if she weren't more circumspect.

"Nay, no fever. You're unused to seeing me a healthy color. Be assured—I've settled comfortably into your household. My lack of poppy juice didn't send me stealing around like a thief in the night, hunting for your brandy-wine. How is your leg today?"

"It has a tendency to ache—I must ask Goody for a salve. So, you no longer feel the need to run away from me, I trust?"

"Not as yet." She chuckled, then sobered. She'd have to leave eventually, though, would she not?

"I'm glad of it. For if you did, I should be forced to saddle up and bring you back. The stakes for which Pike has been playing are higher than I expected."

"Indeed?" She leaned forward. "How is that?"

"I've spoken to Master Bradshaw. You're

not merely an independent woman of means, with her own house and accompanying goods and chattels—you are an heiress."

She gaped, looking for the jest in Will's expression, but the blue eyes were guileless.

"I? An heiress?" Her breath came in odd little bursts. This was incredible.

"You have the house and garden plot, naturally, as well as any funds—though I cannot guarantee Pike has not already sequestered those. But you also have a legacy from your aunt. No, not Hubert's mother, but another sister, Jane, who died before you were born. She left a substantial legacy to Edward, which will now come to you if the terms of her will are followed. Or will go to your husband, should you marry. You have the right to pass the legacy on to another in your lifetime, should you have no need or want of it."

It was too much to take in. "Why did Edward never speak of this legacy to me?"

"He ought to have told you, especially when he decided to seek adventure and preferment as a soldier. Lest anything happen to him, I mean."

"I should not speak ill of the dead, but he

should have, yes." It meant there was enough money to give her a decent dowry and improve her marriage prospects.

Will took her hand and fiddled with the seal ring. She loved the touch of his warm fingers on her skin, though she knew his efforts would be fruitless. She'd already tried butter and goose grease to remove it, to no avail. If only he had worn a ring large enough to wear on his middle finger, all would have been well.

"I cannot answer for Edward's actions any more than you can. However, let us assume it was this sum in particular that Pike was after. I don't know if he meant to marry you for it, or if he deemed your entire fortune would fall to him on your demise—as he's your closest living relative."

"I'm surprised Hubert didn't caper around the room when you told him Edward was dead. For he stood to gain everything, then." A shiver ran down her spine. Pike had planned her murder, she was sure.

Will must have seen her quake, for he stopped toying with the ring and grasped her hand. "Be not affrighted, my dove—that danger is now over and done with. Have I not given my word he'll never harm you again?"

She tried to collect her thoughts, which had scattered the moment Will held her hand. She shook her head. "I wonder if my Aunt Jane had any idea of where her generous thought might lead? She must be revolving in her winding-sheet."

"I'd like to see Pike in a winding-sheet, too." Will's face looked as hard as marble. "But, alas, I don't wish to attract attention to myself, particularly not in light of Mathieson's threat. We must gather our evidence with subtlety, and ensure Justice is on our side."

Isobel shifted on the bench—her thigh was too close to his. She could feel his heat through the layers of both petticoat and skirt. Their discussion was deadly serious, but her thoughts kept wandering to Will himself, rather than what he was telling her.

Why had she poured icy water on his suggestion of marriage? It would solve all their problems. Her fortune would be his, so it mattered not if he was unable to find favor at court. With him as her husband, she would be protected from the machinations of Pike or any other fortune hunters who knew of her legacy.

But there should be more to wedlock than its practical advantages. At least, she hoped there was.

She curtailed her rambling thoughts. "If Hubert was trying to poison me, how did he think he'd get away with it when Edward returned home? He could not have known my brother would die on the battlefield."

"Mayhap he hoped to remain in residence, and convince your brother of your madness. It would not have been *impossible* to fool Edward… even *I* was convinced initially, but then, I had never met you before. Once your madness was made known, Pike might have played the part of concerned friend, and offered selflessly to marry you, or get one of his cronies to do the deed, thus sparing Edward any embarrassment."

"My brother would never have agreed to that. He would simply have found a nurse for me, then thrown Hubert from the house."

"Don't forget Pike had dismissed all the servants who knew you. His campaign was well-planned. Even the gardener, who seemed a decent man, would have sworn to your madness, not having known anything else. You gnashed your teeth at me, you know. Gently bred young ladies don't normally do that."

"And gentlemen don't normally bind young ladies."

He kissed her hand. "The ones that bite, they do."

It felt so delightful to be in good accord with one another. She smiled up at him and caught a twinkle in his eye. It did unpardonable things to her insides.

Looking quickly away, she asked, "How are we to bring that vile man down?"

"Not 'we', Isobel—*me*. You must leave it in my hands for now. I want to be sure you are fully recovered and ready to be restored to the world before you take up cudgels against your cousin. In the meantime, trust me. I'll move heaven and earth to see you take your rightful place as head of the Marston household."

"But you have difficulties of your own to resolve. The Mathiesons—"

"Are not as important as taking care of you. Don't trouble your head with it."

She looked into the intensely blue eyes

that gazed into her own. A lump came to her throat, and it took an effort to find her voice. "I thank you, sir, from the bottom of my heart, for your selfless efforts on my part. I shall owe you a debt of gratitude until the day I die."

A broad grin lit Will's face, easing the tension between them.

"So, no more biting then, nor kicking? And please never tell me you'll hate and despise me as long as you live, and that I'm no gentleman. I was deeply wounded."

He looked so handsome, so appealing, she wanted to fling her arms around him and hold him forever. Perchance she was *still* mad, a little. He'd made up his mind to help her before they'd even met, had acted from duty only. And it was still duty, his loyalty to her dead brother, that motivated him. It would be folly to hope for anything else.

And did she even know what she wanted, or how she felt? She was in danger from Hubert. If she continued to lean on Will, she'd endanger him, too, and that was unforgivable.

She pulled her hand from his grasp and stood. "I must away to the housekeeper's room, or there'll be talk. And I don't want to ruin the marmalade. Pray, excuse me."

A shadow crossed his face, but she ignored it and fled the room.

And berated herself for cowardice every step of the way up to her chamber, where she threw herself on the bed, and gave in to silent tears.

CHAPTER FIFTEEN

SUMMER WAS PROCEEDING apace, and the martins which had nested beneath the eaves and jetties of the London houses now swooped rapidly over the rooftops with their young. Isobel struggled against her new confinement. *Keep away from the windows, don't go out, write no letters, speak no English in front of anyone but Aloysius Maybury*—her life was a series of restrictions.

How she longed for Marston House again! But she knew not what she'd find, or if Hubert had even left anything for her. Her memory was clear enough now to be certain she hadn't been imagining that valuable items—such as her harpsichord—had gone missing. Her evil cousin had evidently not scrupled to steal whatever he chose.

One thing she'd miss when she finally returned home was, of course, Will. Her life revolved around him—when she would see him, if they would have a chance to speak, how he fared, whether or not his leg pained him. She was no better than Paulina Mathieson, thinking always of Will. It must be the fact she was mending his shirts and sewing on buttons, even embroidering his collars, that kept him constantly in her mind.

Once in her own home, she'd feel less dependent on her benefactor. Hubert must be incarcerated soon so she could return, or she truly *would* go mad. The garden would need her guiding hand, and the provisioning and cleaning of the house required her supervision. And all the servants hired by Hubert must be found alternative positions, so her own could be reinstated.

The task was daunting, and she'd agreed with Will when he said he didn't think her ready. He'd assist her, she was sure, but she knew his life was currently in disarray, and hated being a burden to him.

A new servant had recently joined Will's household, a giant of a fellow called Manners.

He made her uneasy—mayhap because he reminded her of Flinders—or because he failed to behave as a servant should. He was something of a mystery. No one was sure of his status, not even Goody Cooper. His complexion was swarthy, and he had a coarse way of speaking—his equally rough hands suggested he'd labored hard in his time.

Manners was involved in a range of activities—he ran errands, answered the door to callers, and pored over documents at the table where Will wrote his letters. Isobel had seen Manners distributing coin to street urchins, and watched them scatter in all directions, like a handful of chaff thrown into the wind, apparently on some urgent business.

Will had reassured her Manners was "safe" but had stopped short of explaining the reasons for hiring him. She suspected it was to do with her, and regretted the amount of money Will must be spending in order to look after her. When, and *if*, she came into her inheritance, she would pay him back. Every last farthing.

This morning, Isobel was sitting in a shaft of sunlight in the old solar, embroidering the cuffs of one of Will's shirts. She knew he was keen to win favor at court, so she'd make sure he outshone all the other gentlemen when he got there. The day's brightness had cheered her, and she was humming contentedly when she heard running feet in the passageway.

Several doors were thrust open and slammed again until Will burst into the chamber where she sat. "Isobel, make haste. Pike has arrived with a constable. We must hide you!"

She stuck the needle into the cloth and placed the garment aside, fury warring with panic. "If he's brought a constable, I'll gladly speak to him and state my case."

"Nay, that will not serve. I have not yet the evidence I seek, although I hope to acquire it now. Pike mustn't suspect a thing—I shall wear the mask of outraged innocence. But you must hide, or all is lost."

"No!" She wanted to confront her cousin. These weeks of pent-up anger and resentment needed an outlet, and to have him taken into custody by the very officer he'd brought with him would afford her great entertainment.

Will swore softly, then swung her up and threw her over his shoulder. The devil! She should struggle, fight, and kick. But he was wearing a shirt she'd finished embroidering just the other day, and that might get damaged. He'd recently bathed, and smelled of soapwort and rosemary. His hair glinted in the golden light.

She swallowed hard. Her breath was coming in such short bursts she couldn't have screamed if she'd wanted to. Even when he carried her down the stairs, her body bouncing with every step, she felt secure in his strong arms.

When he set her by the front door, which was resounding to the hammering of a stick against it, she managed to gasp, "If you want to hide me, why are you taking me to the door?"

He set her down, grinning. "Because of this." Inserting his fingers into a gap in the paneling, he pulled, and a door-sized section of the wood flew open, revealing a deep, dark space behind it.

"Priest's hole," he explained. "Now get in there and don't make a sound until I come to release you."

Entwining his fingers in the lacing of her bodice, he pulled her against him and pressed his mouth over hers. Shocked, thrilled, she flung her arms around his neck and kissed him back and then, her heart pounding, allowed him to push her into the darkness and close the panel on her.

Chinks of light invaded her hiding place when the main door opened, only to be eclipsed as it swung in front of the paneling. Above the thundering of her heart, she heard it being hooked open, thus concealing the priest's hole altogether. And making it impossible for her to let herself out.

Cunning, but would it work? Had Will done the right thing? Had he kissed her to keep her quiet, or to confuse her? Her thoughts were tangled, her chest tight— excited and anxious at the same time.

She heard Hubert's voice and applied her ear to the paneling.

"What do you mean by abducting my cousin, sir? It's despicable and unlawful, and I intend to see you pay the penalty for it. The law, as you can see, is on my side."

How frustrating not to be able to see! But Will had done the right thing in imprisoning her here. Given the chance, she would have thrown herself at Hubert and done her level best to strangle the man. Which, in view of the fact he had a constable with him, would not have been wise.

"You forget your manners, *sir*. This is *my* house, and I have a right to defend it. Manners, my blade, if you please."

Isobel froze. He couldn't mean to fight. And if he *did,* not to let her watch him spike her cousin like the worm he was would be grievously unfair.

"There's no need to send your monkey for your sword. I'm not about to attack you."

"For a man who intends no violence, you have a belligerent aspect." Will's tone was icy. "Manners, I recall you have an errand to run for me. This fellow insists he means me no harm."

Will was sending Manners away? This frightened her. He could best Hubert with both hands tied behind his back, but the constable was bound to be strong. She'd be able to do nothing at all, trapped as she was.

Will was speaking again. "I think, Master Pike, you'd best enter and vouchsafe the reason for this ludicrous accusation of yours.

I've no wish to provide cheap sport for my neighbors."

"I know that you have Isobel. No one else would have taken her—no one else even *knows* she's been out of her mind. I cannot guess what you mean by it. Either you have evil motives for the deed or—and this is scarcely credible—you consider me incapable of caring for her."

The constable had said nothing as yet. Which gave Isobel hope he hadn't come to arrest Will, but more in the role of a witness. She had to hope so, as she'd be in a hideous coil if Will were thrown into Newgate.

He was asking, "What makes you think I have Isobel? I've only met the poor creature once and can have no earthly reason for removing her from your care. Why should I, a man freshly returned to his sweetheart from abroad, want to saddle myself with a madwoman?"

"You have a sweetheart?" Hubert sounded taken aback.

"Indeed. Paulina Mathieson. She lives but a few houses further down the street—pray call on her father if you won't take my word for it."

A dangerous bluff—Will could not afford to give the Mathiesons hope if he meant thereafter to dash it.

"So, I ask again, what cause have I for abducting your cousin?"

"Because you know about the—" Hubert paused. "Because you think you know a better cure for her. Anyway, it doesn't matter what your reasons for her removal are. I've come to insist you return her at once, or you'll take what's coming to you."

Somebody coughed then, presumably the constable. Isobel could imagine him puffing out his chest and looking self-important. But he must also feel uneasy since he was dealing with a nobleman.

"Am I to assume that Isobel Marston is no longer in your care, and that you have no knowledge of where she might be?" Will's tone had changed. There was an edge of barely repressed fury in his voice.

"You know very well I don't have her. Because *you* have."

"What have you done to retrieve her? How long has she been gone? What clues have you to her disappearance? This gentleman here should be raising the hue and cry to find her, not wasting his time on me."

"Sir William is playing games with us, Master Abel. He mocks us because we're both lower than he. Cavendish, I simply want poor Isobel returned to her home. Do as I wish, and no force will be used against you."

"Constable, what's the penalty for neglecting a vulnerable young woman in one's care, and making false accusations against the innocent?"

There was another cough, this time from Hubert, followed by a lengthy silence. Eventually, he said, "Excuse me. I *may* have overstepped the mark. I'm so distraught at her disappearance, and know not what to do."

"Have you made other inquiries? Isobel could not have run to me, as she knows not where I dwell, but there must be others, friends of the family mayhap, to whom she might turn if distressed."

"I cannot believe she has run away. She was much too... um... *ill* to engineer anything herself. She must have been seized against her will."

Why was Will disputing with Hubert? Her cousin was already backing down, and the constable had nothing to say on the matter, so why not throw them both out onto the street? Then she could be released from her stuffy hole and give vent to the hysterical laughter bubbling up inside her.

"So, what steps have you taken to have her found?"

"I've informed the constables and the watch. I have searched the prisons, bride-wells, bawdy houses and hospitals. I'm quite worn out with worry. Forgive me if I acted without thought just now."

Yes, she'd wager he'd searched *all* the bawdy houses. And enjoyed doing so as well. She repressed a snort.

"More good can be done by us working together to find the young lady. Let us not be enemies, sir. I have friends in both low and high places and will use my influence to learn what I can. I must also apologize for so readily accusing you of negligence. It was churlish of me, considering what you've no doubt had to put up with since Edward went away."

What arcane game was Will playing? Why be friendly towards their enemy? Merciful heavens, he'd be inviting the villain to dine with him next!

"Since you've brought a constable with you, I feel obliged to prove my innocence in this matter. You may have the run of my house. Search every inch of it if you will. Then you may be certain I'm your ally in this case, not your adversary."

She froze. Why had Will made such an imprudent offer? As soon as the door was closed, only a thin sliver of oak lay between her and her nemesis. What if she were to sneeze? What if Hubert were to press the wood in just the right place and make the door spring open?

What if Will had changed his mind, and actually *wanted* her to be found? Had he decided she'd trespassed on his life long enough?

CHAPTER SIXTEEN

"OH, YOU SHOULD have seen him!"

Will had rescued a sour-looking Isobel immediately after Pike and the constable had left the premises, and could barely contain his laughter.

"Why? I don't know what's so amusing." She kept her voice low, but there was no one to overhear them.

"Many apologies for hustling you into that niche, but it was necessary. I would have had you out sooner, but hadn't expected your cousin to take a full half an hour hunting for you."

She looked like a peacock whose feathers had been ruffled, so he stroked her back, then escorted her into the parlor where they could speak privately.

"It was a bizarre spectacle. Pike searched every chamber below, peering behind drapes, and even into cupboards. He then insisted on going upstairs and looking in all the chambers. Whether they were inhabited or not, he felt it incumbent on himself to open every clothes chest and look behind every fire screen. He even visited the servants' attic—'tis as well you left nothing identifiable in your room. The constable trailed around after him, his face growing darker with each new piece of folly."

Will pulled her onto the settle beside him, warmed with good humor. If only she would smile. They'd had a fortunate escape and, if Fate favored them, would be well rewarded. "When Pike started opening drawers, I wanted to laugh aloud. I wish you could have seen him. He went down to the pantry after that, then explored the scullery, and even rummaged through the laundry pile. He got a foul look from Cook, and Goodwife Cooper looked ready to beat him about the head with her limestone mortar. My staff are, it seems, good judges of character."

There was still a frown on Isobel's face. Why could she not see the jest?

Wait, he'd kissed her before shoving her into the priest's hole. Was *that* what she was so irritated about? He'd used no finesse at all, just been carried away in the heat of the moment. He'd make a better job of it next time.

Next time?

His vision focused on her ruby lips, now bearing just the hint of a smile. He hadn't given himself time to savor them, to enjoy them. Now, there was no hurry—so long as she was prepared to let him kiss her again.

He held her steady, holding her gaze as he moved closer. She didn't move, didn't blink—just threatened to drown him in the sea-green depths of her eyes. He should have known one kiss would never be enough. Once he'd tasted those lips, he was as much in thrall to them as she had been to her opium.

As he bent his head to hers, what had been intended as the gentlest of touches became something more significant. When his lips brushed over hers, her mouth moved beneath them, and she tasted him, shyly at first, then urgently. He pressed against her, melding his mouth to the delicious softness of hers.

His hands slid behind her shoulders, drawing her nearer, so her breasts brushed his chest. She quivered in his arms, and he reveled in the sweet pleasure of holding her close once more, under such different circumstances to the last time. She wasn't fighting—she was inviting him.

He let his tongue slide along hers, withdrew to tease her, then returned to explore the tempting velvet of her mouth. And she met him, stroke for stroke, her hands tangling in his hair. He forgot himself, allowed the kiss to consume him. Were this moment to stretch out forever, he'd have no objection at all.

Wait, what was he doing? He'd fought temptation for weeks, refusing to take advantage of her vulnerability. Had all that self-denial been for nothing? Heart pounding in his ears, he pulled back, releasing her.

She looked down at her hands and starting rolling his ring around her finger, but she didn't flee, or weep, or strike him. Which had to be a good sign. But internally, he cursed himself for his lack of self-control. How could he call himself a gentleman when he was about to corrupt an innocent? He ran a hand through his hair, struggling for the right words—but there was no point pretending what had passed between them could be lightly dismissed.

Before he could martial his thoughts, Isobel lifted her head, eyebrows raised. "Now then, Sir William Cavendish, what exactly did you mean by kissing me like that?"

He wished he knew the answer to that question himself. "I… um… I didn't mean it to be quite as… thorough as that." Curse it! He sounded more like a dithering schoolboy than a man of experience.

The green eyes regarded him levelly. "Was that an attempt at seduction?"

Yes. *No.* He'd have liked it to be.

"I would never try to seduce a woman I hold in such high regard."

"That is worse than no answer at all."

Aye, he knew it. His words lacked conviction. The awful truth was, now that he'd kissed her, his body wanted to know more of her. It was as much as he could do to hide his desire. It felt as if his carefully laid plans had been shattered, like ice on a pond being struck with an ax. His resolve was in pieces, and all he wanted to do was damn Pike and Paulina to hell, marry this woman, and take her to bed.

Which was—almost certainly—not what Isobel needed to hear right now.

"Then let us agree what happened just now was a mistake, brought on by the thrill of hoodwinking my ghastly cousin Hubert. It will do neither of us any good to dwell on the matter, so I suggest 'tis forgotten. I'm sure you're thinking the same thing yourself."

She stood to leave. Farther along the passageway, the main door was pulled to, and the latch dropped into place.

"No, wait. We need to know who's just arrived."

He laid a hand on Isobel's sleeve. His breath sounded loud in his ears as he waited, hoping his plan had borne fruit.

Someone thumped on the door.

One of these days, he'd teach the ape how to knock properly. "Who's there?"

"It is I, sir—Manners."

He stood, bringing Isobel with him. "Enter."

She glanced up at him, questioning. He squeezed her hand. "It's all right. You may speak English in front of Manners. He knows all my secrets. I pay him well to keep them to himself."

"So, what have you there, sir?" He stepped to one side so Manners could empty his pockets onto the table.

"Let me explain, Isobel. As soon as Pike arrived here, I sent Manners to Marston House to break in and search for incriminating evidence. So, all the while your cousin was poking around in *my* home, my agent was doing the same thing in *his*! Well, *your* home, I should say. Now, do you understand my amusement?"

Manners showed his gap-toothed grin. "It was like taking milk from a babe, sir, so poorly guarded as the house was. There didn't seem to be no one about, and it looked as if someone had already ransacked the place. There was things scattered everywhere, so it took a bit of searching to pick up anything useful. But you'll be pleased with what I got, sir—I know you will. Locked away in a chest, these were, but I got in easy as butter."

Will glanced down at Isobel and saw the understanding dawn in her eyes. A smile played around her lips. "Very clever, Will. I wondered why you were content to have Hubert remain here so long, despite the risk of him finding me."

Good—he'd hoped she'd be pleased. She needed placating after that ill-advised kiss.

He cleared his throat. "So, what do we have, Manners?"

"I think you'll find these documents interesting, sir. Particularly this one." Manners handed him a folded piece of parchment. Will opened and scanned it, then read it again. His blood chilled, and anger roiled in his belly.

"If I'd known about this when Pike came calling, I'd have run him through on sight. I can only hope that I've not left it too late to do so." He dropped the paper to the table.

"There are these as well." Manners carefully tipped out the contents of the scrip attached to his belt, and several glass phials filled with liquid of different colors rolled onto the table.

Will let out a slow whistle. "Look at this, Isobel. Enough medicines to supply an army in the field. Or, viewed differently, enough to poison one person many times over." He removed a cork and sniffed at one of the bottles. It smelled like rotting flesh—henbane. "I fear marriage was *not* the fate Pike intended for you."

Her face had paled. Mayhap he should have spared her this, but he was too angry to think straight. She reached for the folded paper while he unrolled the other document.

His anger was stoked to a blaze. The first paper had been a draft of Isobel's Aunt Jane's will. Proof positive that Pike knew about the inheritance. The second, which now trembled in his hands, was a newly penned document, one Isobel was evidently intended to sign. It stated that, in the event of the deaths of herself and Edward, all the Marston property—including the legacy—should remain in the family, to be administered by Hubert Pike. The paper was neither dated nor witnessed, but Pike had doubtless expected to find some penniless clerk prepared to accept a bribe and give it the seal of authenticity.

Without a word, he handed the document to Isobel.

"There's one more thing, sir, Mistress."

Manners placed a large silver locket on the table. Isobel looked up from the paper she was reading and gazed at it. Will's gut clenched as her eyes brimmed with tears.

"What is it?"

"A miniature painted for me on my seventeenth birthday." She held it out to him, and his heart bled as he absorbed the joyful innocence on the subject's face, and saw how carefree Isobel had looked before her trials. The locket was engraved with her name, and that of her father, presumably because he'd made her a gift of the jewel.

He handed it back, closing her hand around it, then covering hers with his own. "Keep it safe. 'Tis proof of who you are, and to what you are entitled. Just in case Pike hasn't yet given up his pursuit of you, and has some other contemptible scheme up his sleeve."

A sudden loud pounding at the front door made his heart flip in his chest. Manners straightened. "Shall I answer it, sir?"

Will took a deep breath, then swept the papers into a chest beneath the table. "There's no time to hide Isobel properly. If it's Pike, throw him out on his ear. No, detain him. I'd like to get my hands on that scoundrel."

Manners was peering through the panes. "It looks like a lady, sir. Nay, two of them. Shall I admit them?"

"Isobel, behind the drape, if you please. Forgive me—I need to see who this is. I'll not tarry. We must make our plans."

The desire to kiss her pale cheek beat like a storm in his body, but they'd agreed to forget that earlier kiss. He mustn't trespass again—she might not let him off so lightly should he repeat his crime.

Moments later, he stood in the passageway by the front door, as Manners opened it to reveal the gleeful faces of Paulina Mathieson and her mother.

"Will!" Paulina flung her arms about his neck. "I can hardly believe it. I'm delirious with joy—we are to be married after all!"

CHAPTER SEVENTEEN

SITTING ON HER bed, Isobel pulled her knees up to her chest and stared morosely at the flickering candle flame and the dancing shadows it created on the wall. The sleeping house was quiet now, gloomy like her thoughts, dark like her soul.

Today had been one of joy, revelation, and searing pain. Little wonder she was unable to sleep—almost she would welcome the sour taste of poppy juice on her tongue, and the oblivion it offered. But that would be no more than a fleeting comfort, for the issues of the day would remain, and could not be resolved without her action.

Will would take care of Hubert—he had the evidence now, in the shape of those damning documents. He planned to ride out tomorrow, to an honest lawyer he knew, and send out scouts to locate her cousin so he could be arrested for fraud—and attempted murder.

The thought made her shiver, imbued every shadow with peril, made her miss Will's comforting arms all the more.

Yet, she had to leave him. From her hiding place behind the drape in Will's study, she'd heard every word of the exchange between him and the Mathiesons. It turned out Hubert had taken Will up on his suggestion and *had* called upon them. The master of the house had been absent, but it hadn't taken long for the ladies to grasp the significance of what Hubert was saying. After that, they'd cheerfully accepted that Will was engaged to Paulina.

Will's denial when the women called upon him resulted in a deafening fit of hysterics from Paulina. The unfortunate man was in hot water indeed—he couldn't know what the Mathiesons had said to Hubert, whether or not they'd mentioned seeing Isobel on the day of her arrival. Paulina had become incoherent after Will explained

Hubert's assertion resulted from a misunderstanding—and her mother had refused to answer any questions.

If only Isobel could have stepped out and defended him! But who could say they wouldn't have immediately known who she was, and informed Hubert? Will needed time—he must see the lawyer before he faced Hubert again, and must ensure the telling documents were in safe hands. She dared not do anything precipitous.

Will had finally managed to eject the two disgusted females from his house, but he'd sat a while with his head in his hands thereafter, before calling Isobel out from her hiding place. He'd looked drained, tired.

Her candle flickered again, and she came out of her musings with a start. Someone was there, right outside her door. In a sudden panic, she leapt from the bed, blew out the candle and armed herself with the chamber pot.

"Isobel, 'tis Will. Are you awake?"

Shoving the pot back under the bed, she stumbled to the door and lifted the latch.

"Evidently, you *are* awake. I thought I saw a light just now—were you reading?"

"Nay. I was worried you might be an enemy."

He briefly kissed the top of her head, then set about igniting a spill from his tinderbox so he could light the candle. He was carrying a scrip, which he placed on the floor.

"It's late, I know, but I couldn't sleep."

"Nor I." She sat on the bed with her legs curled beneath her. She hoped he wouldn't hear the catch in her voice—or if he did, he would put it down to her initial fright. Having Will here, so vivid and alive, in the intimacy of her chamber, was doing startling things to her, sending her imagination along paths where it had no right to roam.

"What a pass we have come to." His voice was a sigh as he settled at the foot of her bed and leaned forward, his elbows propped on his knees. "We jump at shadows and feel beset with enemies on every side. I regret you were forced to listen to what passed between me and Paulina."

"She's a headstrong young woman, and sadly deluded." Nay, that was unfair. Now, whenever *she* laid eyes on Will, it was as if he filled her horizon from edge to edge and she saw nothing but him. She couldn't blame

Paulina for setting her cap at him. He was an easy man to love.

"I would say the entire family is headstrong and deluded. I trust they now understand I have no intentions towards Paulina."

"She won't let you go that easily." Would *she* fight for Will in Paulina's place? Even if it was not in his best interests? There was the rub.

"But what about your links with Leicester, and your hope of finding favor at court?"

"Mathieson has no proof of any treachery on my part—it is just his word against mine. I'll take my chances. I'm here to discuss other matters."

Her heart pounded. He was going to send her away. She knew she ought to go, but right now, her very soul rebelled against the idea.

"What matters?"

He lifted the scrip he'd brought with him, which she recognized as the one in which Manners had put his spoils from Marston House. "We need to talk about *this*. There's more unpleasantness for you to face, my little dove—you must write an account of all the things Pike and his retinue have done that may be pertinent to the case against him."

"I'll write what I can remember, although it is very little. I was asleep or out of my wits much of the time."

His gaze was soft, pitying. She mustn't confuse his compassion with affection. Steeling herself to pragmatism, she asked, "What manner of actions should I record?"

"If you could note such occurrences as him sacking the servants, or selling your jewels and harpsichord without your permission, that would be useful. Your silver locket was the only item of value remaining in the house when Manners scoured it— perhaps you might write an inventory of what *should* have been there. And if you know the names of your original household, we may be able to trace them, and make use of their testimonies."

A tide of melancholy swamped her. There were so many lovely things she'd never see again. Mementoes of her family, her childhood, her lost brother. Since Edward's demise, Fortune had forsaken her. Only… it had sent her Will, at the time she most had need of a friend. But that friendship was proving to be a two-edged sword. She glanced at him, then dropped her gaze as a treacherous blush invaded her cheek.

There was a rattling at the window, accompanied by a dull roar. A summer squall had arrived. How fitting that the heavens should choose this moment to weep—they mirrored her mood exactly. She shivered.

"You're cold. Shall I light your fire? Nay, by the time it gives off heat, we'll have finished our conversation. Let me warm you."

To her delight and shock, Will pulled her towards him, placed an arm around her shoulders and drew her counterpane over them both. Her resistance lasted less than a heartbeat. She snuggled into his warmth, sliding a hand across his stomach to his waist, savoring the firmness of the muscle there.

She felt him draw in a breath, and raised her head. He was watching her, his expression unreadable, as the candlelight gilded one side of his face and turned his hair to glowing gold. Her whole body became alert, waiting for some sign. But would she recognize it if it came? Could they risk there being more than companionship between them?

"Isobel, have you any female relations or friends who could join you here? I would not have your reputation sullied. And if I am to fall prey to these blackmailers, I would wish the world to know you're guiltless of any complicity in my sins."

"A chaperone?" It was rather late for *that*. A chaperone would not permit such intimacy as *this*. Which wouldn't do at all, as she was enjoying Will's closeness too much.

He pushed a lock of hair behind her ear. Such warm fingers! She quivered, and his arm flexed around her shoulders.

"It would serve our purpose better if I had nothing to hide. So, you cannot remain here disguised as a servant, and the only way to live openly with me is if you are accompanied by a respectable older woman."

Or if she was his mistress. She could live openly with him then.

From whence had *that* thought come?

"Can you think of anyone at all who would suit? A person of stainless reputation with integrity and an open mind. We would be duty-bound to explain to them all that has happened up until this moment."

Wrenching her thoughts away from the

direction they'd been taking, she struggled to bring to mind who might suit. No one had visited since Edward's departure—what had Hubert done to keep them away? Had he burned letters from her friends and relations, turned them away at the door? If only she could remember.

"There is Cecelia Hollingsworth. She was a dear friend of my mother's and used to call regularly. But she dwells some distance away."

"No matter. Where does she live?"

"Hertford. I've been to the house and can show you the way. It's known as Bay House, after the massive pair of bay trees overshadowing the gates."

"Has she a husband who could spare her for a while?"

Isobel searched her memory. "He died, I think. I cannot recall when last I saw her. I trust she's well."

"I'll ride north and find her, and convince her to return with me. If I have your agreement?"

If it meant being able to stay here awhile, then yes. And perchance Cecelia, who had always struck her as levelheaded, could stop her doing something decidedly unseemly.

"You have my agreement. I shall be glad to remain under your protection until my cousin has been brought to justice."

He squeezed her shoulder. "Splendid. I'll leave Manners to watch over you while I'm away. Stir not from here, no matter how convincing a reason you may be given for doing so. Trust only Manners. I'll order the servants to admit no one until my return, so you'll not be bombarded by the Mathiesons."

His fingers caressed her shoulder. Had he any idea he was doing it? Her skin heated where he touched her, a warmth more welcome than any fire. What would happen if she splayed her hand across his stomach, traced the contours of his muscles there?

Her throat grew dry. "The servants will need to be told my true story if they are to understand why I have a chaperone. They'll think we have used them most ill."

He grinned. "Mayhap not. They may relish it. 'Tis not every day that a gentle-woman comes among them in disguise. Besides, I'd like to scotch their thought that you are my mistress as soon as I can."

"Ah. You've heard that, too? They said as

much on the day of my arrival, having no idea I understood their words. I had hoped they'd changed their opinions." She was sure nothing in her behavior would have given her away.

What would they believe if they could see Will and her entangled in the bed covers like this? That they were entirely justified in their suspicions, of course.

"I was such a bedraggled waif when I first came here, it surprised me to hear their gossip about us. A man with your advantages wouldn't look twice at such a one as me."

"Fie! Anyone with eyes would see your quality. I thought you bewitching when you appeared to be a lunatic—now you are well and your own self again, you are utterly enchanting. I'm surprised my male servants aren't trailing around after you already."

"Mayhap I should *not* stay. I could go with you, throw myself on Cecelia's mercy and reside a little while with her." Even though it would tear her heart out to be separated from Will.

His fingers stilled. There was a distinct pause before he said, "Nay, Isobel, that will not serve. I cannot protect you if you decide to stay in Hertfordshire. It is imperative I return to London immediately, to persuade Mathieson to release his stranglehold. Or until the Earl of Leicester is once again the queen's favorite courtier."

"You do too much for me—you risk more than you should."

"Think naught of it. What I did for loyalty to Edward, I now do for you. I will be ever at your service. Now, had I better borrow your locket? It will be proof to Mistress Hollingsworth of my veracity."

She reached under her pillow and removed the silver jewel. "You'll take good care of it? If I can't recover my property, this will be all I have to remember my past."

"I'll guard it with my life, I swear."

Her heart suddenly jerked in her breast. "But what about this? I still have your ring."

"Have you tried to remove it?"

No, she hadn't, not after the first couple of attempts. Now, it had become so much a part of her, she'd ceased trying. Guilt washed over her.

"I'm sorry. Not recently, no."

"Then keep it." His hand stroked her shoulder once more, and his smile was tender. "I won't force you to marry me on the grounds that I've given you what looks like a betrothal ring. I know you're averse to the idea."

He chuckled softly, then eased away, tucked the covers around her, and stood.

"If I'm journeying north tomorrow, I'd best attempt to get some rest. Forgive me if I depart before you wake—I want to be gone as short a time as possible."

"If it's raining now, the roads will be treacherous."

"Jennet is sure-footed, and she'll carry me a good part of the way before I have to hire another mount. I'll brook no delay. Your reputation is at stake, my lady, and I'd be no gentleman if I were to let that situation continue."

He bowed to her, a curiously polite gesture from a man dressed only in his hose and shirt, with his doublet hanging open, and no collar or ruff. He must have been preparing for bed before deciding to come and speak with her. A circumstance that would not be permitted once Cecelia Hollingsworth entered the household. Alas.

It would be far too improper—and provocative, mayhap—to get up and make him a curtsey dressed only in her nightgown, so she blew him a kiss.

Will paused in the open doorway, his bright eyes intense. She half-hoped, half-feared he'd return and kiss her. He did not, though his lips parted as if he would speak. Then he spun on his heel and closed the door quietly behind him.

As the latch snapped into place, a fist of pain squeezed her heart. He wasn't interested—he didn't want her the way she now wanted him. He was going to fetch a woman who would put a wedge between them, destroy any affection that had sprung up.

He was her savior, and what she felt for him was gratitude. Anything more needed to be trampled upon and destroyed.

Or she would, once again, be miserable and alone.

Chapter Eighteen

Despite his intentions, Will had failed dismally to sleep well the previous night. He could so easily have kissed Isobel—he *should* have kissed her. If Mistress Hollingsworth came back with him, he'd never have another opportunity. At least, not for a ridiculously long time.

As he headed out of London in the early morning drizzle, the image of Isobel's green eyes, warm and wide with yearning, flashed across his mind with startling clarity. He'd seen the darkness of desire reflected there after their first kiss. He'd seen the same thing last night as he'd held her in what—so he kept telling himself—was a purely platonic fashion.

And fool that he was, he'd not responded to it. How must that make her feel? He owed it to her to explain his reasons for holding back—Pike, Paulina, Leicester—there were too many complications in his life at present. A man should offer security, both financial and otherwise, to his future wife. He had neither of those, as yet.

A sunburned drover herding a small flock of sheep on the wide grass verge beside the road saluted him. Will tipped his hat and glanced around. Yes, he was still on the main highway—not *quite* so deeply buried in his thoughts that he'd lost his way. He was approaching a coppice he remembered from when he'd traveled this road before, with Isobel beside him.

As soon as Mathieson was off his back, he'd begin the process of courting her properly. Because the idea of her marrying some fumbling youth, or a pot-bellied, middle-aged widower—or even a handsome, dashing blade—was anathema. No one was worthy of his beautiful, entrancing Isobel.

Several pigeons erupted from the trees ahead of him, their wings clattering on the breeze, but he could see nothing that might have disturbed them. He urged Jennet into a canter—with so little traffic, he could give the mare her head. They might as well make good time if they could.

Would Edward be rolling in his grave if he knew the direction Will's thoughts had taken? Will had been charged to protect Isobel, not steal her future by binding her to him in wedlock. Or perchance this was what Edward had hoped for all along, that his comrade-in-arms would fall for his sister.

Will-he or nil-he, it had happened. He'd known her but a few weeks, yet he felt as if he'd known her a lifetime. What did she feel for him? Was there anything in her face when she looked at him that signaled something more fundamental than desire?

Suddenly, he felt pity for Paulina. Was this how she felt when she thought of *him*? Hanging on every word, examining every gesture, to see if he shared the same devotion? It wasn't his fault she'd fallen for him, but neither was it hers. He should be flattered—she was a very pretty woman, and would mature, given time. She might even make some gentleman an excellent wife. He must be kinder to her when he saw her again—she couldn't help the fact her father was a blackmailing scoundrel.

The shadows of the trees merged into one as a rain cloud doused the sun. At the same time, the temperature dropped, and the drizzle turned to rain. A pox on't! He was well past the last village he'd seen, and no other buildings were in sight. He slowed and scanned the trees beside the road, wondering if it was worth sheltering until the worst of the shower had passed.

Galloping hooves sloshed through the puddles ahead as two riders hurtled down the road, doubtless also keen to take shelter. Before he sensed the danger, the first was upon him, yanking his mount to a halt, one arm raised to strike.

Will felt the sting of a riding crop, followed by a savage blow which unseated him. His survival instincts leapt to the fore even as he fell, and he rolled the instant he struck the ground. But when he attempted to regain his footing, he staggered, winded and disorientated by the suddenness of the attack.

Cursing his lack of vigilance, he struggled to fend off the blows that immediately followed. The odds were not good—two masked rogues ranged against one, and having the element of surprise. With all the force he could muster, Will shoved his knee up into the stomach of the man who'd pinioned his arms. The man's grip weakened, giving him a moment's breathing space, so he used his momentary advantage to deliver a kick to the fellow's ankle, tipping him off balance, before spinning around to meet the second attacker.

His blood ran cold. *This* assailant brandished a dagger.

There was no time to lose. Will launched himself forward to catch the man's wrist before he could deploy his weapon, but the fellow sidestepped swiftly. Will grabbed the hand with the knife, but as he tried to shake the weapon free, he was caught from behind.

Summoning all his strength, he spun, bringing the knifeman crashing into his confederate. With a vicious twist, Will forced the fellow to his knees and was rewarded with the sight of the dagger scudding away across the highway, but not before it had grazed along his thigh.

With a yowl of fury, the other attacker landed several heavy kicks and punches to his body, so he was forced to divert his attention away from the man who'd had the knife, praying he could knock his current opponent out before the other regained his blade.

If only he'd had time to reach his sword! He would have spitted them both like suckling pigs by now. Weaponless, he had to fight dirty, so he threw himself at his opponent and punched, kicked and bit any part of the man's sweaty anatomy he could reach. They rolled and writhed on the muddy highway, Will ever watchful for the man with the knife, ready to use his adversary's body as a shield against any blows.

Somehow, Will's foe managed to free a meaty fist and deliver a stunning blow to his cheek. Will regained his feet before the man could get in a second blow, and lurched towards Jennet, determined to arm himself. But his injured thigh refused to support him, and he staggered straight into the arms of the other ruffian.

His arms were wrenched behind his back, and he was held in a vise-like grip against the larger man's chest.

The other stood, brushed some blood from his face, and came forward. With an evil leer, he drew back his fist, then plunged it into Will's stomach.

Will kicked and writhed, fighting for breath. As soon as he recovered, he spat the blood from his mouth and growled, "You filthy coward. Tell this ape to let go of me, and fight me like a man."

The only response was a loud guffaw. The fellow rubbed at his knuckles and looked Will up and down as if contemplating where his next blow would fall. Then he smiled mirthlessly. "Don't expect death ter come too quickly. We're goin' ter 'ave our bit o' fun afore we finish ye off."

Thoughts chased one another through Will's mind at breakneck speed. Was he really going to die here, upon this rain-soaked road? What of his mission, of the promise he'd made to Edward, of the duty he owed to the woman whose portrait nestled against his heart?

He couldn't allow himself to be dishonored and defeated by a couple of lowlife felons. If anyone's bloodied corpse would be feeding the crows tonight, it would be the fellow who stood in front of him, tormenting him with his evil smirk.

Will went completely limp and started sliding through the arms of his captor. Before the fellow could adjust his grip, Will jabbed both elbows hard into his enemy's ribs, jerked his head up until it connected with the man's chin, then wrestled himself free.

He'd left it too late. Before he could take advantage of his freedom, the knifeman threw his fist at Will's jaw and sent him sprawling. His head bounced off the cobbles, and the world blurred, before vanishing entirely.

CHAPTER NINETEEN

I T HAD BEEN four days. Will should have returned by now.

Isobel had become increasingly worried, but what could she do? She was supposed to be a servant who neither understood nor spoke much English, and she couldn't reveal her concerns without exposing not only Will's secrets but her own.

How could one feel so alone in a house full of people? The only person she could confide in, who knew her story, was Manners. Though he, too, was puzzled by Will's tardiness, he refused to go off in search of him, as he was duty-bound to remain in London, keeping a wary eye on Isobel.

After supper on the fourth day of Will's

absence, Isobel retired to the housekeeper's room and took up her sewing, hoping it would calm her. She cheered a little as she surveyed her handiwork on the falling band of one of Will's shirts; the repairs had been done in her finest stitching and concealed entirely with cut-work embroidery. As she ran her hands over the linen, she pictured Will as he'd looked when she first became *really* aware of him, with the lamplight flickering over his face in their room at the inn.

She stroked the soft fabric of the shirt and envied it its closeness to Will's body. What did it feel like for a woman to get as close to a man as his clothing, to touch his naked skin with her fingers?

With a whimper of dismay, she flung the shirt down and stalked around the room. She could not go on thinking about him like that—it was sinful. Nor should she have any hopes where he was concerned—not when they *both* had the sword of Damocles hanging over them.

She shouldn't shed her heart's blood over a man who had simply been kind to her, out of obligation to her dead brother. Admittedly, he'd become carried away and kissed her, but that didn't give her the right to want him the way she wanted him now.

She clenched her fists. "I will forget him this instant. What am I? A green, untried girl, in thrall to the first personable man who shows me kindness?"

Nay. She was Isobel Marston, sister to a war hero. If Edward could find the courage to sacrifice everything for the greater good, then she could, too.

But what if Will was in terrible danger and needed help? What would Edward do in her position? Well, if he couldn't persuade Manners to leave, he'd either go himself, or rally the male servants in the household and send them off on Will's trail.

That was the answer. She must escape Manners' vigilance, obtain a mount and head for Hertford. As he was obliged to look after her, the muscled giant would be forced to follow. Would he throw her over his saddle-bow when he caught up with her, and bring her back, or would he finally see sense and accompany her on her quest?

Praying he would do the latter, rather than cause a scene on the highway and risk the wrath of the law, she made her plans. First, she must pack some essentials, then she must find something to sell to pay for the hire of a horse, and finally, do what she could to leave the house without attracting anyone's attention.

What could she sell? There was her silver locket, but Will had borrowed that. The only other item of value was the gold signet ring. Her lip trembled. It would be agony to sell it, this tiny part of Will, this memento of their adventures together. And there was also the problem of it being stuck on her finger. However… if she went to the stables to hire a hack, would they not have a farrier there? What better person to help remove her ring? Blacksmiths and farriers had innumerable tools and pincers, did they not?

Satisfied that this would serve, she stole from the housekeeper's room, and into the parlor. She must find the documents from Marston House—the copy of her aunt's will and the document Hubert had forged to make her sign everything over to him. He'd be looking for these vital pieces of parchment as soon as he discovered them missing, and would doubtless come to Will's dwelling first. If Manners were absent, there'd be no one to guard these essential pieces of evidence. It was best she take them with her.

There was a loud knocking at the front door. Heart hammering, she threw open Will's chest of papers, and stuffed the two documents down the front of her bodice, then hovered by the door. She couldn't leave now—the hall would be filled with servants, attending to the visitor.

What if that visitor was Hubert? She pressed her ear against the door, her heart in her mouth.

"Sir William, welcome home. Mercy, what has happened to you?" Goodwife Cooper's voice was tight with concern.

Forgetting all else, Isobel charged out of the parlor.

"Will!"

He looked unwell, but his face brightened when he saw her. He was not alone, however, so she had to curb the urge to throw her arms about his neck and kiss him—he was being supported by Aloysius Maybury. If it weren't for the fact there was no smell of alcohol on the two men, they could have been taken for a couple of drunken sots staggering home. But the bruises and grazing to Will's face told a different tale.

"Isobel! Forgive me—I've failed in my duty. Nay, there's no need to fuss, Goody. I've been at Maybury's and, with the help of his doctor, am over the worst of it." He waved a dismissive hand at his housekeeper, then clamped his mouth shut as a startled look crossed his face.

In the heat of the moment, Isobel forgot she was supposed to be a Portuguese seamstress. "I've been so worried. Why is Mistress Hollingsworth not with you?"

Will shot her an agonized look and waggled his brows in Goodwife Cooper's direction. Alas, it was too late. The housekeeper wore a knowing expression.

"I do declare, Mistress—your English is rather superior for one of foreign extraction. And the name Isobel is not the one I was given."

"I'm sorry, Goody." Will sounded breathless. "We've been forced to deceive you. I'll explain why later. Isobel is English, but in grave danger, hence our need for subterfuge. If you could let the other servants know, I'd be in your debt."

Isobel bit her lip. He looked exhausted—there were bloodstains on his thigh and scabs of dried blood on his knuckles. He'd been in a fight. But what manner of skirmish had he fought? And how came Maybury to be with him?

"Mistress." Maybury gave her a bow. "Goodwife Cooper. Following the physician's orders, your master should take to his bed for a couple of days. No broken bones, but bruised ribs, and some blood loss from a wound in his thigh—an old wound reopened in the scuffle. It has been cleaned and looks to have knit well."

Will took a few shallow breaths. "Make up the room next to mine for Maybury. He must stay the night. Ah, Manners. All's well?"

Isobel stepped aside, her face coloring as she remembered the trick she'd been preparing to play on her bodyguard. But that was all forgotten now—Will was back, and nothing else mattered.

"Sir. Permit me." Without waiting for an answer, Manners extracted Will from Maybury's grasp, inserted his own beefy shoulder below Will's armpit, and started to heft him up the stairs.

"Forgive me, Isobel," Will called down as Manners bore him aloft. "I didn't make it as far as Hertford, but shall go another time."

She must go up, too, see him settled into his bed, and ensure Manners didn't hurt him. But she'd barely stirred when Maybury's hand came on her elbow.

"Mistress Marston, may we talk? Do you think Will's housekeeper might order us some refreshment?"

Goodwife Cooper curtseyed. "I can bring forth the remnants of our supper, sir. Will you take it in the parlor?"

Isobel was loath to leave Will, but Maybury's expression brooked no argument. As soon as they were settled either side of the hearth in the parlor, his face softened.

"I thought it meet I explain what happened."

She leaned forward, clutching her hands together. "Is he badly hurt?"

"Not so badly. Ah, I thank you." Maybury took charge of the platter of cold ham, spiced apple conserve, and manchet that was brought in. He poured two cups of ale, handed one to Isobel and asked, "Will you break bread with me?"

"Nay, I thank you, sir." She couldn't touch a morsel—her throat was so dry, any food would wedge in it. Will's reappearance, and in such a condition, had shocked her. The ale, however, was more than welcome.

Maybury sat back and chewed for a moment, then took a deep swig of his drink. She sipped hers. But rapidly.

"I came upon Cavendish on the road, being attacked by two masked brigands. He was giving good account of himself, but two against one is not good odds, and he had no sword, so they must have taken him by surprise. I pummeled one of those gutter-spawn into a heap and relieved the other of his knife. Seemed keen to do Will some damage with it, so I thought it best."

Isobel helped herself to another cup of ale. What if Maybury hadn't happened along when he did? Her heart pumped like a pair of bellows at the thought.

"What happened then?"

"Oh, he grabbed one of the fiends by the collar, and I the other. We brought their heads together with a crack you could hear for miles." Maybury chuckled. "Then I helped Will onto his horse, took him back to my home, and sent for our local constable."

"So, the perpetrators are now in custody?"

"In a cell, aye. But Will was keen to have them questioned as soon as may be. Said he knew 'twas no random attack. Thought he might know who was behind it."

She suspected *she* might, too. The idea froze her blood.

"Take some ham, Mistress Marston—you need sustenance. I understand your feelings—Will has explained your circumstances to me in full."

"I'm sorry you've become entangled in our hazardous affairs, sir."

"Think no more of it. My life has been dull since the death of my beloved wife. Nothing like a little derring-do to add spice to the day. We're now co-conspirators, Mistress Marston. If you have need of me, you'll know where to find me. But knock at the manor house, not the cottage, and I shall find you much better accommodation than you had before."

She rose from her chair. "I should like to see that Will is settled. Forgive my lack of manners, but as it was in my cause that he was thus injured, I feel it my duty to take care of him."

"He won't take long to mend. The worst of it was that his old wound was opened up. Just when it was healing—I could tell from his face, the pain was excruciating, but he bore it well. The blood loss has weakened him a little, but I'm sure you have simples here to strengthen him again. He never did vouchsafe the origins of his thigh injury. I don't suppose you have the answer to that riddle?"

She shook her head. "Alas—'tis not my secret to reveal." She reached for the latch, eager to be with Will and learn the true extent of his injuries.

Maybury tapped the side of his nose. "No matter. Your loyalty does you credit. I hope I shall see you before we retire to our beds this night, when we may talk of lighter matters."

"Indeed." She curtseyed, and left, then hastened up the stairs to see Will.

But it was not to be. Manners had stationed himself outside his master's room, and in response to her look of entreaty, lowered his voice, saying, "He's sleeping, Mistress.

Goody Cooper gave him a draught to dull the pain, so 'tis best not to disturb him. I'm sorry."

Despite the unfamiliar softness in his voice, Manners' resolve was solid as a rock. He folded his arms across his barrel of a chest and gazed at her.

She lifted her chin. Manners knew she was no foreign servant, and it was about time he treated her according to her rank.

"When he wakes, I'd be much obliged if you'd send me word. Whether it be day or night. I shall be in my chamber."

Looking somewhat startled, the man nodded.

She ascended the stairs to the attic, doing her best not to look defeated. If Will had need of her, she would be there, Manners or not. For she knew with utter certainty, she couldn't leave the house on Giles Street without seeing Will one last time.

CHAPTER TWENTY

ISOBEL COULDN'T BEAR to snuff out her candle. She'd been so worried in Will's absence, and her worries had proved justified. Had Maybury not intervened, Will would now be wrapped in a woolen shroud, not tucked up in bed in the room below her own. For she had no doubt Hubert was behind the attack and had paid his henchmen to leave Will for dead.

The thought made her quiver—not just for Will, but for herself. Hubert would stop at nothing to get what he wanted, not even murder.

No matter how often she told herself that she and Will were both safe now, the tremor refused to leave her limbs, and her eyes insisted on remaining wide open and alert. Her ears were strained for any unusual noises—which was why she heard the moan coming from below.

Stealing out of bed, she knelt on the scrubbed oak floorboards and lowered her head. There it was again, an unmistakably human noise, emerging from Will's room. He was in distress, but there was an incoherence about the sounds he was making. Was he in pain, in danger, or having a nightmare?

Silence fell. There was no sound of Manners going into the room, no murmur of voices. This was more unnerving than the moan, and she couldn't bear not to investigate. The night was warm, but she threw a sheet about her shoulders for modesty, slipped into her shoes, and padded to the door.

All was dark and quiet beyond—hopefully, a good sign. She pushed her candle into a holder, seized an empty pitcher in case she needed to defend herself, and tiptoed down the stairs towards Will's room.

The sight of a large shape sprawled partly across the passageway gave her pause, but her light revealed it to be Manners, fast asleep in front of Will's chamber.

"A fine watchdog you are," she muttered as she stepped gingerly over Manners' legs and tried the latch of Will's door.

It opened easily, and her fingers tightened on the handle of her jug. She prayed she was correct, and he was just having a dream, not groaning in discomfort, or crying out because he was being attacked.

Will lay on his back, one arm thrown up above his head. His breathing was labored and, from time to time, his head moved from one side to the other as if evading a blow.

She'd seen this before. He was reliving Edward's death, and the acquisition of the sword wound in his thigh. Or was it now the attack upon the road that haunted his dreams and disturbed his sleep?

"Will? *Will.*" She shook him by the shoulder. "Wake up. You're only dreaming."

He uttered a series of snorts, then his eyes flickered open and focused on the hand shaking him. She increased the pressure, worried that in his half-waking state, he might leap up and reach for his sword.

"Isobel? You shouldn't be here."

No. She shouldn't. "I heard you groaning

and had to come."

He rubbed a hand over his eyes and eased himself up in bed. Laboriously. "Did Manners let you in?"

"He's asleep. I stepped over him."

Will's eyes crinkled with laughter, but his mouth was set in a grim line. "I'll have him flogged, the lazy scoundrel."

"Please don't. He still has his uses, I dare say."

"You look worried. You shouldn't—all is well. We have Pike's confederates in irons—they'll say anything to keep themselves out of trouble. Soon, we'll have your cousin by the collar, and you can live free from fear once more."

He shifted sideways and patted the bed beside him. "If we are to talk, pray, sit. It's been days—what is afoot here? How are the servants coping with your elevated status? I wager they'll be wondering what unguarded things they've said in your hearing, thinking they wouldn't be understood."

She didn't want to discuss such minor details, even though the thought had brought that thrilling dimple to Will's cheek.

"I don't think Hubert's men were thieves.

I fear they were assassins."

Will raised an eyebrow. "Has that wretched dog Maybury been frightening you? Trust me—he has surely exaggerated the danger, in order to make himself out more of a hero. They were thieves who weren't expecting me to put up such a fight."

"What were they after?" She remembered Will had been carrying her locket.

"Those incriminating papers Manners stole from Pike. He must have assumed I was heading off to call the law down upon his head, rather than going to fetch a chaperone for you. I left the papers here—I'm glad to say."

"Oh!" But *she* had them now—she'd pushed them down her bodice when she'd been planning to start the hunt for Will and hadn't had the time to return them. Perhaps now was *not* the best time to mention that scheme. "I was so anxious when you didn't return."

"I'm honored you should care a fig for my unworthy hide. I can only regret I returned empty-handed. As soon as my thigh's mended, I'll make the attempt again— I swear to you."

She'd rather he didn't risk his life on her account. "Take Manners with you, I pray. Or Master Maybury—or, indeed, both of them."

He reached for her hand. "You were truly worried, weren't you, sweeting?"

She entwined her fingers with his, loving the warmth of his hand, hating the torn skin where he'd grazed his knuckles on his opponents. Having him back was so precious, such a blessing, she wanted this moment to last forever, just the two of them, in the heated, muffled summer night, gilded by candlelight.

There was a *clink*.

"Why did you bring a jug with you, Isobel?"

She'd forgotten the jug. Just as well it was empty—it was dangling from her hand, knocking against the wooden bed frame. Setting it down carefully, she replied, "I thought you might be thirsty."

He chuckled, then winced. "Oh, don't make me laugh, I beg of you. My ribs are too sore. You're a poor liar, my darling girl. In the future, should you want a weapon when traversing the corridors in the middle of the night, I'd advise a poker. Far easier to wield than a pitcher."

Her chin went up. "Mayhap you shouldn't be talking, if your ribs hurt."

"Mayhap I shouldn't." He pushed his free hand through his hair. "Did I wake you with my foolish dream?"

"I couldn't sleep." He looked so handsome, lying there relaxed in his voluminous bed, his hair tousled, his nightshirt open at the neck, revealing the shadowy muscle of his chest. If only…

"You must use my bed."

"I beg your pardon?" Had he divined her thoughts?

"I mean, you must have this room. Now 'tis known you are no servant, I can't have you bundled up in that tiny cot in the attic. I'll move into the adjacent chamber— once Maybury's gone—and you shall have this room, the finest in the house. I'll send for a dressmaker, too, so you have gowns befitting your status."

Nay—that way madness lay. It was distracting enough sleeping above him, but to have the width of just one wall between them—how could she cope with the temptation? But it was not her place to set her cap at Sir William Cavendish. She was no Paulina Mathieson, determined to get her man, however low she must stoop to win him. And since when had she given him her heart? Love was a stealthy companion—it had twined around her soul like a bryony stem, and she knew not how she could ever become disentangled.

"Isobel." Will's voice was soft and sent delicious tingles down her back. "I thought, for one bitter moment on that highway, I might never see your lovely face again."

"Fie, sir. You're a soldier. You would never give up hope."

"I never will—not now. Not ever. Kiss me, Isobel. I need to know if you're real, or merely a sprite sent to taunt me in my sleep."

"If I kiss you, you'd best think me a sprite, for otherwise, 'twould be most improper."

"A pox on propriety." His hand tightened on hers, and he pulled her inexorably closer as he leaned to crush her lips with his.

Mayhap she, too, was in a dream, for the touch of his mouth was beyond words, the delight of his kiss beyond imagining. As Will's tongue drove into her mouth, claiming her, she cradled his cheek, stroking it as if it were the most precious thing she'd ever touched. When he released her captive hand, she cupped his face, drinking from his lips, comparing their taste to the sweetest nectar.

He moved, found a position that fitted her against him, cradling her in the crook of one arm while he brushed her hair back from her forehead. Like a mirror to her action, he caressed her cheek, sculpting the lines of her face with his fingers, gazing into her eyes, to the very depths of her soul.

Could he see that new-fledged love? Was it evident in her expression, in the way she responded to his touch? Did he want that love, or was it only the fulfillment of his body's demands that mattered? Heat flooded her cheeks—what if she *was* no better than poor, besotted Paulina Mathieson? Will couldn't possibly respect a woman who responded so greedily to his caresses. Even though he'd asked for the kiss in the first place.

He gave her no time for doubt. Pushing his hand into her hair, he pulled her head against his, demanded her mouth once again, and kissed her thoroughly. Her mind clouded, as dazzling darts of desire shot through her body, and she tilted her head back for him, offering her surrender.

His hand bared her shoulder, and he traced the line of her collarbone. This subtle love-making was more powerful than any drug—she only wished she knew how she should respond, what she might do to please him.

As if in fulfillment of a dream, she felt Will tug her nightgown down, exposing the tops of her breasts. He broke the kiss then, and applied his lips to her neck and breastbone, then taunted her flesh with little flicks of his tongue. Like an opening flower, she gave herself up to him as her own desire met his burgeoning need. Thrilled, she reached up to tangle her fingers in his hair, letting the tawny gold run through her fingers. Now, she understood about possession—she'd had a taste of Will, and now she wanted *all* of him.

But what would become of her then? She was behaving no better than a common harlot.

She scuttled backwards off the bed, tugging the neck of her nightgown up. "I'm so sorry. Whatever must you think of me?"

"Isobel, wait!" He leapt from the bed, then pressed a hand to his side as a look of pain seared his face. "Please, don't go."

She grappled with the door, hurtled out, jumped over the sleeping Manners' legs, and flew back upstairs to her chamber.

He wouldn't follow her there, would he? She was so ashamed. How could she have lost control so easily? Oh, but he'd been right when saying she needed a chaperone—had her time spent in the half-light of madness tainted her soul? Mistress Isobel Marston, of Marston House, Holborn, would never have behaved like that, no matter how strongly she felt for a man.

How was she ever to face Will again after offering herself so wantonly?

CHAPTER TWENTY-ONE

THE HOUSE WAS in uproar. Isobel was jerked from an uneasy sleep by the sound of doors banging and raised voices.

It was full daylight, and no one had woken her, so her status as a guest—rather than a servant—must have been made known to the rest of the household. But surely, if the house were under threat, someone would have thought fit to tell her?

Dizzy from her sudden rising, she shuffled into her shoes, threw her skirt and bodice on over her nightgown, and hunted through the attic rooms in search of a poker, recalling Will's advice of the night before. Thus armed, she descended the stairs until her way was blocked by the sturdy form of Manners, standing with his back to her.

Peeping around his elbow, she saw Will, in nightshirt and hose, being confronted by a mob of his neighbors. Elbow to elbow with him stood Aloysius Maybury, staring blearily at the Mathieson family, crowded into Will's hallway. He, too, was not yet fully dressed, but had managed to fling a doublet on before joining in the fray.

Mathieson was saying, "Then I shall hunt through this house until you produce her. You know how much rests on Paulina's prior claim—I couldn't have made my message clearer."

"For the final time, Mathieson, I have no Portuguese mistress, no matter what tittle-tattle you might have heard. I've become guardian of an English gentlewoman in a time of great peril for her. I'm only telling you this because I see no need to upset Paulina. Despite the fact she has no valid claim on me."

Mathieson, whose face was red as a boiled crab, shook his fist. "You do not take me seriously, sir. You have toyed with the affections of a young and vulnerable woman and now refuse to do the decent thing. You do not deserve the title of knight."

"And *you* do not deserve the title of gentleman, flying into a rage in my hallway before my household is even up. You have roused me from my sickbed, in truth, for which I do not thank you." Will's voice was ice, his body rigid. Isobel saw Maybury place a restraining hand on Will's arm.

Paulina, who stood behind her father, leaning on her mother's arm, let out a wail at this. "Oh, you've been injured. My poor lamb!"

Isobel's mouth twisted. Will was anything *but* a poor lamb. Paulina was deluded in more ways than one.

"You see how upset she is? You should be visiting her, courting her, conversing with her, or she will fade away from misery. There, there, my pet." Mathieson turned and gave his daughter an awkward pat on the shoulder.

"I have, indeed, been injured. I was venturing out on behalf of the lady I mentioned—as I said, I have proof positive she's in mortal danger. Her wellbeing is of greater importance to me than is Paulina's— if you'll forgive me. I'm duty-bound to the lady, and anything you may have heard about her being Portuguese was a deception to keep her presence here a secret. Now, what with *your* gossiping servants, and whichever one of my own revealed the information, I imagine half of London knows. God be thanked you don't know her name *or* her story—and I don't intend to give it to you."

Mathieson pushed his shoulders back. "You have no honor, sir."

"Nor have you, to accuse me of leading your daughter to false expectations."

Will's opponent looked fit to explode. "You'll answer to me for that, sirrah."

"No!" Isobel pushed past Manners, catching him off guard, and rushed down the stairs, coming to a halt between the two antagonists.

"*I* am the English gentlewoman in question, and every word Will says is true." She had the foresight to keep her hands behind her back, so none of the Mathieson family could see the gold ring on her finger. Or the poker she held. "As he says, you shouldn't listen to the gossip of servants. Sir William is, indeed, my current protector—for I have been in need of a champion—and you impugn *my* honor by suggesting there is anything more than friendship between us."

Will would not be hurt by this pronouncement, she hoped—after last night, there evidently *was* more than friendship between them. But for now, she'd say anything to be rid of the troublesome Mathiesons.

Mathieson sucked in a breath, and his shoulders drooped. She'd taken the wind out of his sails, but for how long?

"Forgive me, Mistress." He gave her a curt bow. "You neither look nor sound like a foreigner. I regret to inform you, however, that your presence makes no difference to my daughter's situation."

She felt Will's hands on her shoulders and shook them away, irritated. Why was he giving the lie to what she'd just said by touching her in such a familiar way?

Mathieson's eyes narrowed. "Standing between me and your protector will avail you nothing, Mistress. He and I know that I have the means to ruin him, should I choose to do so."

This man was infuriating. No wonder Will was so angry—she could feel the tension radiating from him, pulsing in his pent-up breathing.

"You do *not* have the means to ruin him. You're mistaken on that score." It was hard not to grind her teeth in annoyance. "I can refute anything you consider proof. That's if you have any at all, which I doubt."

"Isobel, don't say anything more, I beseech you."

Once again, she shook herself free of Will's hands. Her dander was up. She could *not* have these people invading this house and casting aspersions about. "I know you think there is a dubious association between Sir William and the Earl of Leicester. Let me assure you there is none. Sir William has been acting as an agent for my recently deceased brother."

Will groaned softly, but she ignored him. She'd made a decision, and she intended to stick to it. "Edward Marston, of Marston House in Holborn, died in a raid. He was in the service of Robert Dudley in Holland. As Sir William was over there on business, he was chosen to bring back news of my brother's death, and a memento for me—my brother's sword."

"My condolences." Mathieson bowed but looked unconvinced.

"That's enough." Will moved her out of the way. "Isobel, you're upset. Pray, go to your chamber while I make this knave see sense." He stared down at Mathieson.

How dare Will interfere when she was in full flow, and order her about? He didn't know all there was to know, and he certainly had no right to command her.

"I have one more thing to say." She stood beside Will. "Before you make any further effort to blackmail Sir William here, I want you to know that the package you held for him in his absence was intended for my brother. Aye, I appreciate it was addressed to Will Cavendish, but the note inside and the contents were for my late brother, Edward, and have now been passed to me, as his heir. Sir William concealed the fact from you in order to protect Edward's reputation. He deceived you for my benefit, fearing my name would be dragged through the mire along with my brother's."

She paused, allowing her words to sink in, waiting for Will to support her. But he said nothing. Risking a glance at him, she saw his face was pale and set. Mathieson met his gaze.

"Is this true, Cavendish?"

"Do you doubt the word of a lady?" The challenge in Will's voice was fierce, making Mathieson blink, and step away. Isobel remembered she still held the poker and moved it out of Will's line of vision. Just in case.

As soon as Mathieson moved, Maybury joined the wall of opposition, and Manners came down to the bottom step of the staircase. The tension was so palpable, one could cut it with a knife.

Mistress Mathieson broke the silence. "My apologies for having disturbed you, sir. I advise departure, Husband, but not in retreat—only to regroup. We have listened to your case, Sir William, Mistress Marston, and will consider what our next action may be. God give you good day."

Isobel swallowed her gasp of surprise. Who would have thought the lady of the house held sway over her belligerent husband? It seemed she did, however, for although he colored and scowled, he bowed curtly and turned his back on the united front in Will's hallway, and followed wife and daughter into the street.

"Well." Isobel let out the breath she'd been holding. "We seem to have command of the field, Sir William. At least, for now."

Will's face as he turned to her was stark, emotionless, like that of a statue carved in marble. "Excuse me, Maybury—pray, make shift for yourself and don't await my company for breakfast. I need private speech with Mistress Marston."

Without further ado, Will took her by the wrist, making her drop the poker with a *clang,* and pulled her into the parlor.

"Congratulations, Isobel," he ground out as he released her and slammed the door closed. "You've just ruined everything."

CHAPTER TWENTY-TWO

"WHAT? IN WHAT way have I trespassed?"

Isobel looked so shocked, Will immediately regretted hauling her off in front of an audience, even if it *was* only Manners and Maybury. All the same, she should have left him to deal with Mathieson in his own way. He was master in his own house, and he'd devised a plan. Why could she not have trusted him?

"I'm sorry, Isobel, but this is my battle, not yours. I know you meant well, but you should have held your tongue."

"Held my tongue?" Her green eyes sparked, and her cheeks glowed pink. "Don't treat me like a child. I shall say whatever I wish to say."

He hung his head. "A poor choice of words. But I would have genuinely preferred it had you said nothing. Have you no faith in me at all? Have I not preserved both our skins thus far, despite deadly danger? Do you really think I'd let a worm like Mathieson defeat me?"

"Ungrateful cur." She flung her words like projectiles. "I was getting you off the hook."

"I was about to get myself off the hook. If you'd calm down a moment, I'll tell you what I had planned."

"You could have told me last night if you had a plan." Her mouth hardened, and she pressed back in her chair.

Such a beautiful mouth—lips he wanted to ravish, not reproach. He'd like to lift her into his arms and kiss all that resistance out of her, tame her, have her longing for him. If he could only channel all that passionate anger of hers into something else…

"I'm sorry." He pushed a hand through his hair and looked down at himself. He was only half-dressed, barely decent. Little wonder Mathieson had thought them lovers when they both ran around the house dressed only in their nightclothes. He settled onto the chair opposite Isobel and forced himself to relax.

And stop having inappropriate thoughts.

"I know the idea was unpleasant to you, but I meant to ask for your hand again. I planned to make it known to the world that you and I were to wed, and intended Mathieson to see the ring that's wedged on your finger. He wouldn't need to look at it closely—he'd easily be convinced it was a betrothal ring. Once we were known to be a couple, there'd be little point in him attempting to ruin my reputation. Paulina would soon have shifted her interest to some other man if she knew I was taken. And we could have flushed Pike out."

Isobel gazed at him, wide-eyed. Good. At least, she wasn't disgusted by the notion of marriage to him.

"Flushed out Hubert? How?"

"He's gone to ground since I was attacked, apparently. Manners has a network of helpers across London, but none have seen him. He appears to have let all his servants go and abandoned Marston House—too afraid to show his face lest my assailants point the finger at him. My expectation was, that once word got out of our betrothal, he'd do what he could to prevent our marriage, lest he lose his last opportunity of securing your legacy. He'd have to come out of hiding to do that."

"You were going to use yourself as bait, you mean. How could you, Will, when you were nearly killed but a few days since?"

There was a wobble in her voice—her anger had subsided, giving way to distress. She still cared about his sorry hide then—he'd been starting to think she didn't.

He kept his voice soft. "I would be well-protected the next time. I'd have Manners with me, and other men hidden along the route. Aye, I have friends in low places, if you will, and can call upon veterans and mercenaries if required. I'd be in no danger."

"And I'm supposed to be happy about that, am I?" She leapt to her feet, elfin chin raised defiantly. "It's as well you never told me of your plan, Will Cavendish, for I would never have gone along with it. *Never!*"

Before he could stop her, she'd fled from the parlor, and he heard her running up the stairs.

"Trouble?" Aloysius Maybury entered the room, closing the door softly behind him, cutting off Will's chance of racing after Isobel. Mayhap it was for the best—she was in no mood to listen to him now.

"A little. Nothing that won't resolve itself, given time. I'm sorry you had to witness that uncomfortable scene earlier."

"I wouldn't have missed it for the world. Your life is a deal more interesting than mine, Cavendish. Would I had one beauty chasing after me, and another defending me so loyally."

"You think Paulina beautiful?"

"Aye." Maybury settled himself opposite Will. "A most handsome wench. She'll make someone a fine wife—but not you, I take it?"

Will shuddered, his nerves taut after the scene with Isobel. "I'll not be blackmailed into wedlock. No man would."

"Is there no other fellow who could distract yon golden-haired damsel?"

He pondered for a moment. "There's the Comte de Velors, I suppose—he's been visiting them. But the Mathiesons are a traditional family—I doubt they'd smile on any match with a foreigner."

"And what of the winsome Mistress Marston? She has fire in her blood. She'd make the perfect mistress, I trow."

Will's eyebrows shot up, and he gazed at Maybury. Surely the man wasn't contemplating…?

"Are you considering remarrying?" He knew Maybury's wife had died in childbirth in the spring of the previous year, and that the child had been lost as well.

Maybury shook his head. "I know not if I could put myself through that again. We were all much shaken. Her mother took it so hard, she barely lasted until the summer."

"It must have been terrible."

"It would have been worse had it been a love match. But I believe those are rarely come by. And not necessarily for the best. I say, love thy mistress and honor thy wife. You're less likely to break your heart that way."

Will would never have expected to be discussing affairs of the heart with any man, let alone Aloysius Maybury. "Perhaps I can introduce you to a few suitable ladies, once I've won my place at court. 'Tis the least I can do for my noble rescuer. Shall I find you a lady who plays delightfully? I recall you always enjoyed good music."

"I certainly do. I'm particularly partial to the harpsichord. An instrument at which Mistress Marston is accomplished, I understand."

Was that the way the land lay—Maybury was interested in Isobel? Will surveyed his friend in silence, battling to ignore the sudden feeling of panic that clutched at his chest. Maybury had a great deal to recommend him, besides his standing and his wealth. He was well-built, in florid good health, with startling blue eyes that seemed to take in everything they saw and more besides. He was of the same age as Will, and his bulk was accounted for by muscle, not fat. He appeared to have all his own teeth, and there was no sign of thinning in the neatly curled dark hair that framed his brow. Apart from a ready temper, his heart was in the right place, and he was not—as far as Will knew—a philanderer. He would be just the kind of husband and protector Isobel needed.

Will immediately began extolling the virtues of Paulina Mathieson, and every other lady of his acquaintance. The idea of Isobel in the arms of any man but himself was appalling. She was angry with him now, for chiding her, but he'd do what he could to win her forgiveness.

Then it struck him, with a blinding clarity that obliterated all else, that it wasn't her forgiveness he needed at all.

What he needed, above all things, was to win her love.

CHAPTER TWENTY-THREE

I SOBEL HAD SPENT the first half of the day trying to restore her equanimity. The second half had been spent trying to work out how to persuade Manners to fit in with her escape plan. She'd seen nothing more of either Will or Maybury, but when Goody Cooper came to see about moving her into Will's room, she'd refused. She'd created enough turmoil in Will's life—no matter how furious at him she might be, it wasn't right to steal his home comforts.

By the time the household was ready to retire, an unseasonable gale had risen up. This kept Isobel awake, fretting about her scheme to return to Marston House on the morrow. When she wasn't chewing over that, her mind was busy chastising her for her response to Will's caresses the previous night.

How had she fallen so far? Was she so in love with him, that she'd let him do as he pleased with her body? The only explanation for her behavior was that a recently bereaved and lonely woman must be easily moved by the attentions of an attractive man. She wasn't her usual self—she was still vulnerable.

Nay. *Had* been vulnerable. Her mind was clearer now. After that altercation with him this morning, she knew it would be best for all concerned if she were to leave Will's house. He confused and disturbed her. She irritated him—and had put his life at risk.

The howling of the wind against the panes made her increasingly melancholy. How could she sleep with her window rattling so, and the buffeting of the gale outside? She hoped it wasn't going to rain, or she'd be splashing through overflowing gutters *en route* to Marston House. Was there a pair of pattens anywhere she could borrow to preserve the hem of her skirt?

Why had Will kissed her last night? Was she so irresistible that the most handsome man she'd ever met could not deny her? A bitter laugh escaped her at that idea. *She*, irresistible? She couldn't even compare favorably to Paulina Mathieson. Her dark looks were hardly fashionable, and most of the time she'd spent in Will's company, she'd been wearing either nightclothes or the garb of a servant.

Mayhap, having seen the invitation in her eyes, he was simply being gallant—he would not wish to hurt her feelings with a blunt rejection. Perchance, given a moment longer, he would have gently disentangled himself and sent her back to her chamber.

With a *tut* of irritation, she sat up. This relentless brooding was getting her nowhere, and she needed something to help her sleep. Something other than poppy juice, of course—a book would do. There'd be nobody about at this hour and, as far as she knew, Will was still out carousing in some alehouse or playing at cards.

As she crept down the stairs, illuminating her way with a pungent tallow candle, she heard no sound of human activity. The house now slept, oblivious to the gale outside. Below, in the heart of the building, the savage sounds of the wind were muted, and she felt pleasantly secure as she made her way to the parlor.

A flicker of orange light beneath the door made her pause, her hand frozen on the latch. Placing her ear against the wood, she heard the crackle and sputter of a fire and sensed Will's presence therein.

Heart thudding, she turned away, but suddenly the door was wrenched open, and there he stood, gazing at her. He looked much as he had that morning, his hair tousled and his shirt collar untied, but he wore both upper and nether hose and was still shod. How long had he been home?

He went still at the sight of her. Only his eyes moved, glittering darkly from beneath lowered lids as he focused on her face. His body radiated weariness—an empty wine glass hung so limply from his fingers that she thought he might forget it at any moment and let it fall. She needed only one glance to see his soul was as exhausted as his body.

Had that weariness sprung from the same source as her own, an internal battle to deny his feelings? She read failure in his frowning brow, in his downturned mouth, in his mirthless eyes. Had her interference with his plans truly affected him so profoundly? Or was there something else that gnawed away at his peace of mind?

Remorse washed over her. "Oh, Will. Please let us not be at odds. I've been foolish and precipitate. I apologize." She moved towards him and he backed away, allowing her to enter the parlor.

There was a *clink* as he set his wine glass down, then pushed the door closed. His eyes bored into hers and, leaning forward, he seized her chin in his hand, stealing her breath. What was he thinking? His face was so darkly shadowed, his eyes so bright—he was still furious, and she was right to plot her escape. They could never span the chasm that had opened up between them.

"Isobel." To her amazement, he pressed his lips lingeringly against hers. "Sweet Isobel. I would give all the gold in the world to have you feel for me what I feel for you."

Her heart ground to a halt. He was drunk. He must be—unless he meant to punish her with his tantalizing kiss. What meaning lay beneath his words?

"I've detested myself all day long for

dealing with you so ungently. You were not the only one at fault this morn. In my conceited pride, I thought I knew what was best for you, but neglected to share my thoughts with you, and I deserve to suffer for that. I believe you meant well by lying to protect me, and I can only apologize for my lack of gratitude."

Her heart beat frantically as his words filtered through her muddled brain. This was not turning out at all as she'd expected. After their skirmish earlier, she expected him to rail at her. But he wasn't punishing her—he was blaming himself for their fight. Which exacerbated her guilt in the knowledge she planned to run away from him.

"Your way was better," he continued, gazing deep into her eyes. "Mine would have hurt Paulina. Besides which, the very last thing I wish to do is trick or trap you into becoming espoused to me. I wouldn't have held you to it, you know. We need only have kept up the pretense until Paulina's attentions became centered on some other man."

Why did that remark make her heart sink, when only a few hours ago it had incensed her? "There's no need to be sorry. I thought you must still be angry with me."

He brushed his thumb over her lower lip. "Ah, my little witch, how naïve you are." He held her face between his hands a moment longer, then released her.

He was undoubtedly right. She knew nothing of this world of pain and confusion, of power play and politics, of love, hate, and advantageous marriages. If only she could read his heart.

"What are you doing up at this hour, wandering about the house in your night-clothes?"

"I couldn't sleep." She wasn't about to tell him *why*. "I came down here for a book."

"Ah, don't tell me—you're overexcited after this morning's unexpected entertainments."

Excited? No. And she didn't want to be reminded about her blatant lying.

"I regret what I did this morning, Will. At the time, I thought it was for the best."

"As did I. Now, I don't know what to think."

His face was so shadowed, she knew not how to read it. There was an intensity about him that spoke of some deep emotion, tightly controlled. She prayed she hadn't alienated the man who had been her savior.

Although if she had, leaving him would be less painful.

Wouldn't it?

CHAPTER TWENTY-FOUR

WILL GAZED DOWN at the green-eyed beauty. She'd put a spell on him, surely—he was no longer himself. He wanted to rail at her, fight with her, kiss her, and entwine himself around her—body and soul—until they ceased to be two and became one.

He should have been more circumspect in his drinking tonight—at this moment, anything seemed possible, even the most sinful, most forbidden deeds.

Shaking his head, he attempted to dislodge his wayward thoughts. "With regard to this morning, I'd prefer you to tell me what's in your mind if you have a plan, so I may go along with it. Or dissuade you, if I think your idea is folly."

He fanned his fingers across her shoulders, feeling the feminine warmth of her, remembering the silk of her skin when he'd traced his tongue over it last night. The wicked excitement in his belly refused to be banished. Isobel should choose a book and go back to bed. He should choose one for her if it sped up the process—he was so close to forgetting himself and doing something completely reprehensible.

"Let us speak no more of what happened earlier—we have both proved ourselves fallible. Will you forgive my behavior?"

For a moment, he didn't know if he was asking for absolution for his earlier churlishness, or for what he feared he was about to do. Kiss her senseless, then carry her up the stairs and share his great canopied bed with her.

"Isobel, you are so beautiful."

She searched his face. "What? Why would you say that? I look like a stray dog you've picked up from the gutter. After it's been trampled by a flock of sheep. You have never yet seen me at my best."

His heart lurched, and he found himself

grinning like an idiot. "Foolish wench. Come." Collecting a candle in one hand, he steered her into the hallway, then put his light in the sconce beside his Venetian mirror. Placing her in front of him, he slid an arm around her waist and stood her squarely in front of the mirror.

"Look."

"What am I looking at?"

Ah, but it felt so good, holding her against him. He nudged her face around with his spare hand, so she was looking directly at her reflection. "How can you say you look like a stray dog?"

She tried to turn away, but he slipped his fingers into her hair and trapped her there. An impatient huff escaped her. "I'm not fishing for compliments, Will. I have not the coloring nor the curves of Paulina Mathieson, for a start."

He rolled his eyes and lowered his mouth so it was level with her ear. Close enough for her hair to brush his cheek, for him to revel in the sweet scent of her.

"Look at yourself. You *are* beautiful. Those eyes are captivating, and your face is a perfect oval and full of character. Your mouth is soft, vulnerable, and deliciously tempting to any man who sees it. Paulina is like a doll compared to you—a creature of artifice, not flesh and blood. You must already realize the hold you have over *me,* whether I would have it so or not."

He watched her reflection swallow a gulp of air and felt her tremble. His body tensed, waiting for her reaction, searching her face in the mirror for a betraying response, any sign of what was passing behind those sea-green eyes.

Aye, he had definitely quaffed too much Canary wine—it had loosened his tongue. He was saying far more than was seemly, but it was all so blindingly, obviously true, and had been for a long time. So why deny it any longer?

Tonight, Isobel looked more entrancing than ever. Her dark hair hung like a swathe of midnight over her modest white nightgown, and the flickering candlelight produced tantalizing shadows where her feminine curves pushed against the clinging linen. His eyes fastened on the reflection of his hand, still resting gently over her abdomen. One handspan higher, and he could stroke the luscious softness of her breast. But if he did, he would be truly lost.

Cursing roughly beneath his breath, he spun her around, trapping her face between his hands. "Go." His voice was hoarse. "Go, before I do something we'll both regret."

She was frozen in his grasp, neither welcoming nor rejecting him. She certainly wasn't obeying. Her gaze dropped to his lips, and she raised her hands to stroke his face.

"Oh, Isobel." He pressed her hand against his cheek before turning his face to kiss her palm, then ran his thumb over her mouth. This felt like a dream—it was no longer Sir William Cavendish who commanded his actions, but some other self—some untamed, primordial self that responded to the temptation of her body. Without further thought, he dragged her against him, crushing his mouth punishingly against hers.

She whimpered, and he forced himself to retreat. His breathing went shallow as he waited for her response. Then—oh, miracle of miracles—her hands reached for his shoulders, drawing him more deeply into the kiss. Desire flamed hot in his belly, and he murmured meaningless promises as his lips left hers to plunder the ivory skin of her neck and brush softly over the raven sheen of her hair.

Slowly, he brought her closer, until their thighs were touching and he could feel the pressure of her firm breasts against his chest. Soon, she'd be able to feel *exactly* how she was affecting him. What did he intend to do about it? How far dare he take this?

Lifting his head to rub his cheek against her hair, Will caught sight of his reflection in the mirror. The face that looked back at him was drunk with desire, his eyes half-closed, his lips pulled back from his teeth like a stag in rut. With a violent stab of self-disgust, he pulled away from Isobel.

"Why are you still here?" His question was a rough demand. "I told you to go."

He read the distress in her eyes and wondered how he had become so cruel. But honor must persist over nature—he'd made a promise, and was not about to break it by seducing the woman he was meant to be protecting.

When she didn't move, he growled at her. "Go to your chamber, Isobel. *Now!*"

This time, she went, her feet flying up the

stairs as if the hounds of hell were after her.

A thousand curses on Hubert Pike for preventing him fetching a female companion for Isobel! Now, there was no choice. Only one thing would make their situation bearable—they must marry.

He would ask her on the morrow. Well, make his apologies first, for being a brute this evening—and *then* ask her.

He had no idea what he'd do if she refused him. She simply *had* to say "yes".

CHAPTER TWENTY-FIVE

I SOBEL WAS DEVASTATED by Will's abrupt dismissal. On her return to bed, her face still burned from his kisses, her body thrummed with the power of his touch—and somewhere deep inside, a void had been opened that now clamored to be filled. Propriety had been ignored—again. Yet even as she'd unbent to Will's fierce demand, he'd been withdrawing from her. First, he'd enslaved her, then he'd abandoned her, like a grotesque form of punishment.

She'd never imagined a man could wield so much power with a single kiss, a single touch. Kissing was dangerous—*he* was dangerous. Her virtue was at stake, and her heart in peril. To be revered like a goddess one moment, then summarily dismissed the next was unbearable.

Will knew every inch of her shame, every ounce of her weakness, and could play on that vulnerability for as long as he wanted. It was vital she leave at the earliest opportunity.

Hubert hadn't returned to Marston House, so that was where she must go. Perhaps, having ascertained the situation there, she would then go north in search of Mistress Hollingsworth. Cecelia was a mature and sensible woman—she could advise on what Isobel should do about Will. If only she didn't need his help in bringing Hubert to justice! It would be less painful if she could avoid him in the future, but he was far better placed than she to track her cousin down and make him pay for his misdeeds.

There was no possibility of sleep—her mind was in turmoil. By the time a tuneful blackbird proclaimed the arrival of dawn from the gable above her window, she was ready to leave. None of the servants was yet stirring, but she dressed herself, made up the kitchen fire, put some eggs in water to boil, and sought out Will's bodyguard, Manners.

As expected, he was slumped in a chair in

front of the door to Will's chamber. She gave him a gentle shove.

He awoke with a snort, bit back a blasphemy, then wiped his eyes and stared at her. "Good morrow, Mistress. What's afoot?"

"Did your master not say? I *knew* he'd forget. He was too much in his cups last night." She stood, fists on her hips, glaring fiercely at Will's closed door. "I've a mind to charge in and pour something unsavory over his head, the wretch."

Manners scratched his head, then got to his feet and executed an awkward bow. "What was he supposed to have said?"

"Why, that you were to accompany me to Hertford. You recall that was where he was going when he was set upon. The purpose of that journey was to find Mistress Hollingsworth and bring her here. But we decided, as his thigh pains him still, 'twould be easier if *I* were to go to her."

She allowed Manners time to absorb this information. What would she do if he gave her a blunt refusal, or insisted on waking Will?

"I've some eggs cooking, and manchet rolls warming in the kitchen. There's game pie, too, so we may break our fast before we leave. I arranged it all with Cook on the yester, knowing we'd want an early start."

Her appeal to his stomach did the trick. He nodded, requested a short time in which to change his linens and make himself presentable, and agreed to meet her in the kitchen.

She decided it best to say as little as possible. One didn't share one's plans with servants anyway—Manners was more likely to believe her if she kept herself aloof. Besides, what was the worst that could happen? He wouldn't hurt her if he perceived her deception—she was under Will's protection. Most likely, he'd throw her over his shoulder and bring her back here, kicking and screaming, to face Will's wrath.

It was worth the risk. She had put Will in danger by letting him serve her interests. Now, their relationship had become complicated, and she barely recognized the wanton she'd become in his arms. It was imperative she be Mistress Isobel Marston of Marston House again. Not mad, not sick from the brain fever, not hopelessly in love with a man who had rejected her.

"Shall we ride, or hire a wagon, Mistress?"

Manners' rough voice brought her back to herself. "I thought we'd walk, first of all, to Marston House. Then find a conveyance to take us to Hertford."

In response to her companion's questioning look, she explained, "I don't want to be beholden to Sir William. If there's anything of value left in Marston House, I'll sell it to pay for our travel. I also hope to pick up some clothing there."

This was a lie, as she meant to go no further than Marston House—at least, not for now. She needed to be at home, in familiar surroundings, and find herself again. The Isobel aching for Will's kiss last night was not the Isobel she knew—the weeks spent in an opium-induced haze had pushed her to the edge of madness, and she needed to find equilibrium again.

And propriety.

Manners appeared convinced. After all, she wasn't trying to escape him—she'd made it plain he was to be her protector and companion. Quite how she'd persuade him to leave her at Marston House and return to

Will, she had, as yet, no idea.

It took no more than a quarter of an hour for them to eat their fill, leave the house, and step out onto the cobbles in the hazy morning sunshine. Rain had fallen in the early hours—she'd heard it while she lay struggling to sleep. Now, a faint mist arose where the sun struck the stones of the street. It looked inviting, freshly washed, the gutters scoured by the downpour and last night's gale. The muck would, hopefully, have washed away into one of the culverts that bubbled below the roads and buildings, to flow eventually into the cleansing tide of the Thames.

Isobel stood in front of Will's house, relishing the first true moment of freedom she'd had in months. She felt bold and daring, the blood fizzing in her veins at her temerity.

She turned to Manners. "Pray, lead the way. I know not how to go thither, but you have been, have you not?"

He nodded and lumbered off. Her satchel bounced beneath her arm, and she clutched it tightly, eager not to become prey to a cutpurse or thief. For in it, she carried the documents she'd snatched from Will's coffer, including the one with the details of her legacy. He'd be angry when he found she'd taken it, but it was, after all, hers to take.

Her knees creaked from lack of use, and her leg muscles ached as she tramped over the cobbles, but the discomfort soon passed, and she was able to stride out, just about keeping up with Manners as he loped along. There was another pain, however, that could not be eased. The pain of leaving Will.

She shook her head free of the memories, and concentrated on looking around her. Gradually, the streets became more familiar—she recognized an alehouse with a peculiarly carved bear adorning its frontage. There was a costermonger's, with depictions of rare fruit in raised plasterwork between the timber beams; a butcher's, issuing forth a familiar stench; and the apothecary her family used to frequent, its dark interior filled with an array of mysterious bottles, pots, and jars.

The streets widened, the gaps between the houses increasing, until finally, there was space for gardens, their high walls protecting vegetable plots, sweet herbs, and fruit trees bowed with ripening plums, quinces, and medlars.

And there it was—Marston House. It brought back memories of her imprisonment, and she couldn't repress a shudder. How many weeks, months even, had she missed as a result of being drugged? How many friends had she lost as a result of her so-called illness? Her hatred for Hubert increased at the thought of how much of her life he'd stolen, time that could never be regained. If she were a man, she'd have no compunction about running her detestable cousin through.

Her anger buoyed her up as they approached the house, and crushed the nagging worm of fear that he might be within, or nearby, watching them. Standing on the path, grimacing at the straggling weeds that had taken over its edges, Isobel tried the door. It was locked. Of course, it was—and she didn't have the key.

"No matter, Mistress. Wait here." Manners pushed past a trailing rosebush, ignoring the snags on his clothing, and disappeared around the corner of the house. Shortly thereafter, she heard a rattle, and the front door opened.

"A misspent youth," he said in answer to

her questioning look.

As she stepped into the hallway, she was greeted by stale air, but there was no smell of woodsmoke, suggesting the house had been unoccupied for some time. The gloomy darkness within was soon dispelled by Manners, who entered every room ahead of her and pulled open the shutters.

"To make sure there's no one lurking," he explained.

There was no one lurking. Not Hubert, nor Avice, nor Flinders—fortunately—nor any of the servants. She'd have her work cut out in the first instance, trying to get the place up and running. But once she could secure her legacy, she'd staff the house again, and put her nose to the grindstone. Then she'd send messages to every friend she could remember and invite them to pay her a visit—and Cecelia Hollingsworth must be invited, too, and perhaps even Master Maybury. He'd saved Will's life, after all.

As she scoured the rooms, her mood darkened. Hubert hadn't troubled to keep the place tidy or clean after he'd dismissed his household. Everything of value had disappeared, but she supposed enough remained to make the place serviceable, at least for the time being.

It unnerved her to be in her house again, to find it so familiar, and yet so alien. She quelled the frissons of anxiety by concentrating on what would be needed. The remaining furniture had been ill-used and needed replacing. There were crocks enough in the kitchen, and wooden platters to eat from, but all the pewter had vanished. The kitchen hearth was piled deep in ash, and in dire need of a clean, and the tapestried hangings had disappeared from the walls, leaving the plaster looking crude and unfinished.

"I'll clean up the hearth while you fetch your things, Mistress," Manners offered.

Now was the time to see how much further she could trespass on his goodwill. "Thank you. But I feel a megrim coming on—I'm overwhelmed by the condition of my home, I think. I fear I must rest here awhile until I'm recovered."

"Shall I go to the apothecary for a pow-der, Mistress? We passed one on our way hither."

"Nay. There should be feverfew in the garden. If you can clear the hearth and build a fire, I'll make a tisane." She had no coin with which to pay an apothecary, although she hoped the sale of some of her gowns would bring in a goodly return. She had her locket, of course, but she had no intention of selling that to buy physick for an invented headache.

"If you wish to stay here awhile, shall I send for one of the servants from Giles Street? They could put the place to rights while you rest, and help you prepare for the rest of our journey. A wench, I mean—for *I* can do any heavy work that's needful. Or Goody Cooper would come, I know—she would soon have the place fragrant as befits a lady, for all that she keeps house for a man."

Isobel blinked. That wasn't a bad idea at all, although she'd be depriving Will of his housekeeper. Only for the shortest time, however. But no—it would bring him to her door even sooner, and she wasn't ready to face him yet. If Fortune favored her, he'd sleep in today, then go about his business, assuming she'd had her breakfast early. He probably wouldn't miss her until it was time for his midday repast and, even then, he would doubtless be too angry at her to seek her out immediately.

She shook her head. "It is a goodly scheme, Master Manners. But let us see if we can make shift for today—if we need help, or I don't improve, mayhap send for her on the morrow. I shall go and fetch some feverfew."

Unbolting the kitchen door, she strolled into the walled garden, enjoying the taste of the fresher air. Her meandering took her to the place where Will had climbed the high brick wall after he'd been refused admittance—thank heaven he *had* climbed in, or she might have lost her mind completely, beyond hope of ever regaining it. It must have hurt him, with that injured thigh of his. How was the wound now, having been reopened during the attack?

Her stomach clenched, and pain jabbed at her heart as she thought of what had passed between them since that moment. From now on, it must be as if she had never met him. She would learn to stand alone, to rely on no one.

Ah, here was the feverfew. She tugged at the tough stems and filled her skirt with the leaves. Having told Manners she would make a tisane, she'd now have to do it. Hopefully, he'd not watch her drink it, as she couldn't abide the bitter taste, and there was neither honey nor sugar left in the pantry.

Relieved to be outside in the sunlight, no longer in hiding, she continued her perambulation of the garden, then came to a halt by a bank of colorful blooms, nodding gently in the breeze.

Poppies.

Her mouth went dry. There was no place in *her* garden for such monstrosities. Forgetting the feverfew, she fell to her knees, hands tearing at the feathery stems, yanking the white, purple and pink flowers out by their roots, cursing when the stalks broke, scrabbling at the soil to remove every last living shred of poppy flower.

Her eyes blurred with tears and she sat back, staring at her filthy, broken nails, and the heap of greenery and limp petals.

This was not the behavior of a woman who was in her right senses. What had she done, leaving the safety of Will's doors? She wasn't yet ready to be on her own—she wasn't yet cured.

She had just—quite possibly—made the biggest mistake of her life.

Chapter Twenty-Six

I SOBEL PUT ANOTHER stitch into her embroidery, then stared—as she had done every day for the last week—out of the solar window down onto the busy thoroughfare of Holborn. She was sure Will would come, sooner or later, just as she was sure their meeting would not be a comfortable one. He would come because he was too proud to be bested by a woman.

And because he probably wanted his housekeeper back. Goody Cooper had arrived as soon as Manners had sent for her. She had brought tidings of Will—his leg pained him, apparently, and was too stiff to allow him to either ride or walk much distance. The housekeeper came with Will's blessing—allegedly.

Truth was, he'd not want to be humiliated in front of his household, and would have made it appear he had full knowledge of Isobel's removal to Marston House and approved of it. She still hadn't told Manners she had no intention of going on to Hertford in search of Mistress Hollingsworth, though she suspected he'd realized it by now. He'd said nothing, not even when she was up and about and putting the house to rights, clearly no longer suffering from a megrim.

Will must have tacitly agreed to Manners staying with her for the time being. However, she couldn't believe this was the end of their story. Will was too stubborn not to want the last word.

Which was why she was waiting for the first sight of him, so she could ready herself for their meeting. She kept telling herself he wouldn't hurry, even when his leg was better—he must be glad to have her out of the way. She'd caused too much turmoil in his life already, even if most of it *was* accidental.

Despite the compliments he'd paid her, with both his words and his touch, he could never return her love. He'd made that clear enough when he'd banished her from his sight. Yet even after the lapse of a sennight, she could still recall the feel of his lips on her skin. Time and again—when she took a moment's ease—she re-enacted the moments they'd shared, desperately seeking a single grain of proof he truly cared for her.

It was folly to think it—she knew that. Mayhap he had liked the lunatic, untamed Eurydice, with her fantasies and thrilling unpredictability. He barely even knew Isobel Marston, the gentlewoman with a good bloodline, whose family had prospered through the wool trade. She would be too proper for him, too dull, her only accomplishments her stitchery and her ability to play on a harpsichord—which she no longer possessed.

She couldn't see the street below any longer because her eyes were blurred with tears. The sun had passed behind a cloud, sucking all joy from the day.

A sudden knocking at the front door made her pulse throb in anticipation. Before she could regain control of her nerves, Goodwife Cooper was at the solar door, telling her Sir William had arrived to see her.

There was no denying him—she'd known this moment must come. Whatever he had to say to her, there was one point on which she would remain steadfast. If he proclaimed affection for her, even love, she couldn't trust him. If she were ever to unite herself with a man, it would *not* be a ruse to evade the unwanted claims of another woman.

Shakily she rose, then turned so the light from the window wouldn't reveal the pallor in her face, nor the mistiness in her eyes. When she heard Will's familiar uneven tread on the stairs, she grabbed up her needlework and pretended to be absorbed therein.

As he limped into the room, she felt a moment's pity. His leg was clearly worse—he must have taken an infection in it. How could she have left his house without first ascertaining that he was well? Infections could kill.

Her compassionate feelings were soon dispersed by the chill atmosphere that accompanied him. He made her only the briefest of bows, shot her the merest glance from his icy blue eyes, then took up position before the chimneypiece.

"Sir William." She seated herself, plastering a welcoming smile on her face. "I'm sorry to learn you've been unwell."

"Not as sorry as I. I would have come sooner, else."

A wave of delicious awareness coursed down her spine—what a delight to hear his voice again! She was evidently not yet cured of *her* particular affliction.

Her smile was met by a baleful glower. She continued to stare at him, taking in the disheveled state of his hair, the growth of dark stubble on his cheeks and chin. He looked more like a rogue than a gentleman, but the sight of him still made her treacherous heart beat faster.

"Will you not sit if your leg pains you? Did you ride here? Shall I ask Goody Cooper to bring up some wine? We discovered some in the cellar, a cache which my cousin failed to find." She was gabbling, her voice sounding unsteady.

"I'd rather stand, and I don't want any wine. I simply want to talk." His voice was deceptively quiet, but from rage, or hurt?

She picked up her sewing again and began raggedly finishing the seam—it was the best excuse she could find for not looking at him. "Pray, say what you must. I'm listening."

"Why did you leave my protection? Did you not think to discuss your plan with me?"

"I'm sure I'm well enough now to make up my own mind about things." Hopefully, she sounded convincing. "That last night—an exceptional piece of folly on my part that I would not wish to repeat. I assumed you'd have no objection to my leaving."

"No objection?"

His voice was louder now, and he'd moved nearer, but she kept her eyes on her sewing.

"No objection, when there is a would-be murderer out there, after your blood—against whom I've sworn to protect you? No objection, when you've willfully put yourself where he's most likely to find you? If you think I don't object to *that*, Isobel, you do not know me at all."

She flinched, then abandoned her stitching and glared up at him. He didn't seem concerned about what had happened between the two of them—he only cared about Hubert. Why were all men so impermeable when it came to the issue of feelings?

"Well? Have you naught to say for yourself? Do you not understand how much I'm insulted by your thoughtless behavior?"

Raising her chin, she let her anger surface. "My behavior wasn't thoughtless—it was carefully calculated. I suppose I ought to apologize for hurting your pride and your precious honor. But I wasn't going to stay where I wasn't wanted, and where I might be a danger to others."

She dragged in a breath and straightened her shoulders. "I release you from your promise to my brother. I'm now in my own home, and will soon have a houseful of servants to protect me. Nor am I friendless—I just need to rekindle friendships with those my cousin turned away, and to whom he lied."

There. She'd released him, sundered the chain that linked them. Now, she could be free from the complication in her life that was Sir William Cavendish—and must say whatever it took to be rid of him before her resolve wavered.

"It was *you* who sent me away, Will, after

what happened that night in the parlor. I have done no more than oblige you."

A muscle twitched in his jaw. "You *know* why I had to send you away, curse it. But I meant you to go no further than your bedchamber—you understood full well I never intended you to leave the house."

Her head went back, then jerked forward. "What *did* you intend, Will? And what do you intend now? Because you're not winning me over to your cause, whatever that may be." She sounded like a hissing Medusa, full of snakes and venom. A lady should never lose her temper so—especially not when each stab at Will felt like a self-inflicted wound. But nothing she did or said had the desired effect.

He sighed and collapsed into the chair opposite. If only he would open his heart, then the world might be changed. But he was too proud a man. And too devoted to his accursed duty and his loyalty to Edward.

"I was furious when I woke to find you gone. Then, because of this benighted wound of mine, I was forced to keep to the house, and my fears and frustration grew. I'm glad you had the forethought to take Manners with you, and that you accepted the assistance of Goody Cooper. Forgive me for losing my temper—I can't bear for us to quarrel."

His apology was not unwelcome, but there were no signs of tenderness. If he felt so little, if his kisses were just born out of lust and drunkenness, she would *never* tell him how much their encounter had affected her, how she had tossed and turned that night and struggled to understand what it all meant. Her reaction to his nearness now, that coiling of sensation in her stomach, warned her that—despite her best intentions—her heart was still not safe. He must keep his distance, not touch her, or she would never know peace again.

Her hands clasped and unclasped in her lap. She should take up her sewing, ignore his presence, wait for him to leave. The longer he remained, the more desperate her need to hold him.

Lifting her head, she kept her voice as level as she could. "I accept your apology for being unmannerly. There are more things you should do penance for, but I'll not have you think me ungrateful for all you've done for me, so I'll draw a veil over those. Now, if there is nothing further to say, I'm sure you have much to do. God give you good day, Sir William."

CHAPTER TWENTY-SEVEN

WILL COULDN'T BEAR to leave her—neither could he cope with the icy wall she'd thrust between them. It wasn't something one could attack with a cavalry charge, or ranks of archers, or the cunning deployment of troops. All week, on his sickbed, he'd been preparing pretty speeches, hoping to find an excuse for his behavior.

Dare he explain he'd been drinking on that last night because he was trying to make sense of his feelings? What if she were to mock him? Love as deep as this, so swiftly formed, was new and agonizing. Each cold look, each word of censure from Isobel, stung like a thousand lashes. He was a soldier— he'd stared Death in the face many a time, yet here he was, unmanned by a woman.

Could she understand how frustrated that made him? How often had he suggested marriage, and been spurned? If he was to have any hope of winning her, he must be circumspect and bide his time. But he wasn't about to leave the battlefield just yet.

Gazing at the slender line of her neck, and the smooth curve of her cheek as she continued with her needlework, he fought the compulsion to take her in his arms and kiss the coolness out of her, confess that he wanted her with an urgency he'd never before experienced. But what good would it do? She had run away from him, been hurt by him. How could he make it up to her?

"If you have more crimes to lay at my door, then do so. Nothing is worse than simmering resentment. Let us air all your grievances, here and now."

"There's no need. I'm no longer distressed by that final night. You were in your cups, still angry from the morning when I inadvertently crossed you. Let us speak of it no more, for it did not matter one jot. Ouch!"

She had jabbed her needle into her finger. He was out of his chair in an instant, grasping her hand to inspect the damage.

She snatched it away and sucked on the wound. "I'm quite all right, I assure you," she snapped. "You need not treat me like a child."

He stepped back, affronted. "I meant well. But I'm tempted to treat you like a child when it seems to me you behave like one. You rushed from my house on a whim and despite all my warnings, you threw yourself back into the path of danger again. If I seem churlish, 'tis because I care for you—I swore to keep you safe. Don't underestimate Hubert Pike. I've already done it once, to my cost."

"I know. I'm sorry for your hurts. But I didn't leave on a whim—I stayed up all night—"

She broke off and sucked at her finger again, refusing to meet his eyes. There was a hint of pink on her cheeks—she hadn't meant to reveal that, had she? Was that reason for hope?

"Isobel, I'm merely trying to point out that you don't know what you're dealing with. I have lived in the world, experienced its worst side, for a lot longer than you. Pike won't give up easily. Manners has doubtless kept you safe, but you cannot truly relax your vigilance until your cousin is caught and condemned. Manners is not infallible. What if Pike should slip through unnoticed? Once within the grounds, he'd be screened by your high walls and needs but a knife blade to give him entry to the house through a window. Think what harm he could do with that knife if he finds you here alone."

"Once I have my legacy, I'll send Manners back to you, and employ other men to guard the house. I'll have a carpenter check the windows and put bolts on them if need be, and a locksmith will fasten the external doors. Not that I relish the idea of dwelling in a fortress when I have been a prisoner for so long already."

Turning away, she stared out the window as if to reassure herself no enemies lurked without. Then she glanced coolly back at him. "However, if I were Hubert, I'd be well away by now. He *must* know everyone is looking for him. He must also know he has nothing to gain by harming me, now that his scheme has been discovered. *I* have the papers I need to claim my legacy—he does not. Aye, I took them from your document chest before I left. I saw no wrong in it since they were mine."

He hadn't noticed, hadn't even been into the parlor. This was his first day out of bed, and his thigh was already protesting its ill-usage. He ran a hand over it, trying to rub the pain into submission.

"The papers do, indeed, belong to you. I'm still prepared to accompany you when you visit your lawyer, to ensure the funds are made available as soon as possible."

"No need. As you can see, I didn't leave on a whim—I thought very carefully about what I was doing, and adequate precautions have been taken, or soon will be. You need no longer bear the burden of my care—send me a note with your expenditure on my behalf. As soon as I have my money, you'll be reimbursed."

He recoiled as if she'd touched him with a burning brand. *Pay him back?* How could she think so little of him?

She must have taken his stunned silence for compliance, for she added, "Be assured I shall return Manners to you directly, and will pay his wages for the time he's been with me. Please tell me what you've spent on my behalf so I can settle my debt to you."

He stood and turned away, raking his hands through his hair as he tried to compose himself. His breath came in short, panicky bursts as if his lungs were being crushed. "You owe me nothing." It was hard to speak around the lump in his throat. "I shall *not* send you my reckoning. Excuse me, Mistress Marston, but my leg pains me. I must away."

Without a bow or a word of farewell, he limped to the door and let himself out. The stairs were a trial, but it was his heart that felt bruised, not his thigh. He'd meant to stay and win her over. What had he done instead? Stalked out in a fit of pique. How ironic that he should accuse *her* of childlike behavior when it was *him* who was being puerile.

He struggled to mount Jennet, relishing the pain it cost him as a distraction from the agony in his mind. Did Isobel think so little of him that she wanted to pay him back? Did she seriously believe all he'd done had been from loyalty to Edward? How he could prove his love to her—when she appeared to want none of it—was a conundrum of massive proportions and one that could not be readily solved.

He should concentrate on his own position. There were rumors Robert Dudley might be in favor again—he could renew his friendship with the man and see if his dreams of becoming a courtier might still be realized. Yet he had little heart for that now. Something had changed him—*Isobel* had changed him. If only he could persuade her to come with him, he'd be happy to live in obscurity. A friend had recently written to say he was selling a moated house and farm at Foxwell in Suffolk. What better place to dwell quietly, away from faction and favor, and raise his own livestock?

And if it came to the worst, and Mathieson somehow found a way to foist Paulina onto him again, he would sell his services as a mercenary and seek some foreign battlefield upon which to breathe his last.

And sweet oblivion would destroy all memory of Mistress Isobel Marston.

CHAPTER TWENTY-EIGHT

A UGUST WAS NEARLY done, and the current burst of sunny weather after several days of downpours made a welcome change. Having ordered the refurnishing of Marston House to her satisfaction, Isobel had decided to allow herself a moment's ease in the garden.

She'd thrown herself, heart and soul, into the task of making the house once again the family home she remembered. This labor occupied her for much of the day, and it was only at night that she found herself prey to gloomy thoughts. Most of these were centered around Sir William Cavendish, of course, whom she'd not seen since that last dismal encounter. Well, she'd wished him gone and he'd obliged. So why was she still plagued by the feeling there was unfinished business between them?

Sunlight warmed her face as she made her way between the high, headless stalks of lavender, her skirts brushing through them and releasing their remaining scent. She loved the smell, so fresh, so enticing—and she'd harvested the drying flowerheads eagerly, although they'd been left on the stem far too long. A robin loudly proclaimed its presence from the branches of the walnut tree, not yet singing the mournful song that always presaged the change from summer to autumn. Thankfully.

For a rare moment, Isobel was free of her shadow. She'd kept Manners on, at Will's insistence—via letter, as he'd not troubled to come and speak with her himself. Her muscle-bound guardian hung on her heels like a loyal dog following its master, although he tried to be subtle about it. Currently, he was supervising the carpenter drafted in to replace a rotten window frame which had been letting in the rain.

Isobel slowed as she approached the flowerbed where she'd ripped out the opium poppies. She must have still been a little out of her mind then—no English gentlewoman would behave so precipitously. The area had been dug over by her new gardener now and replanted with straggling blue and white periwinkle, which she knew, once established, would challenge anything else to grow amongst its spreading roots. Everyone in the household had been ordered to rip out any poppy seedlings they saw and cast them on the midden.

She halted beneath the espaliered pear tree, her mind's eye full of an image of the dust-covered Will as he'd landed in front of her on that fateful day back in July. He truly *had* been like the hero Orpheus of old, braving everything to rescue his wife Eurydice from the dreaded realm of Hades.

How must Orpheus have felt, when Eurydice was wrenched away from the land of the living? Much as Isobel felt now, mayhap, thinking of Will. Her heart swelled, and the view before her shattered as tears pierced her eyes. Her inability to fall out of love with Will was tearing her apart and, even in his absence, showed no signs of abating.

Stifling a sob, she turned away from the

tree. It had been a mistake to come into this corner of the garden—it held too many memories. She was about to return to the house when a movement caught her eye. Surely, the latch was lifting on the wooden door Will had used when rescuing her?

Shading her eyes, she watched as the metal shaft moved silently upwards. Had Will come to surprise her? Forgetting all her resolutions about giving him no encouragement, she surged forward to welcome him.

And found herself staring at the blade of a dagger.

Her cousin's hand was steady as a rock, his face filled with evil intent. What she could see of his face at least—he had a grimy cloth covering both his nose and mouth, but there was no doubt it was Hubert Pike. As her lips parted to scream, cold steel nicked her neck, and she froze.

The corners of his eyes lifted mockingly. "Such a shame no one ever got around to fixing this lock after your precious Cavendish forced it. You have less wit than you thought, don't you, Isobel?"

She couldn't move a muscle. Part of her wanted to rage at him, to feel her nails rip into his vile flesh. Would he stab her then, or cut her throat and dispatch her quickly and quietly? For he'd gain nothing by it—her will was already drawn up, her money to be donated to the parish for the relief of the poor, particularly the widows and children of soldiers and sailors. He'd hate that—*if* he managed to find it out before he faced the noose.

He yanked at her elbow and pulled her against him. She could feel the point of the dagger pressing against her ribs, even through the layers of canvas and whalebone that supported her tightly-fitting bodice. Knowing Manners would soon be back, would see the open door and come after her, she feigned a swoon, playing for time.

Her captor was having none of it. He jabbed his weapon more firmly against her midriff. "No tricks, Coz. I'm in no mood for your games."

In the street outside stood an ugly covered cart. Flinders issued from behind it—also masked and brandishing a long, white stick—and helped Hubert lift her in. When she wedged a foot against the wooden sides of the cart, someone from within punched it aside, jarring her ankle and knocking her shoe into the gutter.

As she collapsed in an ungainly heap on the floor of the conveyance, she saw another unwelcome face. Goodwife Avice Quill, her so-called nurse. She, too, wore a partial mask and held a long, white stick at her side. When Isobel tried to struggle up, Avice gave her a resounding blow on the side of the head with the stick.

"There'll be plenty more where that came from." She could just make out Hubert's voice above the ringing in her ears. "You've been leading us a merry dance, my fine young lady, and you're going to start paying for it now."

Isobel braced herself for another blow, but Hubert crawled up next to her, his knife blade back at her throat. The dingy cart rocked, and she thought they were about to set off, but the next noise that hit her ears was the sound of a hammer on wood. The cart dipped again as someone climbed into the front of it.

"Have you nailed it firm and proper to the gate?" Hubert's voice was muffled by the cloth over his face.

"Aye." Flinders' voice. It trailed fear along Isobel's spine. "It won't blow away unless we have a gale. No one will be going in or out of Marston House for a goodly while."

Still groggy from the blow to her head, she struggled to understand what was going on, and how best she could escape. There was something else about this cart that was making her feel ill—an ungodly stench, like nothing she'd ever smelled before.

The vehicle lurched off, and she caught sight of Hubert sheathing his knife. But before she could take advantage and try to escape, he had fastened a hand in her hair and dragged her head backwards. Eyes stinging with pain, she stared up at the sagging canvas overhead, wondering if it was the last thing she would ever see. Then her head was jerked still further back, and a cup pressed against her unwilling lips. Terrified, she coughed and spat to stop the familiar-tasting potion burning its way down her throat. To no avail.

They were giving her more of it than they ever had before. Was this what they planned then—to poison her? As her senses started to close down, she wondered why

Hubert hadn't simply stabbed her in the garden, if murder was what was on his mind. Suddenly the agonizing grip in her hair was gone, and she slumped forward.

Waves of nausea and confusion swirled through her brain so she could hardly focus, but she struggled against the power of the poppy juice, the lure of unconsciousness. She was being wrapped in something, like a caterpillar in silk, fastening her arms to her body, trapping and immobilizing her legs. Then she was lying on the floor of the cart, and the appalling smell filled her nostrils.

She was dimly aware that Avice and Hubert had moved away, leaving her in the company of a host of grey shapes, bundled as she was, but with their heads covered, each laid atop the other, like animal carcasses in a butcher's wagon.

The awful realization hit her, just before unconsciousness. The white-painted sticks held by Flinders and Avice were those wielded by the Searchers, people who notified the authorities of the presence of plague.

She'd been loaded onto the death cart.

CHAPTER TWENTY-NINE

WILL HAD INVITED Aloysius Maybury to accompany him to a goose fair on the edge of town. It had rained much of the previous day, driving his mood still further towards melancholy. He needed distraction—he'd failed to pin down Hubert Pike and his associates, he'd failed to secure Isobel's affections, and he'd failed to satisfy the Mathieson family. Though they were no longer attempting to ruin his reputation with blackmail, they knew Isobel had left, and as far as they were concerned, there could be no more perfect partner for him than Paulina.

This visit was supposed to be an antidote to those failures. He would make merry with Maybury, recall fond memories of their young and foolish days at Oxford together, and discuss the shortcomings of their fellow men.

"Thank heaven—the ground has dried out a bit." Maybury prodded the toe of his high boot at the soil. "This would be a disaster otherwise."

Will looked about him at the colorful booths and pavilions reflecting the glaring August sunlight and nodded his head. "Aye. I've barely been out since that infection in my leg. It does my heart good to revel in sunshine and fresh air."

"Not sure I agree about the fresh air, good sir." Maybury wrinkled his nose as they passed a hog pen. "Though something has done you good—I feared I would never again see color in your cheeks."

"What is your meaning?"

"Oh, only that you've hardly had a smile on your face these past two sennights."

What did he have to smile about? Very little, since that last encounter with Isobel. But he didn't want to dwell on that. "Although my leg is healed, it pains me in the damp. Even warm, summer rain brings out an ache in it. I'm becoming old afore my time."

A nearby hurdy-gurdy plucked out its first handful of notes, and young couples rushed to the open space in front of it for a country dance.

Maybury raised a questioning eyebrow. "Shall we go and see? 'Tis free entertainment, after all."

Will strolled over and stood watching while the fairgoers, pink-cheeked and cheerful, kicked up their heels. The dance had none of the stately elegance he'd seen at court, or at Kenilworth when staying with his patron, Leicester. Yet, it afforded him amusement, something he needed rather badly. Taking a firm hold of the coin purse attached to his belt—just in case—he settled next to Maybury to observe.

The dancers comprised a true rag-bag of humanity. Some were children, hopping about gaily and getting in everyone's way. An older gentleman was being steered around— none too gently—by his buxom wife. Will's lip curled. Mayhap she hoped he'd be carried off early by the excitement, so she could become a merry widow. Drovers from the rural farms were wearing their finest clothing, making their stiff-backed bows in front of the rough-faced women who stood watching, in the absence of any obvious husbands. Many a young damsel sported a new ribbon or cheap gew-gaw purchased at the fair.

He should get something for Isobel while he was here. Even better, he should leap on Jennet and ride over to fetch her—she'd enjoy these simple pleasures, too, he was certain of it.

Although, having lived in a quiet part of London, she might struggle with all the noise. The field was awash with it—Will's ears could barely distinguish between the different cries of the hawkers. Tinkers rattled their pots and pans together to prove their robustness while their swarthy-skinned wives clinked their jewels, inviting the unwary townsfolk into their pavilions to have their fortunes told. The whole hubbub of the fair was overlaid by the honking and hissing of the geese that had been driven all the way down from Norfolk.

Maybury glanced up at him. "That's better—showing an interest in life again. I don't know what has been on your mind of late, but it seems to me you need a tonic, something to stop all this unhealthy brooding. Give me your jack, and I'll fetch us some mulled ale."

When Maybury returned shortly afterwards, Will accepted the leather tankard and sipped at the warm liquid. His stomach objected.

"I know you meant well, sir, but this is disgusting. 'Tis is more like mulled small beer than ale. One might just as well drink lukewarm water."

"Nay, indeed. Yon fair damsel informed me people in East Anglia drink it all the time. Are you hungry? Fancy sampling some pigs' trotters? There's a seething vat of them over there, which the vendor assures me are uncommonly good."

Will shook his head decisively and grimaced at Maybury. "I breakfasted well—I thank you. Don't think me ungrateful."

He was, in truth, most exceedingly glad of Maybury's company. The man was irrepressible. Despite the comparatively recent loss of his wife, he refused to mourn longer than was customary. He'd already hinted to Will on more than one occasion that he was in the market for a second wife.

Will took another swig of his ale, then winced and coughed as if he'd just swallowed a pin. "I intend no offense," he told his companion. "But I've had my fill of this."

He emptied the remnants of his drink onto the grass.

"Perhaps wine would be more to your taste. I saw a delightful young lady in command of a half-barrel of the stuff over yonder. Shall I fetch you some?"

"Nay, I beg you. Not unless I can sample it first." He followed Maybury across the sward, neatly sidestepping a tethered bull about to lift its tail, and came to a halt in front of the wine seller.

She gazed up at him, hopefully, exhibiting a gap-toothed grin. Her teeth were stained red with the wine, and her tongue looked black.

Will shuddered, recalling that last night with Isobel, how he'd been in his cups, how he'd kissed her, and turned her away. Little wonder she'd evaded him—little wonder he'd not been welcomed at Marston House.

Why had he not just said what was in his heart? One could be angry with someone, without diminishing the love one held for them. Indeed, that ire might be magnified *because* one loved that person.

He loved Isobel. How could he love her any the less for knowing her own mind, for wanting to do what she thought was for the best? Her stalwart independence, her determination, made her even more of a prize. He didn't want a wife who did nothing but flatter and mollycoddle him. The odd fight made relations between man and wife all the more piquant.

"What is it?" Maybury's voice roused him from his reverie.

"Nothing." He straightened and shook the tension from his shoulders. "There's something I must do. Where might one obtain a trinket for a lady?"

Maybury smirked. "How about a colored ribbon to go around your true love's snowy white neck?"

"That would be perfect—I thank you."

It didn't take long to find a peddler with a stock of good quality silk ribbon. Not sure about quantities, Will bought a couple of yards of the stuff, in dark forest green. Isobel could use it to suspend her locket around her neck, or for trimming her most fancy gowns. Assuming she had some of those—he didn't know. In fact, there was a vast amount he didn't know about Isobel Marston.

How could he have deserted her for so long while he foolishly licked his wounds? He should have returned the very next day and made an utter nuisance of himself, worn her down, convinced her of his sincerity.

Every woman responded well to an ardent suitor. Did they not?

"Cavendish—isn't that one of your servants coming up at the run?"

Will scowled. Aye, indeed—it was Hal, the man he'd employed as a temporary replacement for Manners. What on earth was he doing at the goose fair, when he should be keeping an eye on the house?

"Sir William!"

His grim mood returned. More trouble—just when he'd begun to relax. "Whatever is it, man? No, wait, catch your breath a moment." He drummed his fingers on the hilt of his sword as he waited.

"I beg your pardon, sir. Your neighbor, Master Mathieson, is blowing up a tempest at your house, and you're needed right away."

Maybury rolled his eyes. "That fellow is naught but trouble. I thought you'd silenced him?"

Will felt the anger rise in his chest. "What right has he to do so? He can have no complaint against me now, surely?"

"No justifiable one, sir." Hal took a few quick breaths and straightened. "But he's baying for your blood like a hound on the scent. He says you've run off with his daughter."

CHAPTER THIRTY

WILL FOUGHT THE urge to laugh—this was the most ridiculous thing he'd heard in weeks. But he couldn't have Mathieson disrupting his household. Nor, more particularly, could he allow the man to spread such scurrilous lies. Was it all a sham? Was he being accused of abducting Paulina in order to force him to marry her? The only way to find out was to abandon his outing and race homeward.

Maybury, who appeared to take Hal's news most seriously, insisted on returning with him. Their mounts had had little time to rest, and the highway was filled with country wagons, carts, barrows, riders and pedestrians, all of whom seemed eager to get in the way. Will's progress was infuriatingly slow, giving him plenty of time to brood on the ill hand Fate had dealt him.

What great sin had he unwittingly committed? Not only did he risk losing Isobel, he now looked as if he were going to lose his reputation as well. Rumor spread fast in the narrow streets of London, and if Mathieson were casting accusations about, they would quickly be picked up and embellished.

Will shook his head in disbelief. Had he not been loyal and honorable all his life? Yet he'd lost his younger brother, Simpkin, *and* his friend, Edward Marston. Had he not looked after Isobel according to his promise to Edward? Yet he'd lost her, too. He'd thought he was being patriotic and brave, suffering considerable hardship to promote England's cause in the wars of the Low Countries. All he'd earned from that was a wound that was slow to heal, a stain on his reputation, and a small quantity of coin.

He dug his heels into Jennet's flanks, gritted his teeth, and forged a way through the throng, Maybury following in his wake. This resentment would not do. He'd always been a man of action and had never run from a fight. Somehow, he would vanquish Mathieson. Somehow, he would win Isobel.

The very thought of her sent a wave of despair through him. The longer he was away from her, the more he missed her. At least she was safe at Marston House, and he need only go to war on one front today, not two.

Maybury caught up and came alongside him. "Do you think it true Paulina Mathieson has run off? She's evidently not done so with *you*. Might this be a misunderstanding?"

Will steered carefully around the loaded ox wagon in front of him, then urged Jennet to another spurt of speed.

"Either that or another devious scheme. I know not why both he and his daughter are so dead set on leg-shackling me. I have every intention of living quietly in the country if I can't get preferment at court. There's a farm in Suffolk up for sale."

"Wool country? I can't imagine a bright flame like Paulina wanting to stagnate in the country."

Will snorted. He didn't care what Paulina wanted. Although he *was* curious to know where she'd gone.

As if echoing his earlier thoughts, Maybury came alongside him again and said, "You always were an honorable man, Cavendish. But rather an unfortunate one, it seems. Trouble seeks you out. It even did so at Oxford, despite your best efforts to study hard and make your family proud, God rest their souls. You certainly didn't deserve to lose Simpkin so soon after your parents."

Will tightened his fingers on Jennet's reins. "I may decide to *cease* being honorable. I'm tempted to forget gentlemanly behavior and give Mathieson the thrashing he deserves. And I'll gladly do the same for Hubert Pike and his cronies rather than wait for the authorities. I don't think any of them will be missed, do you?"

Ah, good. Giles Street was now in view. He dismounted, ignoring the twinge from his thigh, waited for his servant, Hal, to catch up, then bade him wait outside with the horses while he and Maybury went within to deal with Mathieson.

Mayhem met them the moment they stepped through the door. Mathieson was there, red-faced and waving his fists. Manners was there, too, trying to keep Mathieson restrained. Goodwife Cooper was bobbing up and down in the background, her face pale, signaling that she needed to speak with him urgently. Why weren't they at Marston House with Isobel?

Everyone tried to speak at once.

"Silence!" He used the roar he'd perfected on the battlefield. To good effect. Even Maybury took a step away from him.

"I'll listen to you one at a time, or I'll listen to no one. Manners, may I suggest you let go of Master Mathieson's coat? You're only making him angry. He's not going to draw his sword on me. Are you, sir?"

He cocked his head on one side and glared at his neighbor. After the briefest of pauses, Manners released his captive and stepped forward.

"Sir. Isobel Marston has been taken."

Will couldn't breathe. He felt the blood leave his face.

"Never mind that. My daughter's been taken. By you, you cur." Mathieson surged forward, but Will's sword was out before he could get within arm's length.

"Don't try my patience any further. As you can see, I don't have your daughter with me. You may search my house if you wish. If you won't take my word for it, take Maybury's here."

He gazed over Mathieson's head at Manners. "What do you mean, Isobel's been taken?"

Mathieson opened his mouth, but Will pressed the tip of his sword more firmly against the man's throat. "You'll have your chance. But I have a more pressing matter. Speak, Manners, damn your hide."

Goody Cooper spoke up. "Please don't blame Manners, Sir William. He was set upon by some people in the guise of Searchers. You know, the kind that seek out houses wherein the plague is thought to be, and shut the people away. He staggered over here to find you, his poor head still bleeding."

Will's gaze switched to Manners. "*What?*"

"They thought they'd knocked me insensible, I think, sir. I'd left Mistress Marston in the garden, but when I returned to it, she wasn't there. The young lady knows not to go out on her own, so I thought the worst. I found the back gate was open—it had a broken catch that hadn't been mended. When I looked without, I saw a lady's shoe lying in the road. And the ungodly scum had nailed a sign to the other side of the gate, claiming it was a plague house. They must have thought it would stop anyone following them, but I tore it down afore any could see."

"Did you look for her? Did no one go after her?"

"They must have had a fast horse, sir. I saw nothing but the death cart."

"*The death cart?*"

There was a clatter as Will's sword dropped from his nerveless hand. He fumbled his way into the parlor and collapsed into the first seat he came to.

She couldn't be dead. It was a ruse of Pike's. He'd feel it if anything had happened to her, wouldn't he?

A shadow came between him and the window. "What about my daughter, sirrah? And now to add insult to injury, you have assaulted my person."

Something snapped deep inside Will. He surged to his feet.

"I don't give a midden clod for your damned daughter, sir—I neither have her nor want her. She's probably run off with that worm of a Frenchman, the Comte de Velors.

Leave my house now. Someone's taken the woman I love, and I must find her—and I'll trample over any man who gets in my way."

"Steady, Will, steady." Maybury's voice filtered through the blood drumming in Will's head. "*I'll* help Mathieson find his daughter. I have a horse still saddled and ready. I'll go first to your neighbor's house and question the servants. Think no more of us. Go and rescue Isobel."

Will felt ready to weep with relief. He patted Maybury's shoulder. "I thank you. Go, both of you. Apologies, Mathieson. I'm certain your daughter will be found."

Someone pressed a pewter goblet into his hand. Shakily, he drank the contents, relishing the fire that coursed down his throat. His best brandy, kept under lock and key by Goodwife Cooper. How well she knew him!

"Thank you, Goody. Now, if Manners needs patching up, pray, do so—he's no use to me broken. I shall make my plans, gather my forces, and devise a strategy for the return of Mistress Marston."

And pray to God in Heaven that he was not already too late to save her.

CHAPTER THIRTY-ONE

WHEN ISOBEL REGAINED consciousness, the first thing that struck her was that she was still alive. But light and fresh air were in short supply, and she couldn't move. There was a riot of sound surrounding her, too, which resembled nothing more than the moaning of miserable souls in Hell.

Mayhap she was dead after all, poisoned by the poppy juice she so abhorred. Although aware of having committed no sin, her soul had gone straight to the depths. Yet the pains in her body felt more like corporeal torment than anything else.

She tested her fingers, toes, arms, legs. All worked, though their movement was restricted, and accompanied by a clanking noise. Looking down, she registered—to her horror—that she was shackled to a narrow bed. Where *was* this gloomy cell? In a prison? A hospital? The madhouse? What had Hubert done, what lies had he told, to have her admitted to such an institution? Why not just kill her—unless this was her punishment for foiling his plans.

Head pulsing with pain, she slid carefully off the bed, her chains just long enough to let her peer through the bars of her cell door. A woman was hobbling past at that moment, dressed only in her under-shift, and continually plucking at her sleeves.

"What is this place?"

At the sound of Isobel's voice, the crone stopped, stared at her for a moment, then let out a high-pitched cackle before continuing on her way.

Isobel rattled at the bars in frustration, but they were solid. If only she could see beyond her door—but it was so dark. She could just make out that she was in a large building, which admitted no daylight and smelled of unwashed humanity and tallow candles. There were other cell doors opposite her own, some open with the beds empty, others tight shut.

A movement caught her eye, and she saw a young woman—clad like the crone in naught but an ankle-length shift of un-bleached linen—following the same route.

Isobel banged her manacles against the bars to get the woman's attention. "Who are you? What are we doing here?"

The girl wandered past, slack-jawed and staring at her feet—as if Isobel didn't exist.

No one else appeared although the cacophony of misery continued. She refused to return to the grim, grey discomfort of her bed—there must be someone in charge, someone who would talk to her. If she and the other women were inmates of an institution, a warden or a keeper would be by soon enough, to bring food and water, or to empty the slops. She hoped.

Struggling to make sense of it all, Isobel remembered both the women who'd gone past had worn coifs, tied tightly under their chins. Not a single lock of hair had been visible, and the coifs were skull-tight. Heart sinking, she raised a manacled hand to her head. Aye, she, too, wore a coif of coarse unfinished material. Not her own, then, for those were all of embroidered lawn. Fighting the rising tide of panic, she wrenched the cap off, shuddering as cool air met her scalp.

No hair. A soft stubble only—shorn more closely than a sheep. *Merciful heavens!* Her long, raven-dark hair was gone—without it, she was a fright, an outcast, no longer herself. In her shift and regulation cap, she was faceless, characterless, nameless—just like every other poor soul that moaned out their days in these ranks of tiny cells.

This was not to be borne. She wasn't ill—except for the headache and her understand-able confusion. Hubert had manufactured her illness, her so-called brain fever, just as he'd done before. But now she knew his methods. Now, she would fight to the very last drop of her blood to defy him. There must be someone in authority, someone who would listen and release her. She had money at home—would her keeper accept the promise of a bribe?

The sound of hobnailed shoes reached her ears, footsteps drawing closer. Here was someone *not* shuffling along in bare feet like the women she'd seen. Hope kindling anew, she yelled out as the man passed her door.

"Sir, good sir. Pray, grant me a moment of your time."

As he stopped and saw her, he gave a mirthless grin. "Awake at last, are we? I hope you're not thinking of making any trouble."

"Nay. Why would I? I simply wish to know where I am."

"In a hospital—of sorts. The Bethlehem Hospital. Here you'll be cared for you until you're better, and your family is ready to take you home."

The man didn't seem unkind, just matter-of-fact. Though his clothing was simple, it was cut from good cloth, and he had a large loop of keys suspended from his belt. He must be someone in authority, and therefore her best chance of escape.

She made sure he was looking directly into her eyes as she said, "I assure you, I'm not ill, sir. I was given too great a dose of poppy juice."

He shrugged. "They *all* say they're not ill. 'Tis one of the problems with sickness of the brain—the sufferer himself doesn't realize there's anything awry. I've observed this time after time. 'Tis usually the family or loved ones who notice when lunacy has struck.

That's why our ladies and gentlemen have been committed here by thoughtful relations. You mustn't worry—your keep has been paid for a month in advance. You shan't go hungry."

He turned to leave, but Isobel clung to the bars of her door. "Wait, I beg you. Believe me—I'm not insane. I've been deliberately drugged by a greedy relation who wants to get his hands on my fortune. He has no scruples whatsoever—I know it was he who brought me here."

The man raised an eyebrow. "Aye, Mistress. I understand. There's naught to concern you—all that is needed will be provided. You'll be cared for much better in this place than you could be at home—we're used to your kind."

Panic clutched tightly at her stomach, but she couldn't give in to hysteria. She must remain calm, collected, as sane as possible. Just because she now looked like a lunatic didn't mean she intended to act like one.

"What must I do to make you believe me? You keep records, I assume. I know the man who committed me is Hubert Pike. Or possibly a Master Flinders—or even Goodwife Quill. I swear on my life, they abducted me. Send to the house of Sir William Cavendish on Giles Street, and you'll find out all you need to know and be rewarded for your trouble. If *my* word is not enough, perhaps the word of a gentleman such as Sir William *will* be."

The warder pushed his hat farther back and scratched his head. "I wish I could say I'd heard of Sir William Cavendish, but I haven't. Is he a wealthy fellow?"

She nodded vigorously, then wished she hadn't. Her head still thumped as if being beaten by a blacksmith's hammer. "Wealthy and well-connected. He'd see you were rewarded for helping me. Will you send for him?"

"Are you hungry, Mistress? You'll feel better for bread and ale. Then, perchance, we can talk more of this William Cavendish."

Before she could utter a protest, the man had gone.

She slumped onto the bed, sick, dizzy, and battling not to give in to despair. If she could only keep her head, she might yet escape this place. She'd heard of the Bethlehem Hospital, knew it was operated by the same authority who ran the Bridewell House of Correction. She also knew that the lunatics housed in Bedlam were often paraded as a source of entertainment, like the animals in the Tower of London menagerie. If she could maintain her sanity—not easy to do under such circumstances—either Will would find her or she'd be spotted by someone who knew her, who would help get her out.

Having decided to behave exactly as one might expect an English gentlewoman of good family to behave, she politely thanked the drudge who brought her food. This consisted of a wooden platter bearing bread and cheese, and a large cup of a dark liquid that smelled like strong ale.

"Tell me, good mistress, am I not to be unshackled while I eat? It is most awkward, else."

The servant looked at her dully. "I can't do that. Only some gets unchained."

"Why might I not be one of those?" She did her best not to sound belligerent.

"You've not been here above a day, and no one knows what you might do. There'd be trouble if you harmed yourself. The shackles will come off if you're quiet—in time."

The door thumped shut, and a key rattled in the lock. Isobel was left alone once more to contemplate her fate and try to stop listening to the noises of human suffering and confusion that continued to break out all around her.

She chewed on the bread and took a sip of ale. The bread was gritty and grey, and the ale bitter, but she'd expected no different. The cheese was palatable, a hard Suffolk cheese, full-bodied and salty, which made her drink more freely of the ale. Though the quality of the food was disappointing, it offered some comfort and familiarity. At least she was not to be left to starve in this new prison of hers.

When she'd cleared her plate, drowsiness crept over her. With a wash of horror, she realized her ale had not been as innocuous as she'd thought. Poppy juice again? Or some other soporific? Was it just for her at Hubert's request, or did all the inmates receive this doctored ale, to keep them from making nuisances of themselves?

No! She must stay awake, alert, or she'd never get out—she'd be as helpless as when she was confined at Marston House. But it was too late now—she couldn't help but give in. As she sank back on the bed and closed her eyes, someone stared in at her window and started laughing.

It was the last sound she heard before sleep took her.

CHAPTER THIRTY-TWO

THE LAST WEEK had felt like a year. Will barely recognized himself on the few occasions he saw his reflection—he'd developed the lean look and haunted eyes of a man obsessed. Which was doubtless true— he'd sworn to find Isobel, or die in the attempt. He'd scoured the streets day and night for her, coming home only to change his clothes and collect more coin for bribes— rarely to sleep or eat.

Despite his efforts in combing the city, asking at every tavern or meeting place whether anyone knew Pike, or had seen a young lady in distress, he'd failed to locate either of them. He cherished the hope they were yet in London, for that was where the

Marstons' man of business, Bradshaw, was to be found. No matter what cunning swindle Pike had up his sleeve, he'd still need to deal with the man who held the purse strings.

He prayed this was the case, for if Pike took Isobel out of town, then all hope of finding her would dwindle to nothing.

Will had done everything he could think of. He'd sent Manners to Hertfordshire to question the rogues who'd set upon him on the road. Despite Manners' persuasive powers of interrogation, neither knew the whereabouts of the man who'd hired them. From the description they willingly gave, it was Flinders who'd dealt with them. A huge disappointment, for if Pike were found, they couldn't bear witness against him.

A brief spark of hope had flickered in Will's heart when one of his team of urchin-spies had described a felon known as Goodwife Quill, brought to book for stealing a chicken from a street vendor. Will had rushed to the jail where the wretched woman was being held, only to discover that she'd bribed her way out—shortly after a visit by a well-dressed gentleman. Despite this blow, Will soldiered on, now asking after not only

Pike and Isobel but Avice Quill and Flinders as well, in the hope that if *one* were found, they could lead the way to the others.

Today, he'd been working his way along the river, hoping one of the ferrymen might remember carrying Isobel and her captors, but he was well-nigh exhausted now, and Jennet, too, must be tired of the punishing cobbles of the streets. Though none of the taverns he'd passed looked enticing, he must refresh himself in one of them, and use the opportunity to ask around.

He gestured to a small boy armed with a shovel, who'd been gazing hopefully up at Jennet. Sliding off her back, Will waved a coin in front of the urchin's nose. "Here's a groat for you now, and a second one shall be yours when I return to find my horse unmolested, and still in this place."

The tow-haired child nodded and tucked the coin into the depths of his soiled coat. "Aye, my lord, we'll be here. On my ma's grave, I swear it."

Will ran a hand over his sword hilt as he turned away—money could buy one anything one wanted in the crowded streets edging the docks, but it could also attract unwelcome attention. For good measure, he touched the handle of his bollock dagger, as if to reassure himself it were still there—in case anyone happened to be watching.

He turned his back on the river and surveyed his surroundings. Even a week spent searching the most degraded hellholes of London's poor had not inured him to the misery and suffering he found in such places. At least down by the Thames the air was a little better—or would be, until the tide went out, revealing the banks of slime and muck on either side of the river.

Choosing the most salubrious of the taverns in view, he marched into the taproom. It was busy, packed to the gunwales with boatmen, mud-larks and doxies, drinking or gambling away their money, or plying their trade.

Will scanned the gloom for the landlord and approached him. "God give you good day, sir. I seek a thin, reedy gentleman, a bit of a cockscomb, who goes by the name of Master Hubert Pike. He may have been in company with a young gentlewoman, striking to look at, with green eyes and black hair. 'Tis possible they were accompanied by an ugly giant of a man named Flinders, and Goodwife Avice Quill, who is a portly dame of some five-and-thirty summers. If you can lead me to them, my gratitude will be considerable."

The tapster stared back from narrowed eyes before his face relaxed into a smile. "Mayhap I have, and mayhap I've not, but I *do* see a fellow in want of a cup of ale. Why don't you sit here and tell me more?"

Will glanced around him. None of the other customers seemed interested in him, and if he sat with his back to the barrels facing outwards, he was less likely to be knocked on the head and robbed. Settling onto a bench, he gratefully accepted the offer of a drink.

"So, you're on the track of some gutter scum, are you?" The man held Will's leather jack under the spigot and filled it. "Is there a reward on offer?"

"Not officially. But three of those I mentioned are gallows bait, and it would stand you in good stead with the authorities if you help find them. And I have access to gold, should I receive information leading to their capture."

He fished for a shilling and pressed it into the landlord's hand. "This is for a pitcher or two of ale, and a roast beef dinner for you, if you can help me."

The landlord grinned. "You've bought my time until the moment that pitcher runs dry. I'll ask around—better the question comes from me than gentry like yourself." Taking a gigantic swig from the jug he'd just filled, the landlord heaved himself across the room to interrogate his customers.

Gazing out the window, Will listened to the keening of the kites and gulls as they floated on the breeze from the river, looking for scraps. He swilled the dregs of his ale around, then followed the progress of the landlord, his spirits sinking further as each customer, in turn, responded to the question with a shake of the head. The landlord returned to his seat and took another draught of his ale.

"Not a soul has seen them. You could ask every mortal in Christendom if they'd seen your friends, and still not find 'em. If a man in London means to stay hidden, he'll generally succeed—unless he's a fool."

"I don't know that Pike can remain hidden forever. If the lady I seek is still alive, she can be useful to him, as he can force her to sign certain papers. He'd need to visit a lawyer for that, but I'm having a watch kept on the one most likely."

He sighed and pushed a hand through his hair. She must still be alive. She *had* to be, for how could he live without her? If only they hadn't parted on such bitter terms—he'd give all he had to take back his harsh words.

The landlord leaned forward, subjecting Will to a blast of his rotten breath. "If I had a troublesome relative who I needed to keep alive and easy to persuade, I'd stick 'em in the Bridewell or Bedlam. Folk would sign or seal anything to get out of there, afore they were driven mad."

Before they were driven mad…

Will's mug hit the counter with a *clunk*. What if Pike had no imagination? What if Pike used the same methods as before, drugging Isobel to send her out of her wits? What better place to hide a madwoman than amongst others?

He seized the landlord's hand and pumped it vigorously. "You have it, sir! That is just what he'll have done. Can you give me directions from here to the Bethlehem Hospital?"

The directions were duly given, in exchange for another shilling, and Will hastened out of the tavern and stood blinking in the sunlight before calling for his horse.

"We've got a little farther to go, old friend, just as far as Bishopsgate," he announced, patting Jennet's neck. He dutifully paid the boy who'd looked after her, stepped off the mounting block into the saddle, and turned the mare's head towards the east.

If he didn't succeed in finding Isobel this time, despair would tear him apart. And he'd end up consigned to Bedlam himself.

CHAPTER THIRTY-THREE

WILL REINED IN at the Hospital of St. Mary of Bethlehem, breathless, but hopeful. He was cursing himself inwardly for not having looked here sooner, because the more he thought about it, the more logical it was that Pike would secrete Isobel in such a place.

The hospital, it seemed, was used to visitors. He was met by the principal keeper, a well-fed gentleman by the name of Cartwright, and his wife, who told him anyone might view the inmates for a fee.

He ground his teeth. If Pike had made a spectacle of Isobel, he'd slice him into quarters, then throw the pieces in the Thames. It was disgusting that the insane should be exhibited for the amusement of visitors—but he couldn't let his feelings show. He needed the Cartwrights on his side.

He asked after Isobel, describing her minutely and wishing—as he had time and again—that he'd held on to the locket which contained her portrait, instead of returning it to her.

Cartwright exchanged glances with his wife. "A young lady, sir? Alas—we have several of those. Whatever mixture of the humors promotes madness, it can occur in persons of any age."

"Do you keep the women separate from the men?"

"Nay. 'Tis thought best to keep life as normal as possible. The women seem happier to be in the company of men."

As Will followed the couple through the massive locked and bolted door, he wondered what could be considered "normal" about being kept in such a place. If Pike had wanted Isobel safely locked away, he couldn't have chosen a better prison for her.

A female servant came running up and spoke to Master Cartwright. He bowed to Will. "My wife must take charge of you, sir.

Another visitor has just arrived."

"I'll let you in, sir, so you can look in the cells. It's quite safe. The inmates are only allowed out for exercise, which they take on the sward on fine days. The dangerous ones are shackled, the harmless ones not, but their doors are locked—for the most part. Not just to keep the patients secure, you understand, but because some of the visitors are most unsavory—if you take my meaning. They have been known to abuse, or even to try to abduct some of our patients."

"If I find the woman I'm looking for," Will said grimly, "it will be because she's already been abducted, and placed here under false pretenses."

Goodwife Cartwright blanched. "Not with our knowledge, good sir, oh, no, indeed. We keep full records of all admissions."

"Then mayhap, Goodwife, you might go and fetch those records. I'll pay you a half-angel for a look at them—I'm certain I'd recognize the false admission document if I saw it."

The woman's eyes glowed as he showed her the coin. "I shall be back straightway, sir. Now, you will understand that I must relieve you of your sword before you enter, and bolt the door behind you."

Will nodded his acquiescence, but couldn't escape a quiver of unease as he heard the bolt pushed to.

The hospital reminded him of a parish church, with a high roof and arches to support its span. But whereas a church would have had great glass windows, this building was more akin to a barn. What little light there was came from slots and wind-eyes high above. At ground level, the space was lit by rushlights and hanging lanterns.

Either side of the central aisle stood what could best be described as cells—too small to be considered chambers—each with their own door and slatted window. There was at least a score of these. The building resonated with noise—low murmurs, weeping, tuneless humming, and even the occasional laugh.

He wasted no time, but set to, peering through the slats into the cells—but the light was so weak, he could barely make out faces. Some of the inmates were sleeping—mere humps beneath their coverings, while others sat rocking on their beds with their blankets pulled over their heads. The few lunatics who were currently wandering freely up and down the aisle had noticed him and were starting to congregate.

How was he to find Isobel this way? He'd need every door unlocked so he could take a proper look, since both men and women were dressed only in shifts and shirts, and had their heads either shaved or covered by coifs.

The manic stares of the people surrounding him were unsettling. Clearing his throat, he summoned the voice he used for issuing commands in the field, loud enough to carry to the far corners of the room.

"Isobel. Isobel Marston. 'Tis I, Will Cavendish. If you're here, answer me, I pray."

For a second, the whole room fell silent. Then one of the women nearest Will exclaimed, "I'm Isobel."

"Nay, fool," responded an elderly man with no teeth. "You're the Queen of France—you told me so. You can't be her *and* this Isobel the man is calling for."

There was a clattering from one of the closed doors, and Will turned his head to see a middle-aged woman running a wooden platter along the bars. "I think I might have been called Isobel once," she said, in a quavering voice.

"Nay, *I* am Isobel!" This came from the adjacent cell.

Will rolled his eyes as the whole hall erupted into shouts and screams as the poor wretches in the cells and the aisle, both male and female, claimed to be the woman he was seeking. Whether it was simply that they were deranged, or they were still sane enough to see a chance to escape from their captivity, he couldn't tell. Had their response not been so pitiful, it might have been amusing.

"Silence! Be still!" He'd have the keepers back in minutes, and they'd eject him for certain for disrupting the residents thus.

The racket ceased, followed by a few mutters of complaint. There was one last thing he could try, while he waited for Goody Cartwright to return with the records. Lowering his voice this time, he called, "It is I, Orpheus, come in search of my wife, Eurydice." And as he looked about him, at the empty stares and miserable confusion of his audience, he felt as if he *had* descended into Hades, searching among the damned souls for his Eurydice.

The hubbub began again, with everybody speaking at once.

"I'm Yoori… 'tis I."

"Orpheus. Come and fetch me—your Idiocy awaits you."

"I'm your Medici, sir, I'm the one you seek."

The poor wretches' attempts to pronounce the name were so ridiculous that Will nearly laughed aloud. Then he drew his hands over his face, and groaned inwardly, realizing he must be patient and await the return of Goodwife Cartwright. There was nothing he could do alone.

A movement caught his eye. Someone in a cell at the far end of the room had pushed their fingers between the bars. He could just make out a gold ring on one finger. Odd— because none of the inmates he'd seen thus far had any personal adornment.

His heart beat a rapid tattoo in his chest. The little circle of people surrounding him scattered as he raced the length of the room One glance at the ring was all he needed.

Isobel clung to the bars in her door, her green eyes filled with tears.

"Will? Oh, thank God! Is it really you?"

He kissed her fingers. "Get this door open, someone!" He looked over his shoulder and saw Goodwife Cartwright bearing down on him, clutching a ledger in her hands.

"Goodwife, I've found her. Now, where is that benighted key?"

"I cannot just let you—"

"The key, Woman." He had to get Isobel out of here—the sight of her in her tiny prison, like a rat in a trap, was killing him.

When Goodwife Cartwright looked as if she were about to refuse again, he growled at her. "Open this door, and you get a whole angel. Open it not, and I'll see the queen's closest ministers are informed, as this woman has been unlawfully confined. You'll lose your position—as will your husband."

After barely a heartbeat, the key was produced, the door opened, and Isobel was in his arms, clutching at him like one drowning. She held him so tightly that he could hardly breathe.

"*Isobel.*"

"Will." She was running her hands over his face, stroking his hair, her green eyes wide with wonder and relief. He couldn't stop grinning.

"You seem pleased to see me. Does this mean I'm forgiven all my sins?"

"I can't for the moment remember what they were. They drugged me again, you see."

"So, there's hope for me yet." Hope that blazed like the sun in his heart. Forgetting the many eyes trained on him, he sought Isobel's lips in a frenzied kiss.

She stilled against him, her hands settling tightly around his waist as she opened her mouth to his and drew him in, drinking from his lips as if she would never be satisfied. He rocked her, clung to her, and kissed her. When he felt moist tears on his cheek, he knew not from which of them the tears had come.

Gradually, a sound began to filter through his miasma of joy—a strange, happy gurgling sound. Reluctantly, he dragged his lips away from Isobel's and stared around. All the inmates in the cells had their faces pressed against the bars, some grinning and laughing, others open-mouthed in shock.

Will's little group of admirers was bearing down on him again.

"Let us conclude our business outside." A

red-faced Goodwife Cartwright led them back to the main door and called for a servant to go in and quieten everyone down.

As the clamor of the inmates faded behind them, Will kept tight hold of Isobel's hand. After so many frustrating days of searching, he wasn't sure he could ever let it go again.

Goodwife Cartwright took them into a small building on the opposite side of the exercise yard.

Eager to avoid any further delay, Will said, "I've found what I came for. What do I need to sign?"

The keeper's wife ignored him and turned to Isobel. "Do you know this gentleman?"

"I most assuredly do." Isobel's voice sounded weak, shaking with emotion.

"He wants to take you away from here, without your family's consent, and before you are well. It is most irregular."

Isobel's head snapped up. "There was never anything wrong with me. I kept telling you, but you refused to believe me and continued pouring some kind of soporific elixir into my ale. How much did Hubert

Pike pay you, I wonder?"

Goodwife Cartwright frowned. "You were in a complete stupor when you came in—it was impossible to get any sense out of you. The soporific was to calm you, when you became too excitable. You've seen yourself, sir," she added, turning to Will, "how little it takes for the whole hospital to be in an uproar."

"Of course, I spoke no word of sense at the start." There was an unmistakable edge to Isobel's voice. "I'd just been abducted, stolen from my own back garden and drugged, then smuggled away in the death cart before being dumped in this dreadful place."

"That was not my understanding." Goodwife Cartwright looked uncomfortable. "This lady was brought in by a concerned relative, a respectable-looking gentleman who made a generous donation to the hospital. The young lady was in a pitiful state, physically exhausted—the man said he'd been caring for her at home, but she'd run away. As soon as she came to her senses, she started raving about abduction, and legacies, and the death cart. It just sounded too fantastical. The inmates here are prone to all kinds of imaginings."

Will held the woman's gaze and raised a questioning eyebrow.

She swallowed and looked at Isobel again. There was a long pause before she said, "So, he lied to me?"

He nodded, his lips pressed together in stark disapproval. Call it what one liked—this woman had accepted a bribe to ask no questions about Isobel's condition. He'd risk the queen's displeasure and ask Leicester to pull some strings to get this place looked into. Particularly the way it was run, and the moral fiber of its officials.

"Goodwife Cartwright—the man in question is a trickster of the worst kind. To call him mean, grasping, and vicious would be to understate the case. He's already made one attempt on *my* life and is even now being sought by all the constables, street children, and watchmen in London. I can bring you written testament to that fact, should you need it—and let me assure you, I'm far better connected than Hubert Pike. Now, give me a paper to sign, and we'll be gone."

The keeper's wife made a great show of

shuffling through documents. "I'll send for the young lady's clothes, that she came in with. She can dress in there." She pointed to a side door.

At least they hadn't sold Isobel's things. Will looked down at her feet and was shocked to see she wore no shoes. These lunatics were deprived of all comforts, everything that might be familiar to them. How could there be any cure, any recovery, when they were treated like this?

Isobel gave Will's hand a squeeze. He clung to her delicate fingers, not caring what anyone thought. He never wanted to let her out of his sight again. The self-recriminations, the guilt, loss, loneliness—all these things had eaten away at his soul until it was in tatters, and he'd no idea if he'd ever be whole again.

A girl appeared, was given her orders by Goodwife Cartwright, and disappeared off. Will shuffled one-handed through the papers that had been laid out on the table, refusing to relinquish his hold on Isobel. He had to, however, when she was taken off into the neighboring chamber to be dressed.

He took up the quill and signed the paper placed in front of him, then met Goody

Cartwright's eyes. Aye, suitably cowed, as she should be. However, he must remember it was not the institution at fault, as much as those who ran it—and quell his ungentlemanly urge to take the woman out onto the sward and dump her in the fishpond.

"Had you more in the coffers, could you improve the lot of the inmates here?" he queried.

Her chin went up. "Changes could be made to their diet, and their clothing replaced more frequently, I suppose. One might be able to afford sweet rushes for the floor more regularly, also. I could think of many other things, given time."

He'd expected to see her eyes narrow with greed, but they did not. He removed a gold angel from his purse and placed it on the table. "Then allow me to make a donation. Be certain, if you accept it, another visit will be made, either by myself or one of my connections at court, to ensure the money has been spent wisely."

She gaped at him a moment, then—for the first time since he had set eyes on her— smiled.

"Forgiveness is a virtue, and righteousness is its own reward. I bless you for your generous gift, and humbly apologize for our mistake. We endeavor to do our best here—both by God and by our patients—but we're not infallible. Only the Lord can see through deceit, and He will doubtless punish Master Pike in his own way, without you needing to lift a finger."

He held her gaze, refusing to release her until he was assured of her sincerity. He only blinked when the click of a latch presaged Isobel's return.

She was still wearing the rather grubby coif beneath her wide-brimmed straw hat. It took him a moment to realize the reason for it, and when he did, he was tempted to seize back the coin he'd offered to Goody Cartwright.

Pity moved him so powerfully, it was all he could do not to crush Isobel into his arms and run his hands over that shorn head, kissing every inch of exposed skin. Pike would pay for all he'd made her suffer—by the rood, he'd make him pay! Giving Goodwife Cartwright a curt nod, he seized Isobel's hand and strode to the outside door where he could suck in the air he so badly needed.

Beside him, Isobel, too, was gasping for air.

"I don't know how long I was in that place, but I ofttimes feared I'd never see the sun again. Others were released for exercise, but not I. Doubtless because I insisted that I was innocent of insanity, I was considered troublesome. Having you here with me now, feeling the sun on my face, is all I believe I will ever need."

She had such courage. And possibly more faith in *him* than he had in himself. "I'm so sorry we argued. You should never have been put through this." He raised a hand to her head, his thumb caressing her brow. "Your beautiful hair. How distraught you must have been, my poor darling. But it will grow back. Even if it does not, our queen has set a fashion for wearing wigs."

He looked deep into her eyes, translating every nuance of her expression. He knew he could kiss her again, and she'd not object—he knew he could offer her his love, and that it would be returned.

But before he could speak, she was pulling away from him, her body tense, her green eyes wide. Following the direction of her frozen stare, he saw a familiar figure stalking towards him across the grass.

Hubert Pike.

CHAPTER THIRTY-FOUR

I SOBEL WAS THRUST behind Will as he squared his shoulders and felt for the hilt of his sword. Which, she saw with alarm, wasn't there, and nor was his sword-belt. Yet he was prepared to defend her with his body—which made her love him all the more. If they could but survive the next few moments, they might find true happiness together.

Which was something worth fighting for. She peeped out past Will's shoulder, setting her chin at her cousin.

Hubert's eyes narrowed. "What's this? Who let you out, you mad bitch? I shall have words with the authorities about this."

"Stand off, cur." Will bristled with fury.

"You'll do no further damage here."

"Why? It is *you* who should stand off, interfering again where you're not wanted."

Ah! She'd forgotten how tight and whining a voice her cousin had. She tensed, ready to leap to Will's defense if needed. She'd use her teeth, her nails—whatever it took. Aye, and scream a good deal, too—nothing on earth would induce her to enter Bedlam again. Death would be infinitely preferable. She stepped around Will and folded her arms, glaring at her cousin.

"Pah!" Hubert spat on the ground. "A fine pair you make. Stand back, girl. Only a desperate man would want you now." He looked her up and down in a way that made her sick to her stomach.

He turned his attention to Will again. "You'll regret this, sirrah," he sneered. "She's broken, ruined. There's nothing you can do to help her. Get away now, before she drags your name into the mire along with her own."

How dare he! She'd done nothing wrong, done nothing to deserve the cruelty with which Hubert had treated her. He was a black-hearted villain, and she loathed him.

"You impugn an innocent and honorable lady, and must pay for it." Will's voice was thick with fury. "Isobel, pray, return to the Cartwrights' room of business and remain there until I tell you otherwise. Your cousin and I have a score to settle."

She didn't move. This was *her* fight, too.

"You love *that?*" Hubert jabbed a finger towards her. "She had no beauty or skills when first I found her, and she has none now. Why, she doesn't even have hair! She looks like a gutter whore."

Anger swamped her. She threw herself at Hubert and, summoning all her strength, slapped him on the cheek. He growled and lunged at her, but she sidestepped him. The next moment, he was on the ground with a furious Will on top of him.

No! What had she done? She'd put Will in danger by antagonizing Hubert. But as she gazed about for anything she could use as a weapon, she saw Will knock Hubert's head sideways with a powerful blow. As the blood began to trickle from her cousin's mouth, he freed his hands and struggled to throw his opponent off.

Will had just clenched his fist for another

blow when she saw sunlight flash on cold steel. She screamed, but it was too late—Hubert had sunk a dagger into Will's arm. Grunting in pain, Will rolled aside and scrambled to his feet, dealing Hubert a savage kick in the stomach as the man tried to rise. While Hubert gasped for air, Will squeezed his wrist with such force, the fingers around the knife went white, but Hubert refused to relinquish his blade.

There were shouts and running feet, but she couldn't tear her eyes from the fight. With a great yowl of fury, her cousin heaved himself up, still brandishing his weapon, then crashed back to the ground in an awkward twisting motion as Will knocked his legs out from under him.

There was a gurgling noise as Hubert landed on his front, and the air screamed out of his lungs. Suddenly, the fight seemed to have left him.

Someone took hold of her arm, but she shook them off. As her cousin remained unmoving, Will knelt, fists still raised in case of some trick. Master Cartwright, who must have followed his visitor across the sward, reached out and rolled Hubert over.

His own knife protruded from a bloody wound in his chest. His face was pallid, his eyes already dimming.

"Call a surgeon, someone." Will's voice was ragged, shocked. "You must have bandages here or something."

"Too late, I fear, Sir William." Cartwright was leaning over the body.

Nausea rose in Isobel's throat, and she struggled not to choke. Her knees went limp, and she put out a hand to save herself from falling, but Will was there, supporting her.

"I'm so sorry—I never meant that to happen, nor for you to witness it." His voice was rough with emotion.

"It wasn't your fault. I should not have goaded him."

He held her close. "None could blame you, after what he's done."

Cartwright was still examining Hubert's body, inspecting it for any sign of life. His wife stood by the door to their office, her face as white as death. "Shall I send for a constable?" Her tone was abnormal, high-pitched.

"There's no hurry. We'll need to fetch the coroner in due course." Her husband glanced up. "No crime has been committed here. Yon fellow died upon his own dagger—we all saw it. Sir William drew no weapon and acted to defend himself when this man pulled out his knife."

Will eased away from Isobel. "A moment, I beg you."

She stood there shaking as he examined the body, and pulled a gore-stained paper from the corpse's pocket. Stern-faced, he scanned the contents, then stood and returned to her side. "This is your will, Isobel, leaving everything you own to Hubert Pike. All it lacks is a signature. No doubt he was hoping to force you into that when he came to see you today."

The faintness threatened to take her again. But as Will reached to catch her, she saw a gout of blood course down his arm, staining the sleeve of his doublet.

"Oh, Will, your arm!"

"Your apron, Wife." Cartwright took the garment and covered the dead man's face. "You may send for a surgeon after all, but to aid the living, not the dead. I'll seek a constable, so we may all be exonerated of wrongdoing. Now, take Sir William and his lady to our private parlor, and see they receive succor while waiting for the surgeon."

Not sure how long they'd have to wait, Isobel kept Will talking, mainly to reassure herself his wound wasn't serious, and he wasn't likely to faint from loss of blood before the surgeon arrived.

"Does it hurt very much?"

"Hardly at all—I have better things to think about than pain." He gazed deep into her eyes.

Flushing, she turned away. He was looking at her just as he had that night in the parlor—only then, he'd had the excuse of drunkenness.

He kissed her, a gentle salute on the cheek, then kissed her again, all over her face, her mouth, her neck, as if he couldn't quite believe she were real. Even when a servant brought a costrel of wine and a cold pigeon pie, he didn't stop, shamelessly caressing her with his lips.

"I want to wipe away all foul memories," he said as soon as the wench was gone.

"I'm sorry I didn't take your advice, didn't protect myself properly." She ran a hand over the tawny gold of his hair, thinking it one of the most precious things she'd ever seen. "I need no further illustration of the folly of pride and stubbornness."

"Hush, sweeting. It is *I* who must take the blame. For was it not my knife that broke the lock on the garden door in the first place? I should have reminded you of it, not stormed away in high dudgeon. How much less you would have suffered had I insisted you return to my protection until Pike was apprehended."

She pushed a lock of his hair behind his ear. What a thrill it was to be able to touch him like this, and to appreciate him—showing him with her hands how greatly she valued him.

"Ah, but then, you would have dented *my* pride, and my freedom would still have been curtailed." And he would still have had the problem of Paulina Mathieson's jealousy hanging over his head.

"Perchance we're *both* at fault, but have each now learned our lesson. We shall call a truce, and be friends again. What think you?"

His wicked grin as he stared down at her melted Isobel's heart. He must have seen something in her eyes, for the smile immediately faded, and he brought his mouth hard against hers. She gave herself up to his passion, savoring every last searing drop of his desire, kissing him back as if each taste might be her last. She must look such a fright—no hair to speak of, her shift smelling of dirty rushes and close confinement, her fingernails chewed to the quick with anxiety.

Yet none of this mattered to this extraordinary man. Would it not be heaven to be loved by him? She'd rather die a thousand times over than see him with any other woman.

He drew away a little, giving her the chance to catch her breath. "You cannot know how relieved I am to have you back—I've been driven demented by your loss."

"Then there can have been little to choose between us. I was subjected to the poppy juice again, and some other soporific they use in the Bethlehem Hospital. I would truly have been driven mad by my treatment had I remained there."

Will's breath hissed between his teeth. "You might not have lasted that long if Pike had had his way." He kissed her again and cupped her face tenderly.

"But you were there to save me. It was more than foolish of me to hit Hubert like that, but the moment he threatened me, you were there—without hesitation, without thought for your own safety. I thank the stars you are the better fighter, else I'd have had your death on my conscience forever."

He smiled. "I never start a fight I cannot win. Have you not learned that by now?"

Before she could answer, a gentleman bustled in, accompanied by Goodwife Cartwright. He bore a leather bag which rattled—she, a basin of steaming water.

"Here is the surgeon, Sir William," Goody Cartwright announced. "You had best leave the chamber, Mistress," she added, turning to Isobel. "You may see things no young lady of quality should see."

Will shot Isobel a look that made her blush and picture what he looked like with his shirt off. To the surgeon, he said, "I assume you are speaking of the indignities to which you will be subjecting my wound, sir. The lady may decide for herself if she wishes to watch—she has looked on death this day and shown no weakness."

"May I be of any use?" Isobel asked.

The surgeon shook his head. "Now, no. But later. When you take your husband home, Madam, I'd advise a long soak in the tub before he has his supper. His wound may be dressed again when his flesh is dry."

The dimples appeared in Will's cheeks as he winked at her.

"May I secure myself an invitation to spend the night at Marston House, that you may take good care of me, my lady?"

"Indeed." She would enjoy a bath herself, after the unsanitary places she'd been—she'd remember the stench of the death cart until Kingdom Come. A change of clothes was also essential, and a prettier coif, to cover her shorn scalp. She'd send for Goodwife Cooper to bring Will's things to him, and have her new maid, Annott, make up a room for him, and clean and mend his torn clothing.

She left the room to wait outside in the bright August sunshine. Turning her back on the activity going on around Hubert's body, she walked along a pathway edged with neatly trimmed rosemary bushes, enjoying the clean scent given off as her skirts brushed the leaves. The sun's heat warmed her, as though bringing her back to life, and she thrust aside her memories of what had happened, pondering instead on what was to come.

Most of all, she thought about the man being treated in the Keepers' residence, who would shortly be joining her at Marston House for the night. Wickedly, she wondered what he'd look like in his bath, his golden hair sleek and dark with water, the candle shadows flickering over his smooth, naked body.

The sudden arrow of desire that lanced through her made her bite her lip in consternation—where on earth had such unladylike conjecture come from? It was none of her business what Will looked like naked—in fact, it was the last thing she should be thinking about right now.

Only… after all she'd been through, she couldn't help herself. Her fears, her frustrations, all needed an outlet, and she knew Will could help her release her tensions.

So long as he felt the same way about her as she did about him. Why had he not yet spoken any sweet words of love? Was it because Paulina and her father had a hold over him still?

CHAPTER THIRTY-FIVE

WILL COULDN'T WAIT for their evening repast to be over. Though it seemed there were almost as many of *his* servants in Marston House as there were of Isobel's, he had happily let her take charge of the arrangements, knowing how much she valued her independence.

There were so many things to discuss, away from prying eyes and curious ears. Goody Cooper, having forged a particular bond with Isobel, seemed ever to be dancing attendance on her, almost to the point where Will started wondering if he should just gift the woman to Isobel, and find himself a new housekeeper.

He needed to tell Isobel what had happened with Paulina. He had to hope that, since the woman had run away, she must no longer carry a candle for him, and that her father would stop trying to blackmail him into marrying her. He also needed to sound out Isobel about moving to the countryside. Initially, he'd thought of his rescue of her as restoring to London society one of its brightest jewels—but now his hopes were selfish ones. He didn't want to share her company with anyone else, didn't want to see her corrupted by the false fancies and flatteries of life at court, could not stand the idea of her being manipulated by fashion and faction.

What had once seemed exciting to him had now lost its gloss. He'd seen Leicester strive, and fall. How quick his former comrades had been to condemn him to his queen! Such hypocrisy turned Will's stomach—he couldn't help but feel good men like Edward Marston had suffered and died pointlessly because of the poison poured into Queen Elizabeth's ear by others. That poison had had the effect of making her remove financial support from Leicester's Dutch campaign because it looked as if he were accruing too much power.

These were weighty matters, indeed. He hoped and prayed Isobel would understand his feelings and accept what he had to offer. As the last of the dishes were cleared away from the board, he moved his chair next to hers and reached for her hand.

"How do you feel? Not too tired, I hope."

She smiled at him. "I feel much refreshed for having washed away the stink of that place."

And replaced it with something most compelling—a musky scent, sweetened with the smell of roses. He thought he'd never smelled anything more enticing.

"Is your wound troubling you, sir?"

He rested their joined hands on his knee and stroked her palm slowly with his thumb. "Barely. With the wine and peerless company, I've hardly thought of it."

"I ask, because your eyes seem brighter tonight than usual—as if you were feverish."

In a sense he was, but not because of that.

"May I keep Manners with me a little longer?"

Why were they talking about Manners? He'd not been a great deal of use when it came down to it, had he? Besides, she'd have *him* to take care of her—if he could persuade her.

"You need no longer worry about your cousin." He stroked her fingers, then noted, with a flip of his heart, that she still wore his seal ring.

"Let us not forget that the odious Flinders is still at large," she reminded him.

"Oh, there'll be no danger from that quarter—the authorities are on the lookout for both him and Goodwife Quill. They are nothing without Pike—cut off the head and the body will die. But of course, you may have Manners if you wish."

Isobel shivered, and he immediately tightened his grip on her hand. "My apologies. I don't mean to conjure up vile images. You were courage itself, today, Isobel. You have been since I met you, in truth."

He gazed at their entwined fingers and toyed with the ring. It moved easily.

"Isobel, this has loosened. You could take it off."

She looked up at him, her eyes moist. "So I could. I confess I've not eaten well since I left Giles Street."

"That won't do at all." Now was as good a time as any to make his declaration, but his voice felt like a boulder in his throat. "Isobel, what do you plan to do next?"

She looked away. "I don't know what you mean."

"You are free now." Why had he mentioned that? It was the last thing he really wanted. Could he marry her, yet convince her she was free?

"You're a wealthy young woman, most eligible. There'll be a line of suitors a mile long at your gates. Shall you stay at home, here in London, or will you go to court?"

She removed the ring, then put it back. Were her hands shaking?

"I know not. I feel as if I might like to bury myself in obscurity a while to collect my thoughts. I don't know if I should write to my friends and more distant relations and tell them what has happened. I could go on a peregrination, I suppose, and visit them all, yet I feel ashamed for having been duped so easily by Hubert. And I'll need to tell everyone of Edward's death."

Will's breath became shallow. An idea had sprung into his head, one that might tempt her to remain with him. For he could countenance no other outcome.

"If you wish to defer that decision, why not remain under my protection a little longer? I have my eye on a property in Foxwell, in Suffolk, with a farm attached. The roads are good enough for an occasional visit to London, but bad enough to prevent London folk making unnecessary journeys to Suffolk."

She turned to him, her eyes bright. "When could we go?"

"As soon as your affairs here are concluded. You may keep Goody Cooper to manage Marston House in your absence—I'll find another housekeeper. I'm sure Mistress Mathieson keeps a very good house."

Excellent—she was laughing. Though she'd not mentioned it, he understood the loss of her hair made her unwilling to seek company. He could bury himself in the country, away from court intrigue and scandals, and she could live in quiet obscurity while her hair—and her confidence—grew back.

But there were one or two things that still needed to be settled.

Releasing her hand, he got to his feet. "I'm wearied. Shall you tell the servants they may shut up the house and retire for the night?"

"Aye." She tilted her head, looking at him intently as if suspecting him of having an ulterior motive. Which, of course, he had.

He gave what he hoped was an innocent smile. "But please return when you've spoken to them—I have something to give you."

Her cheeks pinked charmingly as she left the room, and he returned to his seat, unable to wipe the smug grin from his face. It looked as if the dice were finally loaded in his favor. Reaching into the space between his doublet and the clean shirt he'd borrowed from Edward's clothes press, he pulled out a folded object, wrapped in linen. It was the green silk ribbon he'd bought for Isobel at the country fair—how long ago that seemed now!

He wondered how Maybury had managed with his attempt to rescue Paulina Mathieson from the Comte de Velors—he hadn't even told Isobel about that yet. It seemed unimportant compared with his current mission.

Before her return, he extinguished all but two of the candles and the walls of the room seemed to close in around him, wrapping him in a warm cocoon. Perfect. He needed her to feel relaxed and secure.

When she came back, the color in her cheeks was still there, and she moved awkwardly, stiffly, avoiding eye contact with him. Crouching by her chair, he unwrapped the ribbon and handed it to her.

"Not much of a gift, mayhap, but it comes from the heart."

She ran her fingers over the green silk, but her expression remained guarded.

He'd hoped for a more positive reaction. Surely, he could not have misread the signs, the moisture in her eyes earlier, her delight at the thought of accompanying him to the country? Anxious, he placed a gentle finger beneath her chin and tipped her lovely face to look at him. Was it a trick of the light, or were those tears brimming in her eyes?

"I had not expected my love token to be a harbinger of melancholy." He gave her a shaky smile, but her lips drooped. Whatever was wrong?

Then realization hit him.

He rose, pulling her into his arms. "I am the greatest, stupidest, blindest fool in Christendom. Please forgive me, my darling Isobel. Yes, I bought that ribbon for your hair. I have kept it next to my heart ever since, awaiting the right moment to present it to you. When I saw your ring was loose, I thought you might use the ribbon to suspend it about your neck, as I have no expectation of taking the ring back. It's yours now, whatever you choose to do with it. In my eagerness to give you my lover's token, I quite forgot you had lost your hair."

"You've said that twice now." Her voice quavered but she wasn't trying to pull away.

He ran his hands down her arms. "Said what twice?"

"That the ribbon was a lover's token." Her voice was little more than a whisper.

"That is the simple truth. Don't you know how precious you are to me? How much I long to know that your heart beats only for me? Dearest, bravest, most beautiful Isobel, only tell me that my feelings are returned."

He seized and kissed her hand, aware he was trembling. He prayed she could feel it, could read the powerful longing in his eyes. How he ached to kiss her now! But words were more vital than kisses.

"I... I don't know what you mean, sir." He read a mixture of joy, doubt and confusion in her face.

"Here." He removed the ring from her finger and tucked it into his coin purse.

"I regret to deprive you of this, having said you might keep it. But have no fear—I will have it reworked and inscribed by the very best goldsmith, and presented to you again under more auspicious circumstances. Before the altar."

CHAPTER THIRTY-SIX

I SOBEL WAS TOO stunned to breathe. Then the air rushed back into her lungs, and her breast rose and fell with alarming rapidity. *Could* they marry? What of the Mathiesons' threat to besmirch Will's name through exposing his activities with Leicester? And even if that plot failed, a besotted woman like Paulina would think of some other nefarious plan to tie herself to Will.

Then there was the issue of her own financial independence. Her legacy would become her husband's as soon as she wed. Would she have to give up Marston House? If Leicester were to be exonerated, Will would want to go to court. Did she have the confidence to go with him, or would everyone laugh at her for being gulled by her cousin?

Will held her firmly, giving her a little shake. "You're not going to deny me now, I hope, or I shall have to kiss you mercilessly until you capitulate."

She scanned his face and was arrested by what she saw there. His eyes were deep pools of desire, of need.

"You want to marry me?"

He held her more tightly. "Haven't I made it clear enough? I've loved you for a long time, sweet Isobel. It seems like forever. Only my desire not to clip your wings has stopped me declaring myself. Well, that, and a few impediments, like the fact you kept disappearing, and Pike was after my blood. But none of that matters now."

He leaned in and subjected her to an assault of kisses. Like the soldier he was, Will was storming the bastion of her heart—and her surrender was not far off. When it came, she knew it would be complete—there would be no turning back.

She wriggled in his grasp, tearing her lips from his. "But what of your reputation? Aren't you afraid that Master Mathieson—"

"Hush, my dove." Will bent his neck and nuzzled her cheek. "It is of no matter to me, so long as I have you. My honor may remain untainted yet. I can't say the same for Mathieson since Paulina has run off with the Comte de Velors."

She pushed away from him. "*What?* When did this happen?" How could he not have told her? She'd been so anxious.

"About a sennight since. Maybury offered to help recover her. I had other things on my mind."

Her hands clutched the front of his doublet as elation soared through her. Sir William Cavendish was—to all intents and purposes—hers for the taking. Unfortunately, this revelation had stolen her voice. She could do little more than stare at him.

"I've come so close to losing you, Isobel. Had I not found you in time, I'd have lost the greater part of myself. I will do whatever it takes to make you happy."

He kissed her lightly on the forehead, then nudged at her cheek. "Every man has his pride. Before mine is destroyed utterly, will you not favor me with an answer?"

Her whole being wanted to cry out "*Yes!*

Yes!" but she schooled herself to caution. Every woman was entitled to a little thinking time in such circumstances.

"I'll give you my answer on the morrow. I'm *almost* certain it will be favorable, but your declaration, after the excitement of today, has overset me. I think it would be only fair to us both if I were to—"

"Sleep on it?" Will suggested.

She felt a wave of color swamp her cheeks. That image of Will stark naked was back again, a pox upon it!

Seeming not to notice, he relinquished his hold on her and stretched, then winced.

"Forgive me—I had quite forgot my wound. I'll receive your answer tomorrow then since you mean to torture me. But that is your prerogative as a woman, is it not? Now, let us take a candle each and ascend to our chambers together. Two candles light the way better than one."

Taking possession of his uninjured arm, Isobel was relieved to feel the solid muscle beneath his sleeve. Since his declaration, a sense of unreality had swept over her, so profound she needed reassurance that he was, indeed, there and not some mad dream sent to torment her. She was a mass of confusion—jubilation warred with caution, and she strove to maintain a balance between them. Her whole being wanted to whoop with joy, but she didn't trust in her good luck. Dame Fortuna had smiled on her too little of late.

Will gave her his candle to hold as he pushed open the door to the chamber which had been made up for him. Then, to her surprise, he drew her inside as well and closed the door behind them.

"What are you doing?" Her voice sounded shaky and high. He smiled slowly, then removed both candles from her trembling fingers, and placed them on the linen chest.

"I have an injured arm, and the servants will all be abed by now. I may need help undressing."

She could rouse one of them, couldn't she? But did she want to?

"Come, I only need a little help undoing my points. I'll do as much as I can by myself."

"But 'tis most unseemly."

Will pressed a finger against her lips. "After all we've been through together, I think we can overlook this slight breach of propriety. Who is there to judge us? Besides, I have this wound on *your* account, so the least you can do is help me."

"Sir William Cavendish, you are the veriest rogue."

"I know." He didn't look at all contrite as he started undoing the points of his doublet one-handed.

"Oh, for goodness' sake—that will take you all night."

He didn't bother to hide a feral grin as she took over the task, rapidly undoing the bows that tied his leather laces. All the while, she felt his eyes on her and the caress of his breath on her cheek. His gaze was a tangible thing—it was as if he touched her wherever he looked. Her body resonated in response.

Soon all the laces—except those which fastened his upper hose—were undone. She helped him shrug out of his doublet, resisting the urge to run her hands appreciatively over his broad shoulders.

"The shirt, too, if you will—the knot at the neck is too tight to manage one-handed."

She ought to leave now. He could sleep in his shirt, could he not? All the same, she went to him, bade him lift his chin, and undid the knot in the linen cord.

"Thank you. It's hot tonight, so I'll take this off." He pulled the tail of the shirt free from his hose and tried to bring it one-handed over his head.

"Help!" His voice was muffled as he got stuck halfway. Isobel had to smother a laugh as she rushed to assist him. But when the shirt came away, the laugh became a gasp, and she stared, mesmerized, at his torso.

Who would have expected to see the perfection of Italian sculpture made flesh? But now the proof was before her, the finely honed muscles rippling with strength beneath the marble-smooth skin. Will's chest was covered with a down of fine blond hair, darkening over his breastbone and beneath his throat, and swirling in little eddies around his nipples. Silvery scars marred his skin, tokens of battles long past. It took all Isobel's self-control not to stroke her fingers over the marks, and press her lips to them.

She felt Will watching her, assessing her response to his naked flesh, and flushed.

He didn't seem to mind. Instead, he reached for the lace that secured the front of her gown and started undoing it.

His voice was soft but determined. "Now it's *your* turn."

CHAPTER THIRTY-SEVEN

WHEN ISOBEL AWOKE from her light doze, she felt the change in herself. She had become a woman, having spent a magical night in Will's arms. His gentle wooing had gradually overcome her reluctance. Before the clock struck midnight, her naked body was pressed against his, every part of her thrumming with a heady desire instilled by his touch. From the moment his mouth closed over her erect nipple and suckled at it, she'd been lost.

When she'd felt that secret part of him, potent and aroused, she'd drawn back in fear, but he'd soothed and consoled her, then stoked her to a writhing passion which had nearly vanquished her. Something had snapped inside her, and a rush of hot sensation in her loins had given way to an overwhelming desire for fulfillment.

The moment of Will's possession had consumed her. Despite the initial sharp jab of pain, she'd clenched her legs around his body, clinging to him frantically as he surged into her, driving her wilder with every thrust until she felt ready to explode. And explode she had, at the same moment that he went rigid inside her, then moaned out his release and buried his face against her neck.

As she'd lain holding him, feeling his comforting weight and the still ardent pressure of his body inside her, she thanked every Power she could think of for the joy of their union. She knew he did not lack experience of women, but felt no jealousy for her predecessors—instead, she silently blessed whoever had taught him so well to discover and arouse a woman's most intimate parts.

It had almost torn her in two when he'd eased himself out of her body but, instantly, he was back, shifting position to tuck her closely into his side while he murmured breathless thanks and compliments in her ear.

She hadn't meant to stay all night. She hadn't expected him to make love to her at all, and even when he did, she'd thought once the deed was done, she'd be permitted to escape.

But it was not to be. Will had held her, talked to her, told her of his hopes and plans for their future. Then he'd caressed her until her whole body trembled with desire for him, and he took her again, slowly, deliciously—until she feared she would faint from the pleasure.

Becoming more fully awake, she was aware of the grey touch of dawn around the edges of the shutters and could hear the sound of a robin trilling from a nearby tree. She couldn't move—her body was entwined with Will's, the sheet thrown haphazardly over them.

It was vital she go to her own chamber now before the servants started scampering around. But first, she must rouse Will.

She ran her fingers through his tousled hair. He stirred but didn't wake. She thought, sorrowing, of her own missing locks, and loved that it had made not one whit of difference to Will's feelings for her. In fact, he'd insisted she remove her coif and had gently kissed her scalp, telling her she had a beautifully shaped head, and he'd still love her, even if her hair never grew back again.

She ran a hand over her scalp and felt a rasping softness there. Her hair was growing back already—a wash made with blackberry leaves might encourage it. If she remembered rightly, rosemary made an effective hair tonic. She could try that, too.

Will's hand moved against her thigh, then began a rhythmic caress. He was awake. And interested.

"Tell me, Will, do you want children?"

The hand paused for a moment, then continued its stroking. "I shall be happy to have some, my love, if you are. Especially if they're dark and beautiful, like their mother."

"Nay. I would prefer them to be noble and golden, like their father."

"Noble and golden?" She could hear the smile in his voice. "That is a compliment to treasure. But you won't think that in thirty years' time when I'm wizened and grey."

"I shall still love you then." She paused, teasingly. "Assuming you've proved a good husband."

"I'll do my best to keep you satisfied." His hand moved up to claim her breast. "In as many ways as you can think of."

She swallowed and tried to moisten a throat gone suddenly dry. "Why did you do it? Why did you want me to stay with you?"

"Because I wanted to be sure of your answer. 'Probably positive' wasn't good enough for me. I thought if I ruined you, you'd have no choice."

"Damned scoundrel." She twisted in his arms to make a pretend slap at him, then saw blood soaking through the bandage on his arm.

"Will, you're bleeding!"

He examined his bicep. "'Tis but a trifle. In my enthusiasm last night, I quite forgot about it."

She frowned, concern mingling with annoyance.

He pulled her closer and brushed a light kiss on her temple. "Don't worry—I shall have the banns called immediately. We'll be wed before anyone knows what we have done this night, and then we can do it all again, without a stain on our conscience. You know as well as I how many brides are no longer virgins on their wedding day."

He stroked her with undemanding tenderness, running his hands over as much of her naked body as he could reach—as if teaching himself her form so he could remember it always. She wanted to do the same to him—he felt warm, relaxed, and totally, utterly desirable. How had she even managed to doze with his tempting body pressed so firmly against her?

Yet somehow, she must have fallen asleep, because the next thing she knew, bright sunlight was flooding through the gaps in the shutters, and someone was banging on the chamber door.

"Sir William, I regret disturbing you." It was Goodwife Cooper's voice. As Will stirred next to her, Isobel leapt from the bed, dragged her shift over her head, and started hunting for her coif. Where could she hide? She mustn't be found here!

"Sir William."

Isobel glared at Will and shook her head. He looked grim, but rose from the bed with the sheet around his waist and strode to the door.

"Goody Cooper. Forgive me—I slept

badly due to my injured arm. What's amiss?"

"It's Master Maybury, sir. He says he needs to see you urgently. He has Paulina Mathieson with him."

Isobel's heart sank. Just when she thought the Fates had decreed she might be happy, they'd changed their minds. Both she and Will were about to be vilified.

CHAPTER THIRTY-EIGHT

WILL SMILED AT Isobel with a reassurance he was far from feeling. What could possibly have brought both his friend and his nemesis to Marston House demanding to see him? And what a morning to have chosen!

He put his head close to the door. "Have you roused the mistress yet?"

"Nay, sir. We thought, after yesterday's events, she should be left to sleep. Shall I wake her now?"

At Isobel's frantic head shaking, he replied, "Nay. I shall dress first, then wake her myself. I can see if she'd rather I dealt with the matter alone or, as this is her house, request Maybury wait until she's dressed. I'm sure he'll understand if she's not in the mood for visitors at present."

Isobel whispered, "Tell her to show them into the parlor. I'll run to my room as soon as she's gone down."

Will relayed the message and listened until Goody's footsteps dwindled into silence. "Go. Can you dress yourself or shall I come to you as soon as I'm ready?"

Her face was pale, but she shook her head. "I shall manage. What about you?"

He gave a wry smile. "Much as I would rather be *undressed* by you, I think your help in putting my clothes on would be most welcome."

After a brief tussle with his shirt, doublet and hose, he felt fit to be seen, poked his head out the door, and made sure it was safe for Isobel to return to her chamber unobserved. It took considerable strength of purpose—what he really wanted to do was shout to the world that he had just enjoyed the most perfect night of his life and that all his dreams were coming true. Why did reality have to intrude with such brutal insistence? But once Maybury and Paulina were dealt with, there was always this afternoon.

He took care over his toilet. If Maybury had bad news, he was in no hurry to hear it. As soon as he was ready, he hastened to the kitchen to request that some manner of repast be sent into the parlor. Whatever he and Isobel must face, they might as well do it with full stomachs.

Both Maybury and Paulina got to their feet when he finally entered the room. They looked somewhat sheepish, though he couldn't help but think Paulina looked particularly splendid today with her golden curls artfully coiled on top of her head and a starched lace ruff emphasizing the length of her neck. A pity he knew her to be so spoiled and selfish—though perchance she would grow out of that in time.

The door opened behind him to admit Isobel. She'd donned a low-cut gown which accentuated the white flesh of her breast, and had a charming cap in green velvet over the top of her coif. She, too, wore a high collar edged with lace, all of which concealed the fact her hair had been shorn.

He thought her the loveliest thing he'd ever seen and was rendered temporarily speechless.

Maybury broke the spell. "Ah, Cavendish. 'Tis a relief to find you here. We have already been to your house, where they denied all knowledge of your whereabouts. And Mistress Marston—God give you good day." He made a low bow and Paulina bobbed a curtsey, much to Will's surprise.

"I am delighted you've been restored to us, Mistress. Did Sir William recover you, or did you rescue yourself?"

Paulina tutted, and whispered something Will couldn't hear.

Maybury thrust his shoulders back and continued. "I daresay there's a long story attached to your reappearance, Mistress Marston. I should be glad to hear it if you're prepared to impart it—I like to think we might consider ourselves more than mere acquaintances. Hmm." He glanced around the room, then caught Paulina's intense expression, and cleared his throat. "However, I… er, that is, *we* have news for you both that cannot wait."

Will indicated a chair, and Isobel took it. He stood behind her, pleasantly surprised how at home he felt here. He was already ordering Isobel's servants about and entertaining her guests as if he were master of the house.

He'd have to make sure he didn't do that too often or she'd punish him for it. But today, he was so happy, he couldn't help but behave like a lovesick idiot. Aye, he'd use that as an excuse if she reprimanded him.

One of Isobel's serving wenches elbowed open the door and set a pitcher, some horn beakers and a loaded platter on the table. She bobbed and left, then returned almost immediately with a whole cooked carp, beautifully filleted and laid out on a bed of ground rice with cow-cumber and chive decorations.

Will exchanged glances with Isobel, who looked utterly puzzled. The servant bobbed again. "Goodwife Cooper ordered it, my lady," she informed Isobel. "She thought there was something to celebrate this morn."

He had to force himself not to laugh as Isobel colored up. "Your retrieval, Mistress Marston," he said. "Evidently, your household is glad to welcome you home." He helped Isobel to a plateful, then offered some to their guests. When Maybury stretched out a hand to accept some bread and ham,

Paulina gave him an unsubtle kick on the ankle.

"Forgive me. I must waste no time. Paulina—I mean, Mistress Mathieson, has exhorted me to tell you this story myself as she is somewhat embarrassed. But she has been brave enough to come and face you in person, Cavendish, so for that, we must all applaud her."

He gazed at Will hopefully, then Isobel. She was stifling a smile.

"I hope you don't mind if my hostess and me break our fast while you speak, Maybury. I was injured on the yester, and have slept late. Mistress Marston has kindly waited for me."

"Indeed. As you can see, I helped find Mistress Mathieson and bring her home. She was crying her eyes out, poor creature, when we finally came up with her, and the blackguard who ran off with her. She fell on her father's neck and told us the Comte de Velors had treated her abominably. It wasn't long before she suspected him of having a financial motive for making off with her, rather than a passionate one. Said she'd rather the shame of being a runaway than marry a man whose main motivation was greed. My, but she was plucky to stand up to that cowardly cur. She said she regretted her behavior towards *you*, Cavendish. Now she knows what 'tis like to be pursued for the wrong reasons, and to be the victim of what can only be described as blackmail."

"Forgive me, Sir William. My father made a fool of me. Or, should I say, allowed me to make a fool of myself where you were concerned."

Paulina didn't meet Will's gaze, but her apology stunned him. He *had* underestimated her, *and* she'd matured rather sooner than he'd expected. Even if she was trying to lay all blame at her father's door.

Maybury swilled his small beer around his beaker. "De Velors has gone into hiding. Despite his alleged skill with a blade, I disarmed him, broke his jaw and, finally, his nose. He won't be charming any more ladies with his handsome face unless he can afford to pay a good bone-setter."

"I shouldn't imagine he'll be much missed. Well done, Maybury. It seems Mistress Marston and I are not the only ones to have been involved in adventure of late."

"Indeed, indeed." Maybury took a covert glance at Paulina, but she seemed to have retreated into herself again. Most unusual. Her experience with de Velors had left its mark—Will began to feel pity for her.

"So, Mistress Marston, Cavendish has found you. I'm right glad of it."

"He has." Isobel shot Will a coy look that made him want to puff out his chest. He grinned.

"And he's removed any further danger to my person."

"Excellent news. And you're both friends again, I hope?"

Where was this leading? Why did Maybury seem so awkward? He was a man who usually got right to the point. Will rested his hands upon Isobel's shoulders in a proprietary gesture. That ought to satisfy the man.

"I should say we always have been, Maybury. Now, will you stop paddling around the pond and tell us what you *really* want to say."

Maybury drained his cup. Paulina wound her hands together and stared at him.

"On the journey home, Mistress Mathieson and I were thrown much into each other's company. As you know, my wife died. I mean—I'm not averse to marrying again. Paulina and her father spent a night at my house and liked it a good deal. A pox on't! What I'm trying to say is… she and I are now betrothed."

Will felt an ache around his heart. This news was exceedingly welcome but, at the same time, reminded him he'd not yet received Isobel's answer. How could he bear to congratulate his friend on the prospect of domestic felicity when his own future was far from certain?

Isobel had risen and, bless her forgiving heart, was embracing Paulina. "That is splendid news and gladdens my soul. May I embrace you, too?" She turned to Maybury, who was out of his seat in a second. Will felt the bitter sting of jealousy as the man wrapped his arms around Isobel's slender waist and kissed her cheek.

This would not do at all. He waited until Maybury had released Isobel, then knelt before her, to a chorus of gasps.

"My lady. I believe that we, too, deserve such happiness. Will you do me the honor of agreeing to become my wife?"

He steeled himself for her answer—how many times had he asked her now? Surely, she could no longer refuse him, not after last night. But by asking her in front of witnesses, he was putting still further pressure on her to agree. She wouldn't like that. But he'd make it up to her—tonight if she'd let him.

Tender arms wrapped around him, and he felt her kiss his hair. He closed his eyes and waited, feeling as if he were poised on the edge of a cliff, looking down at dark, choppy waters. If she said "no"…

"Of course, I will." Her voice bubbled with laughter. "You foolish fellow—how could you think I would not?"

He rose then, and—not caring about the company—kissed her thoroughly.

Someone clapped their hands, and a masculine roar of laughter was accompanied by a feminine giggle. Still entranced by the nectar of Isobel's lips, Will refused to pay any attention—until Isobel gently eased herself away. Even then, he couldn't let her go but slid his arm possessively around her waist as he turned to face their audience.

Maybury was still laughing. "You two, despite adverse circumstances, have found each other, as have we. Fate is a fickle mistress, but I believe she has smiled on us undeserving mortals this day."

"Amen to that." Will shook Maybury's hand, and kissed Paulina's, silently forgiving her all the trouble she'd caused him. Then he indicated the table.

"Goodwife Cooper was right. We *do* have something to celebrate today, and how better than to celebrate in good company? Let us now enjoy our betrothal feast. Is it too early to call for wine, Eurydice?"

Isobel gave him a look that warmed his soul and heated his blood. "Nay, good Orpheus. You have my permission to do so."

He glanced at Maybury and Paulina, who were watching him and Isobel in slack-jawed puzzlement.

"A private family jest," he explained as joyous laughter bubbled up in his stomach once more. Isobel was his, his heart was whole, and every day would be a blessing with her by his side.

And he'd devote the rest of his life to proving that Edward *had* made the right decision when he'd asked Will to care for the incomparable Isobel Marston.

EPILOGUE

THE WEDDING HAD taken place in the small church at Foxwell. Isobel was already carrying little Edward by then—the announcement had been her wedding gift to Will, who was ecstatic.

Maybury and Paulina had had a grander time of it when they wed. Of course, the new Lady Cavendish and her dashing husband had been invited to their massive bride feast, there to mingle with the cream of London society and the brightest lights of the court. And to bid them all farewell, so that Isobel's lying-in could take place in the fresher air and quieter surroundings of Foxwell Hall.

It was high summer, almost a year to the day since Isobel had first met Will. Sheep grazed in the surrounding meadows, and the hedges bordering the lane which led to the house were a tangled display of rampant dog rose, green elderberries, and hawthorn.

Little Edward dozed in his cot, his nurse near at hand. Will had ridden off on one of his mysterious ventures, leaving Isobel to the garden planning which had—after young Edward and Will—absorbed much of her energy since their acquisition of Foxwell.

She gazed down at the spindly young branches of the rosemary she'd planted, reaching up towards the early afternoon sun, and wondered how long before Will returned, and what news he'd have to relate.

As if reading that very thought, he clattered into the courtyard and swung himself agilely from Jennet's back. His leg was so much better—after she'd made an ointment of arnica and boneset to rub into it—and his limp had vanished altogether. She waited, her stomach prickling with anticipation, as his energetic footsteps came up the stairs.

"Isobel." He nodded at the nurse to resume her seat by the cot. "Is Edward asleep?"

"Aye, Husband."

"How long do we have?"

She chuckled. "Half an hour at best." Though Will loved his firstborn dearly, he liked to make the most of whatever time he could spend alone with his wife.

"That should be long enough. Come, fetch your sunhat and partlet—I have something to show you."

She rose and collected her things. "Where are we going?"

"Only to the church. For a little stroll."

"Around a graveyard?" There were plenty of other lanes, fields and coppices through which they might take a very pleasant walk. They'd have to go through the village to reach the church, which might mean running into some of their tenants. That would be no bad thing—she'd discovered a lot of pleasure could be had from village gossip.

"Stop interrogating me, and come." He held out his hand.

"Aye, Husband." His grip trembled with contained excitement. There was something special he wanted her to see, though she'd no idea what it might be. From the tension in his body, it meant much to him. She must be sure to react favorably, whatever it was. A goat, a new calf, a rare orchid, a newly thatched roof for one of their tenants?

When they got down to the courtyard, he said, "I'll put you up before me on Jennet. We'll get there faster if we ride."

"You'll do no such thing. I now have a fine grey mare called Molly, as well you know. The lord and lady of the manor must always ride in state through the village."

Will rolled his eyes. "Forget it—we'll walk. Give me your hand."

So, they walked, she raising her skirts a little to avoid the dust of the lane, Will striding onward with a look of intense urgency on his face. Swallows swooped above, and the scent of honeysuckle hung heavily on the afternoon air. How different this was from London! Though Marston House was still hers, she no longer wished to live there—the memories were painful and poignant. Instead, she'd let it out, and brought her servants to Foxwell. All her life was here now, and she could not have been happier.

"Do you tire, Wife? Would you have me carry you?"

"I am not quite worn out with bearing your son. I've had three months to recover my strength."

"Hah! He's *your* son, too, and you seemed to enjoy his conception just as much as I did."

"Merciful heavens! No gentleman should say such things to his wife when in public." She gave his arm a playful pinch.

He cocked his head at her, eyes twinkling with amusement. "But then, I am no longer a gentleman where you are concerned, *Wife*. That would be far too dull."

She battled the flush that threatened. Will had never tired of touching her, holding her, even when she felt herself bloated and ugly with child. She was eternally grateful for it.

"Nay, we are almost there. What was it you wanted me to see?"

He pushed open the lych-gate and ushered her through. "It is at the far end of the churchyard."

"Where the masons have been at work, behind that canvas?"

He came to an abrupt halt. "You haven't looked, have you?"

"Nay. Why should I? I assume they've been making repairs to an ancient tomb or monument."

His handsome face relaxed. "Not quite. Come around the corner, and you'll see the canvas is gone."

It was, in truth. But what it had concealed was no old monument being resurrected, but a new one, freshly carved. When she came closer, she saw an inscription in Latin, a date, a number, and the name "Edwardus Marston".

"What does it say?" Her voice was a mere whisper.

Will held her hand. "His date of death, his age, the fact he fell in the service of his country. He lies beneath the slab, Isobel. I had his body brought back."

"He's here?" She moved forward, eyes blinded by tears, and laid her hand on the sun-warmed stone.

"An odd bride-gift, I know. But I had so much for which to thank him. It seemed only right and fitting he return to England, and be near us, and his namesake." There was an odd catch in his voice, and she wondered if Will were weeping, too. But her eyes were brimming and she couldn't see.

"Here." Will handed her a handkerchief she'd spent much of the winter embroidering for him. She dabbed at her eyes and saw that, down by her feet, a freshly planted rose bush was growing, bordered by sweetly scented chamomile.

She lifted her head, a new warmth invading her heart. Now, beneath the open sky with the larks singing high and loud above, her grief for Edward began to fade. Nature would always take over, instilling new life where there had only been death and sorrow before.

Her husband had given her a great gift, one that came from the heart.

"We must bring little Edward here to visit his uncle. I know the babe won't understand the significance of this place, but if Edward's spirit lingers here, I'm sure he would be glad to see his nephew."

"What are you talking about, you little witch?" Will's voice was steadier now. "Don't tell me you can feel ghosts?"

"Perhaps I can. And I know you feel them, too, for all you're being so noble and brave about it."

He dipped his head and shrugged in acknowledgement. "I can never hide anything from you, can I, Lady Cavendish?"

A slight breeze whipped up, stirred by the hot summer air, and he shivered slightly. As if for warmth, he wrapped his arms around Isobel's waist and rested his chin on the top of her head.

She gazed at the beautiful scrolling on the stonework of Edward's monument. "Do you think he planned this?"

"What, you and me? You think he might have guessed I'd be perfect for you?"

She chuckled. "I know not how he could have when I knew it not myself."

Will's chest flexed at her back as he let out a sigh. "Aye—I never knew a man needed to ask a lady so many times before she accepted him."

She lifted his hands and kissed them. "What do you think we should call our next little one? I can't think of a female form of Edward."

She sensed Will's grin as he said, "How about Eurydice if it's a girl? Or Orpheus if it's a boy?"

"You can't call someone Orpheus in this day and age—he'd be a laughingstock."

"Then I'll suggest something more suited to present times. Avice is a popular name for a girl. Or if it's a boy, what about Hubert?"

Isobel spun around, jaw dropping, and stared at Will for a moment, then hit him hard on the arm. "Vile creature! You jest with me."

"Ah, but I so love to tease you." He pulled her into his embrace until her clenched fists were pressed up against his chest. "You look so wild and wanton when you're angry."

She capitulated immediately. "Will, I'm so grateful for Edward's monument. It can't have been easy to have him brought back."

He smiled softly. "I used Leicester's influence in the Lowlands. Shameless, I know, but the end justifies the means. I'm glad you're pleased."

"More than pleased. I can't thank you enough."

She was about to try, but the heated caress of his lips silenced her. Her hands splayed against the firm muscles of his chest as she gave herself up to his kiss. He ran his tongue temptingly over her lips, then plunged deep into her mouth, pulling her fiercely against him as he did so.

She lost herself for a moment in the luxury of her husband's love, then eased away.

"I think, mayhap, a churchyard is not the place."

He raised a mocking eyebrow. "No, indeed. As you reminded me, Lady Cavendish, the lord and lady of the manor must show dignity and decorum when in public."

She gazed up at him, her handsome, golden-haired husband—and knew a need so deep, it threatened to consume her. "Will?"

"Yes, my darling?"

"I never dreamed love could be so wonderful."

"Nor did I, my sweet, nor did I. But then, I had never met a nymph before, my Eurydice."

"And I had never met a demi-god, my beloved Orpheus."

He took her hand and turned her away from the churchyard, with its solemn silence and mourning souls, and led her back into the blazing sunlight of a promising summer's day.

About the Author

Elizabeth Keysian is an international bestselling author of heart-pounding Regency romances, set mostly in the West of England. She is working on a fresh series for Dragonblade Publishing called Trysts and Treachery, which is set in the Tudor era. Though primarily a writer of romance, she loves to put a bit of mystery, adventure, and suspense into her stories, and refuses to let her characters take themselves too seriously.

Elizabeth likes to write from experience, not easy when her works range from the medieval to the Victorian eras. However, her passion for re-enactment has helped, as have the many years she spent working in museums and British archaeology. If you find some detail in her work you've never come across before, you can bet she either dug it up, quite literally, or found it on a museum shelf.

Social media/web links

Newsletter
eepurl.com/cxe369

Amazon page
amazon.com/Elizabeth-
Keysian/e/B06VVL9JMB

Twitter
twitter.com/EKeysian

Facebook
m.facebook.com/LizKeysian

BookBub
bookbub.com/profile/elizabeth-keysian

Website
elizabethkeysian.com

www.ingramcontent.com/pod-product-compliance
Lightning Source LLC
Chambersburg PA
CBHW070733190726
48292CB00002B/245